S0-ABB-457

Heart To Heart

Book Two

in the

Angelica Brown Series

By

IFÈ OSHUN

YA
FIC
OSHUN

Copyright © 2014 by Ifè Oshun

All rights reserved. No part of this publication may be
reproduced, distributed, or transmitted in any form or by any
means, including photocopying, recording, or other electronic
or mechanical methods, without the prior written permission
of the publisher, except in the case of brief quotations
embodied in critical reviews and certain other noncommercial
uses permitted by copyright law.

ISBN-10: 0-9859235-5-5

ISBN-13: 978-0-9859235-5-6

Papa Grace Publishing

NOV 26 2018

To my father, Hal.

Your soul flew away to the sounds of Chopin.

Peace be still as you continue on your travels.

RIP

♪♫ CONTENTS ♪♫

FLOATING

The light of the full moon disappeared as he closed the front door. Darkness enveloped us, and soon his arms encircled me in an arc of coolness.

"Angel Brown." He whispered my name fervently, like a prayer…and I wanted him more than almost anything: more than sunlight, more than even music.

But despite the intensity of my love for him, there was still one thing I wanted more than Sawyer Creed.

Blood.

"Getting thirsty again," I whispered, trying not to breathe in his maddening scent.

He picked me up and cradled me in his arms. "Let's take care of that." I relished the haven created by his lean, muscular chest as his long legs moved a few strides to the Grand Room, named for, and host of, the two grand pianos we'd played endlessly over the past six months.

He touched me as if I were the most fragile thing on earth, as if I'd break from the slightest movement of air. But I was Shimshana—a newborn immortal blood drinker from the ancient race that had sired vampires. And he was mortal—a novice wizard and medium just coming to grips with his magical abilities after a lifetime of being kept in the dark about who and what he was.

We'd just said good-bye to the last of our session guests after spending the past ten hours recording tracks. Included in the crowd were the other members of my girl group Kat Trio—Julietta and LaLa; guest musicians and rappers; our group's manager, Nina; and various people from our Boston record label, House Quake.

"I'm glad we finished recording all of our songs with you today," I said while stroking his five-o'clock shadow. "But I thought they'd never leave."

"Been wanting to do this all day." His raspy voice was next to my ear. "Get you alone."

Shimshana is what we are *and* what we have— an unraveling intestinal tube that extends up through the throat and out of the mouth to draw blood from people or animals. It shivered in my stomach as he gently set me down on the piano bench.

Unlike my heart, which banged against my ribs, his heartbeat was as steady as it always was. But the glint in his emerald-green eyes gave away his excitement.

At six foot four, he was a full foot taller than me, but was able to pick me up only when I lightened my body weight. I could easily overpower and crush him with the smallest amount of applied pressure. And right now the sound and smell of the blood coursing through his body almost drowned the sounds of my own heavy breathing.

We were in dangerous territory for two reasons. First: I was capable of losing control and draining him dry. And second: my once-mortal, now-immortal blood donor, Justin McCarthy, was capable of sensing my hunger from wherever he was and, within seconds would materialize to feed me.

Since we became girlfriend and boyfriend, Sawyer made sure there was no need for Justin. The latter boy hadn't been in my life since the two of them had a heated exchange, which ended with Justin cockily reminding me that my time with Sawyer was limited due to his mortality.

I never drank a drop of Sawyer's blood and vowed it would stay that way; there was no guarantee I had enough self-control to stop myself before killing him.

"Wait," he said gently. "Play our song until I get back." He ran to the kitchen.

Swallowing my quickly growing need to devour, I placed my fingers on the keyboard and began to play the song that we heard in our heads every time we kissed. The notes progressed like a soothing stream for my soul as the tune's structure ebbed and flowed through the piano's keys. It was a ballad that came to us in small segments like a mystical gift, a musical puzzle chopped into pieces and shuffled around.

Sometimes, as our lips moved together, we'd hear eight bars of this mystical, musical puzzle; sometimes we heard part of the chorus. I played all we'd heard so far, rearranging the pieces, stopping when it didn't sound right, and starting again at the place where it went wrong.

While playing, I watched the musical notes— brightly colored and dancing before my eyes, the same way music had appeared to me all my mortal life and since I experienced The Change that transformed me into a Shimshana six months ago. It's second nature to remember the musical arrangement of every song I hear, and the challenge of "solving" the puzzle kept me occupied enough to forget my waxing hunger.

My mind wandered to how life had changed since Sawyer became my producer and boyfriend. When not in school or doing boring tenth-grade homework, I spent most of my time at his brownstone, in the new studio, which encompassed the entire ground floor of the three-level home and had French doors opening onto a garden full of wildflowers. Sometimes I'd pull studio all-nighters alongside Sawyer and go to school the next day; sometimes I'd crash at home. On weekends, I'd just stay at Sawyer's. He had spare bedrooms, and there was never pressure to sleep with him (he was a virgin, too). We'd insulated ourselves in a world of music, melody, note and rhythm, even as a steady stream of people came in and out.

Life had also changed in the wake of our first hit song. The Sawyer-produced "No. 8," featuring Little Wolf, went viral and hit number one in download sales a couple of months ago. As a result, all our Kat Trio dreams were starting to come true; we'd even been invited to perform on the USA Music Awards, one of the most important music awards shows in the business.

Continuing to play, I shook my head slightly, still not completely over the awe of landing that gig. It was a huge deal to me, but not to my anti-awards-show boyfriend. Although a song he'd produced for another artist was nominated, the only reason he planned to attend was to be my date. Despite Sawyer's lack of desire for accolades, Nina and House Quake wanted the Kat Trio/Sawyer partnership to continue because Sawyer, dubbed by *Billboard.com* as "Pop's Teen Genius," was one of the most prolific young producers in the industry, and Kat Trio had officially become "a group to watch."

But there were other reasons why our partnership was good…

He returned carrying two gallon-size jugs of stored donor blood.

"Thanks." I took one from his hands—not stopping to read the name label on the jug to see who the blood was from—and proceeded to down the contents rapidly, rabidly, and without shame.

I stopped chugging once to savor the taste and envision the source in my mind's eye: she was older, AB-negative, with white-blonde hair and a long neck. She, too, was a singer. I ignored the rest of the information my core was extracting about my donor and put the jug back to my mouth to down the rest.

"My pleasure," he said, producing a second jug and watching me as if he wondered what was going through my mind.

In support of my mission to glut myself in order to quell all impulses to drain the guy I loved, the second gallon was soon finished down to the last drop. Feeding this way didn't require or stimulate my shimshana, but it got the job done. Remembering Mom's endless lectures on manners, I swallowed the need to burp.

"Heard from your parents?" I asked, wiping my mouth with the back of my hand. He nodded.

His mortal mom and stepdad had visited a couple of times to check the new house (he paid for it with cash, but they'd helped with the legal stuff) and they'd voiced concern that he was growing up too fast, seeing as he was already a homeowner and a millionaire at the age of eighteen, but still not in control of the errant magical powers that frightened them.

Since they found Sawyer frightening, it was a good thing they didn't know everything about me. He took the empty jug from my hands, placed it on the hardwood floor next to the first jug and sidled up to me on the bench.

"If my parents knew you were a blood-drinking immortal, they'd thank you for satisfying your thirst so completely."

"If your parents knew I'm a blood-drinking immortal, they'd drag you back to Georgia." My lips stretched into a mischievous grin, but his small frown deepened slightly. He usually frowned with the concentration it took to regulate his heartbeat— his mechanism for keeping *me* safe.

He'd practiced regulating his heartbeat for a couple of years under the tutelage of his grandmother, an immortal witch and the matriarch of his family, with whom he'd lived for the past two summers. Her guidance helped ensure that the strong emotions—fear, anger, love—that caused an accelerated heartbeat wouldn't cause what he called "witchy incidents."

In the past, these incidents took many forms—from shoelaces of girls he had a crush on tying themselves (hmph!), to murder (his mom's second abusive husband dropped dead), to the permanent disappearance into thin air of his alcoholic dad as he tried to strangle Sawyer's mom. Sawyer still didn't know how to control the witchy incidents, but he'd become a master of controlling his emotions.

"Speaking of Georgia," I continued, "are you feeling better about your summer plans?"

With back-to-back projects, he was booked to the end of the year. It'd be the first summer in two years that he wouldn't live with Nana or receive her guidance in getting the witchy incidents under control.

"I'm good as long as I can do this," he said, kissing one cheek, then the other, before his lips hovered close to my mouth so that his cool breath fanned my parted lips.

Opening my eyes, I reached for his hand, intertwined his long fingers with mine and reveled in the contrast of our bodies; his pale skin was just starting to tan as June set in; my milk-chocolate skin was flushed with a red undertone that gave away my current mood. His shoulder-length, dirty-blond hair mixed with my brownish-black hair, which flowed over my shoulders in fluffy waves as he took it down from the messy bun I'd hurriedly pinned it into this morning.

"You're so beautiful," he murmured in a way that caused the room's temperature to rise and the air to turn a shade of red.

The rising temperature and red-tinged air was a direct result of my excitement—typical Shimshana passion reaction.

I wrapped my arms carefully around his shoulders and pulled myself closer to him until our bodies curved into one another and my heart threatened to jump out of my throat. Still his heartbeat remained even.

"I want you." The words fell out of my mouth before my lips gently covered his.

I'd never been so close to a boy. A few months ago, right after I'd matured into a newborn Shimshana, Mom had the "talk" with me and clued me in to the way we show love. With our entire beings, she'd said. Now it was clear what she meant. I wanted him on every level—wanted to feel every angle of his body pressed to mine and lose myself completely.

He sighed as my lips pressed against his Adam's apple and my hands gently tugged his silky locks. My eyes were half-closed when I saw one of the empty blood jugs floating behind him...

"Good thing I'm from the South," he said. "It's crazy hot in here."

Oh, no. I had to bring the intensity down, or my mortal boyfriend would burn. I pulled away from him and sucked in a couple of huge breaths to bring down the heat my body was generating.

"Come back here," he growled, clasping his hands on my hips and pulling me so that my behind slid along the smooth surface of the wooden piano bench. "I can take your heat."

"No, Sawyer, you can't."

"Like hell," he said before kissing me again, this time urgently. As if there was a band in the room with us, the ballad started to play in our heads—a bittersweet cascade of notes that sounded like it would work well as part of the chorus.

Suddenly, the temperature dropped several degrees. I immediately suspected Sawyer even though his heartbeat remained steady.

I pulled away to question him about it, but the words remained unformed on my lips; Cici was calling me.

It wasn't the way most big sisters call, like on a phone, for example. She was locked to me. After The Change, and the development of the abilities that came with it, the family demanded a blood ritual, a spell called a mind lock. Linking Cici's mind to my mind, the lock's purpose was to keep me on damage control twenty-four/seven just in case I went berserk with bloodthirst, killed someone with the sound of my voice or accidentally stopped time again.

Thankfully the latter hadn't happened since my Mahá, the ancient, ritual-laden coming-out party for immortals. It was there that the immortal world saw I wasn't too dangerous for Mom and the other Council members to allow me to live. Since then, Cici's unwavering calm had been the perfect foil for my anxiety-ridden fumbling with my developing abilities.

She was tugging again. This time it was uncomfortable…

Angel.

My hands automatically stopped wandering over Sawyer's back as I clearly heard her voice in my head. Cici knew what was going on with me at all times and, under normal circumstances, would never butt in on a moment like this. Her delivery was still characteristically soothing but with an unusual undertone of urgency.

Come, now.

I was standing before consciously making the decision to do so. Something was wrong. Even though Cici didn't say where, I knew she was at home. For the first time in months, anxiety set in, and my feet lifted off the floor.

Sawyer stood, too, his green eyes level with mine. "What's wrong?"

Before I could answer, Cici continued. *Angel, it's Mom.*

My breath caught in my throat. Mom! I had to get to her. But my anxiety had me floating just below the ceiling.

Control. My feet couldn't move forward to Mom any other way. Closing my eyes, I took several calming breaths until my toes touched the floor and my feet set down firmly. I opened my eyes and returned Sawyer's worried gaze, craning my neck to look up at him.

"Something's wrong with Mom." The color drained from his face. As my boyfriend, and mate, he was considered a family member, and my parents treated him like a son.

"Right behind you," he said as I pivoted and headed for home.

Ifè Oshun

REST IN PEACE

I took off with one mission: to get home as soon as possible.

For the past three months, so much of my time was spent at Sawyer's, people referred to it as "Sawyer and Angel's place." However, publicly and legally, my home was still with Mom and Dad. Like all Shimshana, the first part of my life, before The Change, was spent as a normal mortal. My parents treated me like a new adult, but I had to keep up the appearance of life as a sixteen-year-old.

Putting into overdrive my new ability to go through solid objects, I chose the most direct route—a little under a mile—from Boston's Back Bay to the historic neighborhood of Beacon Hill, where Mom and Dad lived. I decided to run northeast—right through the line of brownstones attached to Sawyer's.

Taking a deep breath, I ran rapidly toward a closet door and passed through it as if it weren't there. I shot through the next brownstone (as well as its inhabitants and their belongings) and the next one, so fast everything, and everyone, was a blur. I continued this way through to the end of the block of buildings. Without pause, I propelled my legs even faster and leaped from someone's living room, through their wall, over three lanes of traffic, and directly into the Boston Public Garden across the street.

I'd never run like this: so fast it felt less like moving forward and more like being pulled through space by my intended destination. Passing through mortals whose eyes and senses were unable to detect me beyond a small gust of wind, I went straight through the massive, stone pedestal of the George Washington monument before skimming the top of the pond that housed the Swan Boats. The night air was cool, but I burned in urgency to get home.

What could possibly be wrong with Mom? I tried to see what Cici was seeing. Our mind lock allowed her to see everything I saw, and sometimes the ability was reversed. But, like Dad, Cici was a powerful telepath. They didn't technically read minds; instead, their minds were wired in a way that enabled the thoughts and brain waves of living beings to be attracted to them like metal shavings to powerful magnets.

They also could block people from seeing into their minds. And Cici was blocking me now.

Angel, just get here. You'll see everything soon enough.

She was protecting me from something. Something having to do with Mom! Heart racing with fear, I jetted forward faster, pushed by adrenaline and momentarily blinded by a haze of blood-red tears. Hurtling through speeding vehicles, tree trunks, and people sitting on park benches, I cut a razor-straight path through the northwest corner of the Boston Common.

Frustrated my speed couldn't compare with Mom's or even Cici's, who flew at the speed of light, I crossed Beacon Street before racing up the hill to my parents' brownstone mansion, where they'd lived since the early 1800s. Its red door at the top of wide, stone steps loomed ahead for a fraction of a second before it bared down on me and, like every solid object I'd approached within the past couple of minutes, succumbed to my ability to make it of no consequence.

My sneakered feet skidded to a full stop in the foyer, where Cici stood waiting for me.

She was dressed in tattered jeans and a dirty T-shirt—highly unusual as she had the tall, willowy build of a runway model and always took pride in dressing accordingly. Shocked, I steeled myself for the worst.

"Mom's going to sleep," she said.

I drew a blank as my unspoken question caused my eyebrows to arch. My head cocked in anticipation of an answer that made sense. "Wh-what…?"

She took my hand while her other hand gently cupped the side of my face, the way she used to do when I was small and had skinned my knee or had some type of accident that caused me pain. The gesture was once a surefire way to calm me down, but now it caused me to stiffen.

"Sleep, Angel. Mom's about to go to sleep."

And then it was clear.

The older immortals get, the less sleep we need until after a few thousand years when sleep might not be needed at all. But there was one exception. The Great Sleep.

Every seven hundred years or so, The Great Sleep causes immortals, including Shimshana, to sleep for an indefinite period of time—anywhere from months to decades. It affects the entire human/fallen angel race, and short of being destroyed, is the closest thing to death an immortal can experience. I'd never seen either of my parents—or anyone in our family—go through it.

Cici, knowing that I finally understood, grabbed my hand and whisked me up the stairs to stand outside the door to one of our parents' bedrooms. They had several in the house, and this one, the India Room, was Mom's favorite.

"Brace yourself," Cici warned before opening the door. I took another deep breath.

The first thing my eyes focused on was Mom. Surrounded by hanging jewel-colored saris and richly dyed Indian fabrics, she looked fragile as she lay in the California king-size bed.

Jetting over to her, I noticed the rest of my family; around the richly appointed room, monitors allowed all my siblings to be present via videoconference. My oldest siblings, 1851-year-old twins Menelik and Memnon, were each on their own monitor, and for a moment it felt weird not to see the two of them together since they are telepathically linked to each other and move like two halves of one person. My oldest sister, 349-year-old Aurora, and her husband/mate, the cold-blooded, day-walking vampire, Roman, broadcasted together from their home in Sweden. And 581-year-old Adrian—my only non-Shimshana sibling—was linked in from Paris, finally in human form after having spent the past couple of weeks shape-shifting into a variety of insects.

Cici's eyes followed my gaze. *In order to get him here, it took me hours of flying around searching for him.* Her lips pressed together. *After figuring out what hole he'd crawled into, I had to cast a telepathic net to find the bug thinking human thoughts.*

Mom lay underneath the embroidered, silk comforter despite the fact that the weather was unseasonably hot. "Angelica?" Her voice was thin, and her eyes—usually bright, sharp, and penetrating—were unfocused. The irises were darker than usual, almost black, and instead of its healthy dark-caramel color, her skin was ashen as if she hadn't drunk blood for days.

You're right. She hasn't had a substantial amount of blood for three days now. She's literally wasting away.

Mom was more than two thousand years old, and one of the most powerful of immortals, known for her ability to rearrange anything, or anyone, on the molecular level. But here she lay, weak and frail. I sobbed and fought back more tears. "I'm here, Mom."

I was a selfish idiot who hadn't seen this coming. There were signs over the past year—times when Mom seemed tired, even exhausted, but I'd stupidly thought it was about my transformation and what *I* was going through—had never even considered that maybe *she* was going through something. To make things worse, she'd barely seen me during the past few months and even had to visit me at Sawyer's a couple of times just to say hello. My face burned with shame.

I crawled onto the bed and lay down next to Mom. Putting my head on her chest, I swallowed my shock as her cold hand stroked my cheek.

Shimshana are never cold.

Except when they're going to sleep. She'll stay cold until she wakes up again. At least, that's what Dad says. It's my first time seeing Mom go to sleep, too.

My eyes met Cici's. She was sitting on the opposite side of the bed, on the edge. Next to her was Dad. Six foot eight, bald, and with skin the color of dark chocolate, his usually jovial expression was sorrowful as he carefully propped Mom's head on a mound of silk-encased pillows.

For the sake of the family, Cici held her back straight and her head high, but her main emotion, resounding grief, was clear to me. *I will cry for us,* I transmitted to her. As the youngest, it would be more acceptable for me to cry.

The comfort of Mom's arms touched a part of me that longed to be little again, a part of me that needed to feel her love surround me. Life was so simple when I believed the world was a safe place, and I had Mom to thank for that. She and Dad protected me so completely, my mortal years were spent in blissful ignorance of how messed up the world could be. How could I thank her for such a gift?

I recalled the sound of her voice at my birth, seeing her face for the first time, and my point of view when, as an infant, I gazed up at her face while she rocked me in my nursery for hours that felt like lifetimes. I recalled the song she sang and felt the same joy of seeing her smile radiate above me.

I sang what she used to sing to me during the first year of my mortal life:

> *Go to sleep, dear Angel/*
> *Go to sleep for me.*
> *When you awake, you'll find me here/*
> *So go to sleep for me.*

Instead of "Angel," I sang her name, Cleo, short for Cleopatra, the popular name for girls when she was born in Alexandria, Egypt around 12 BC.

Around the room the monitors showed my siblings listening, their faces reflecting the recollection of their own infant memories with Mom. I imagined her singing the same song to Menelik and Memnon in the ancient language of Aramaic, and hundreds of years later in Chinese to Adrian and Aurora in Asia where they were born.

I sang in a clear soprano and packed all the love that was humanly possible into the simple lyrics designed to be sung repeatedly until the subject fell asleep. Since learning my singing voice had the power to affect the emotions of everyone within earshot, I was careful not to cry and plunge everyone into more grief. Instead, I focused on the joy and peace Mom's smile brought when I was a child and she was the center of my existence.

Joy shone on the faces of my family, including Dad as he leaned over to kiss Mom and give Cici a bear hug. Even the dual long faces the twins usually wore were slightly happier. Roman's fangs were revealed as he smiled, too. The song's pastel-colored notes gracefully wafted through the room, and soon even Mom was smiling.

After singing the lyrics repeatedly, I hummed the melody.

Dad says she feels at peace but there's something she wants to say.

I lovingly ended the humming on a drawn-out, lavender-tinted note. Through her monitor, Aurora sighed peacefully.

Mom was whispering something. I leaned in to hear, but couldn't understand what she was saying. She was speaking another language, possibly Aramaic, but I couldn't be sure; whatever it was, it sounded archaic.

It's an ancient Egyptian dialect she spoke as a mortal child.

"She is delirious." Dad's voice sounded hollow as he gave me a sad smile. "Your song took her back to memories of being a baby." He leaned down to kiss her again. "In her mind, she is with your grandmother who, at that time, was still a priestess in the Temple of Isis."

"Yes," Menelik concurred. I was still taken aback to hear him and Memnon speak even one word of English. They usually spoke in the Aramaic dialect of their youth.

Cici caught my eye. *They're making a great effort to speak only English today. For us.*

Menelik continued. "Grandmother sang a similar song to her and later to us when we were born. Mother held one of us, and Grandmother held the other to get us to sleep at the same time."

"Mother held me more than you," Memnon said.

"That is unnecessary at this moment," Menelik shot back.

"Who cares?" Adrian said. His voice sounded strangely metallic, as if the experience of being an insect had not completely worked its way out of his being. "Our mother lays on her deathbed, and you two remain locked in eternal stupidity."

"Adrian," Aurora chided, "show empathy for your brothers. Mom is the only parent they have." She was alluding to the fact that the twins' father and Mom's first husband, Levi, had been destroyed more than six hundred years ago.

Levi died protecting Mom from their firstborn son, Tunde, as he tried to kill her during her last Great Sleep. Like me, Tunde had displayed enormous abilities, but he turned evil. Mom eventually overpowered and dismantled Tunde. The event destroyed the twins' natural immortal ability to adapt with the times; they talked and dressed the way they had when their dad was still alive and their big brother was still their best friend.

We sat in fretful silence and listened to Mom babble.

"What's she saying?" I asked.

"She now thinks she's in the Temple of Isis." Cici closed her eyes. "I can see what she saw, the temple. So beautiful...Ha, Grandma looks younger!"

"Yes," Memnon agreed. "She would because she stopped visibly aging only a couple centuries ago."

"Grandma's wearing white and a headdress that's shaped like an asp. She's carrying something…a device. Mom's asking her what it is, but Grandma smiles and doesn't tell her. Mom keeps asking, though."

We listened as Mom repeated the same questioning phrase a few times.

"It would seem her predilection for inquisition was honed at a tender age." Dad's joke was like an eggroll: love wrapped in humor and dolloped with a garnish of chide. We all laughed.

Mom's voice grew louder as if she was upset. Her heartbeat grew slower.

"It's like the immortal equivalent of Alzheimer's," Cici said. "She doesn't even know where she is. All the images in her mind are now jumbled."

Mom's quavering hand stretched toward me, and I leaned back into her. "Mom, I love you." My brothers and sisters repeated the words. As if buoyed by the sound of our declarations, Mom opened her eyes. The weight of her gaze pinned me. I *knew* that in that moment she was aware of where she was and what she was saying. She drew in a deep gush of air and gripped my hand.

"Be not afraid," she said. A loud exhale…her body relaxed onto mine, her eyes stared at me, open, yet empty…and everything in my world crashed to an end.

Afraid of what?…Mom?

With one massive hand, Dad closed her eyes.

My face crumpled as I kept my promise to Cici and wept for the both of us. Stoically, she rose from the bed and then, with immortal speed, opened Mom's giant, mahogany armoire and extracted a gown fit for an Egyptian queen—pure-white, embroidered with gold thread, and accompanied by gold undergarments. Throwing the comforter on the floor, Cici proceeded to dress Mom in the royal-looking clothing. Roman was no longer on the monitor, as if he was giving her privacy, but the rest of the family looked on as if to officially witness the process.

"We have no time to waste," Dad urged as Cici worked. She nodded in response before he turned toward his own massive armoire and drew a curtain, blocking him for our view.

"Hurry," Menelik and Memnon said simultaneously. "They know as soon as she goes."

"Who?" I asked while helping Cici put the final touches on Mom. I affixed an amulet, a family heirloom older than our grandparents, around her neck while Cici painted Mom's eyes with black eyeliner and her lips with red lipstick. "What did she mean by 'Be not afraid'? Who knows as soon as she goes?"

Dad's voice, vacillating as if he was engaged in a vigorous activity, sounded from behind the curtain. "The Council, Angel."

Mom was also a senior Council member of the Body of Restoration. Established by the Ancient Ones, the fallen angels who sired immortals, B.O.R. was an ancient organization established to maintain law and order among the international immortal community. Mom, along with the other senior Council members, represented the AOs, who used to walk the earth in ancient days but now were rarely seen. As a result, she was highly regarded and, in some parts of the world, revered by other immortals.

Dad continued. "They will come to claim her body as their eternal sister, bound by the Oath of the Ancient Ones—the oath they took to serve as Council members for eternity. They will come to take her."

"Why?"

"For her own protection," Cici said. "Or so they claim."

"Can they do that?" I asked. The thought of the Council taking Mom filled me with many emotions; anger was the most prevalent. The room took on the red tinge and higher temperature accordingly.

Cici finished her ministrations and now Mom looked like a sleeping, ancient-Egyptian queen. "They will try," she answered, turning her palms upward in a gesture of helplessness. "They may try to exercise their rights of eternal blood bonds."

Wearing a long, black tunic sheath and a cloak, Dad emerged from behind the curtain. On his arms were thick, black leather bands inscribed with our family seal and ancient Nubian which translated to: Power. Protection. Loyalty. Forever.

I'd seen him wear ceremonial dress for the first time at my Mahá, but never all black. His usual warm, easygoing nature had vanished as surely as if he'd taken it off with his modern clothing and stashed it in the armoire. All that was left was a steely, seething determination.

"Let them come." His voice sounded deeper and its resonance bounced off the walls of the room as if we were in an echo chamber. "Let them try to take her." It was a warning and a summons emerging from the silence her departure had brought. His brown eyes turned ice blue, and his rarely unsheathed wand was ready in his right hand.

"Let them fail." His words were still conversational in tone, but now reverberated throughout the house. "Power."

Through tears of awe, I stared at my father. *No one* was taking Mom. My eyes went to Cici and to each of my siblings. "Protection," I repeated with resolve.

"Loyalty," Cici said.

"Forever," we said in a unified voice.

And then there was a loud knock on the front door.

SEPSU KHA

As soon as the knock sounded, I whooshed through the house's structure to get to the front door. Dad and Cici were already there; he'd positioned himself at the foot of the staircase, right at the perimeter of the foyer, and she was walking toward the door. My sense of smell told me who was there before she opened it.

Sawyer stood wild-eyed and panting as if he'd run up the hill at maximum speed. His eyes took in me (and my rage), then Cici's alert posture, and finally Dad before they came to rest on his wand.

"Come, son," Dad said. Sawyer came inside and stood with us, took his place by my side and pointed his chin toward the door.

Council members now stood in the doorway. They were the same ones who'd advocated for my execution during my Mahá—Charleston and two others whose names I'd never learned and didn't care to know. Instead of following Sawyer inside the house, they stood in the vestibule facing each other as if they'd just materialized there before turning to face us.

Like Sawyer's, their eyes took in the fact that we were ready to defend Mom to the death. They peered at Sawyer, no doubt wondering who he was. Aside from longevity and superior healing ability, most immortals looked and smelled like mortals, due to our shared humanity. For all they knew, Sawyer was immortal, too.

Charleston addressed Dad. "Brother Abraham, may we come in?"

"You may," Dad answered without budging from his spot at the foot of the stairs.

Why are we letting them inside? My question was a silent shriek.

So they can't say we didn't offer them access. Cici was as still and expressionless as a museum sculpture. *To deny them access would be a tool they could use to garner sympathy from other Council members and build a movement against us.*

They wore immaculately tailored silk suits, diamond-studded watches, and highly polished leather shoes. They took their time stepping over the threshold; as they came inside, not one of them lifted a foot at the same time as another and, as a result, the visual effect evoked an image of people walking under a Chinese dragon costume, or worse—the moving feet of a centipede. Their sharp facial features were reminiscent of weasels, and their heads moved back and forth with purpose as if trying to find something.

They've tracked Mom's scent and are now listening for her heartbeat.

A low sound rumbled at the back of my throat. Charleston's black gaze swiftly shifted to where I stood next to the entranceway mirror.

No doubt he recalled the time during my Mahá when I used my singing voice to bring him to his knees. It would be so easy to give a repeat performance, to simply open my mouth and direct deadly notes straight at his head.

Don't, Angel. They'll use that, too. Any excuse to challenge our claim to Mom's body. Don't give them the ammunition. They must attack us before we can do anything.

Frustrated at how slow this battle was taking to heat up, I looked for the "click": a concave impression in the space around me that, when engaged, would enable me to freeze time. But for the first time since I turned immortal, the click wasn't there.

Cici, I can't do the time freeze. I'm trying, but nothing is happening.

Abilities come and go during the first year, remember? It may not have been a permanent ability. I'll let Dad know.

I felt useless. What good was I if my abilities to defend Mom weren't working?

Charleston, as if he understood the conflict raging within me, gave me a chilling smile, before turning to face Dad on the other side of the circular foyer. "We have come for our sister's body," Charleston said politely.

"We claim her by right of the Sacred Blood Bond instituted before she mated with you," said the second Council member.

"Our claim predates yours," stated the third.

"Your claim is noted," Dad answered. "And rejected. Cleopatra stays with me. I am her mate."

The second Council member took one step toward Dad and extended his hand in a gesture of explanation. He obviously was the diplomat of the trio. "Surely you must agree that we are better equipped to protect her." His tone was humble. "We have massive resources at our disposal to ensure her safety and well-being during the Great Sleep."

"Besides"—Charleston threw a derisive glare at me—"you have this newborn to control." He spat the word "newborn" as if it were used toothpaste. "She may have survived Mahá, but she is reckless, and you cannot keep her out of your sight." His eyes traveled down the length of my body. Sawyer stiffened at my side. The room grew hotter. "As I said," Charleston added, referring to the growing heat with a smirk.

I took a deep breath in preparation to hurl a B-flat at his head.

No, Angel. He's picking on you. Don't give him ammunition.

Sawyer squeezed my hand as if silently saying the same thing.

"You dare to suggest I am incapable of protecting my family?" Dad's voice was ominous. His wand's engravings, an ancient spell of power carved by the hand of his mentor, a Nubian high priest, now burned a brilliant ice blue that matched his eyes. Charleston took a step back. Dad took a step forward.

They're giving him some ammunition. Now he needs a bit more.

Unable to initiate a time freeze or use my deadly voice, I racked my brain for a way to help. Then it came to me…

Long ago, in the ancient kingdom of Kush, where Dad was born, it was an offense for a man to look at another man's daughters for as long as Charleston had just looked at me. It was ancient—and a long shot—but it was worth a try. I turned to Dad.

"Daddy." My voice was frightened as I backed away toward the stairwell and pulled the neckline of my sweatshirt up toward my chin. "I feel uncomfortable."

Dad jumped on it. "Not only do you insult my ability as a man to protect my mate, you also insult me as a father by your offensive behavior toward my daughter." He took another step toward Charleston. The third Council member (obviously the smart one) pulled the other two back toward the door before he spoke. "He did not mean to disrespect you in this manner, Sepsu Kha."

Cici, what did he just call Dad?

Sepsu Kha. An ancient term of respect for renowned practitioners of magic.

The third guy continued. "These times are less formal, and sometimes the ancient laws are forgotten when emotions are strong."

"I assure you," Dad continued, "I possess the resources to protect my family and my blood."

As he spoke, he took small steps forward. With each step he seemed to grow a few inches and— although he stood directly under the crystal chandelier that hung from the ceiling—his face grew obscured by shadow, until he resembled an eight-foot-tall silhouette, black and foreboding, with the ice blue of his eyes and wand now glowing brighter than the light fixture.

As if that wasn't scary enough, the walls of the house glistened with a luminescent, bluish glow and seemed to stretch to accommodate his new height.

"This very house will prove there is nothing that will stand between me and Cleopatra. She is mine."

The house reverberated with his voice like before, and then something truly frightening happened—the walls moved in and out as if they were alive and breathing.

The house is a fortress infused over the centuries with Dad's magic. It will fight with us if need be, Cici explained.

I knew Dad was a formidable wizard from the tales I'd been told of his prowess—like the time he leveled an entire town, or when he marshaled millions of locusts to attack oncoming Roman forces—but I'd never witnessed this side of him.

Smart One now pulled the other two, each by the arm, backward toward the door. "Of course, Sepsu Kha," he agreed quickly. "Your claim as mate is stronger in this instance. We will take our leave. Please accept our apologies."

And with that they continued to back out of our front door, down the front steps and into the darkness of the night that swallowed them like a vacuum swallows dust. Cici shut the door.

I turned to Dad to ask him why the Council members had left so easily, but he wasn't there. A faint *swoosh* indicated Cici was also gone.

"Come on!" I grabbed Sawyer by the hand and led him up the stairs as fast as his mortal feet would allow.

MAGIC SPARK

By the time Sawyer and I got upstairs, Dad's normal size and facial features had returned, and he was once again by mom's side; only this time he was urgently chanting something under his breath and into her ear.

"What just happened?" Aurora asked.

"They retreated," Cici answered.

"I'm surprised our little sister let them live," Adrian said.

"I did nothing." I still held on to Sawyer's hand. "It's Dad they're afraid of."

"As well they should be." Aurora's voice was dark.

"They're scared of Angel, too," Cici added. "They baited her relentlessly, but she held her ground."

"She has shown admirable self-control," Memnon acknowledged with a big-brotherly nod in my direction.

"Cecilia," Dad said. "Help complete Uzuzu Mitu."

Cici flew to Mom's side and chanted something into her ear as Dad continued to chant into the other.

"What are they doing?" I asked no one in particular.

"Uzuzu Mitu is an ancient protection spell going back to Sumerian times," Aurora explained. "It taps into Mom's molecular-manipulation abilities to act as a layer of protection for her body, mind, and soul. After that is put into place, we take Mom to a place where she can rest in peace."

"I've heard about this spell," Sawyer murmured, entranced as he watched Dad and Cici work. He turned to me. "Your dad's mighty powerful. Nana told me tales of legendary wizards and witches. I just realized he's one of them."

The two most important men in my life had grown close over the past months. The few times that Sawyer left the studio to come to our house, I'd find him hanging out in the basement with Dad, talking sports in his workshop. Sawyer had clicked right away with Dad, but now as I witnessed the reverence on his face, I saw their relationship was deeper than I'd realized.

"One legend says he resurrected dead Ethiopian soldiers to fight against and defeat the Ottoman Empire."

"My dad?" I watched him as he worked on Mom, saw the determined set of his jaw, and the magnitude of Sawyer's words hit me. My father could raise the dead. "That's why the Council backed down so fast," I said.

Sawyer nodded. "I bet the guy who apologized is the oldest. He seemed more familiar with the repercussions of messing with your dad."

"Whad'you mean?"

"Nana taught me magic has nothing to do with being mortal or immortal and everything to do with the supernatural." He absentmindedly ran his forefinger along my arm. "Even the most powerful immortal can be brought down by strong enough magic. The only advantage immortals have is time;

they have longer to hone their craft. The core of a wizard is what Nana calls the Magic Spark. You either have it or you don't. Some have more than others. Your dad has lots of Spark. That's what makes him incredible. Magic trumps all powers, everything. Magic's king."

Magic Spark didn't seem to be hereditary, though. Cici always struggled with simple spells and usually got help from Dad. Not wanting to distract her, or hurt her feelings with this thought, I focused on my own lack of Spark. As a mortal, I could do basic glamours Dad had taught me, but since The Change my Spark was just a memory.

And then there was Sawyer, who spent every waking hour trying *not* to do magic.

"If that's the case, what does that say about you?" I asked him.

He looked at me as if the mention of his dilemma was something new and we hadn't talked about what would happen the day he stopped regulating his heartbeat and just let himself be.

But he didn't get a chance to answer. Copious amounts of black mist seeped through the windows and walls before dripping to the floor like atmospheric molasses and moving with purpose toward a clearing in the room where it formed a large cloud puddle. Figures rose rapidly out of the vapor, one after the other, until the nebulousness was gone and four people, dressed in black hoods and cloaks, stood in its place. They were my aunts and uncles on Dad's side of the family—all wizards and witches.

In the middle of greeting us, Aunt Alpha swiveled her head in Sawyer's direction before taking in the sight of him with an ice-blue stare and inclining her chin in his direction. I assumed she was surprised to see a mortal in our midst.

It was a rare pleasure to see them, but it was clear they weren't stopping by just to say what's up.

They're here to escort Dad. They'll form a wall of protection and use everything within their power to protect Mom as Dad carries her to her resting place.

Uncle Solomon, Dad's older brother, watched Dad and Cici working on Mom. "Uzuzu Mitu," he said. "Amplify." He extended his hands toward Mom and the others followed suit. Soft bluish light emitted from their hands as they chanted words in an unfamiliar language.

"Amazing," Sawyer said. "They're injecting more power into the spell."

When they were done, Alpha turned to us. "Know this. Your mother is well-protected." She placed a strong hand on my shoulder. "This is our bond."

Lovingly, Dad picked up Mom's body and went to stand among the aunts and uncles. They quickly dissolved back into the black mist, which completely enveloped Dad before it disappeared and they were all gone.

They'll lay Mom to sleep in the same underground tomb where Dad had his last sleep—it's been in Dad's family since antiquity. Cici collapsed into an overstuffed armchair and released a huge sigh. *Our older siblings already know the plan. Dad's parents are waiting for Mom's parents in the tomb right now. It's hidden with very old magic, so it's never been discovered like most of the other burial tombs in that part of Africa. Mom will be safer than before and under the care of all of our grandparents.*

Knowing Mom was under the care of our combined families filled me with relief. Through political power (Mom's side of the family) and high magic (Dad's side), our grandparents had kept our collective family intact through the ages despite the upheaval of empires. I had no doubt Mom would be safe this time around.

There was another knock on the door. Had the Council returned? My eyesight clouded with red.

No, Cici said, already downstairs. *It's Satchel.*

Soon Cici's electric-channeling fiancé from L.A. joined us in the India Room.

"Got the first flight I could." He folded her into his arms.

"She's gone," I told him. The words dug a trench in my heart.

Mom was gone.

Sawyer held me as my bloody tears stained his green T-shirt. Cici held on to Satchel so tightly her knuckles turned white. I really wanted to throw my head back and bawl, but I swallowed the impulse, knowing it would affect everyone else. The mood in the room was somber as the older siblings gave us time to collect ourselves.

Eventually Cici straightened and cleared her throat. "I've been formally charged with Angel's care during Mom and Dad's absence," she announced. The siblings murmured approval as I looked around the room in confusion.

"Dad's absence?" I pulled away from Sawyer and wiped my face with my hands. "Shouldn't he be back soon?"

Aurora's lips pressed together in Mom-like disapproval. She looked to Roman, whose face seemed more unreadable than usual, before launching her glare in Cici's direction.

"Aurora…" Roman warned.

I got nothing from Cici's mind. She was blocking me again. "Cici, what aren't you telling me now?" I asked.

"We must stop this Inc thing," Aurora said from between clenched teeth.

She was referring to the two factions of immortals: Incs (short for Incorporates), who embrace the rules of mortal society and live within its parameters; and Trads (Traditionalists), who live outside the rules of mortal society. Mom and Dad were Incs, while all my siblings, except Cici, had chosen to embrace the Trad lifestyle. Almost every immortal we knew identified with one or the other. There were a number of subgroups in both camps, who subscribed to various points of view ranging from the practical to the radical—from advocating complete integration into mortal society to "live and let live" to destruction of mortal society and everything in between. Even B.O.R. and its Council were not immune to the partisanship.

"Roro," Cici answered, "I realize our way of life doesn't agree with yours, but this is how our parents raised Angel."

"Angel is an adult now," Aurora said. "She needs and has the right to know what is going on. She is too powerful to be babied."

"Ro is right," Adrian said. "Angel can decide how she wants to live her life."

"She's still a newborn." Cici spoke through gritted teeth. It was rare that she showed anger, but sure enough the room started to feel warm and look pink. "She still needs care. After the window closes at the end of her first year, then she can do as she pleases."

"That moral window is a foolish Inc notion," Memnon retorted. "Trads are encouraged to be true individuals from the first day of their existence."

"Oh, really?" Cici's usually sweet tone was cutting. "Trads throw their newborns into the fire and say 'fend for yourself'. Besides you and Menelik, none of us were raised that way. Why would we want that for Angel? I'll tell you why in one word: Tunde."

Silence.

"She is right," Menelik said. "This is Mother's wish."

"Our mother is not here," Aurora shot back.

Dead silence.

"Well, I'm here," I announced. "And it's a fact, I'm not a Tunde repeat."

While their initial fears had lessened since my Mahá, there was still a small amount of uneasiness among my older siblings when it came to the enormity of my abilities. I stepped toward each monitor to meet their eyes measuredly before turning to Cici.

"Tell me everything, Cecilia." My tone of voice was no-nonsense. "No more secrets."

Aurora smiled, and all the older siblings nodded with approval. Cici held up her hands as if to say she was surrendering to the will of the family at large.

"Dad needs to protect Mom from possible attack. He plans to pool his resources with the others. He needs to be there in order for it to be stable. He isn't coming back today, and he may or may not come back until Mom wakes up."

Life without both of my parents? Both of them gone in one day? Fresh tears pricked the back of my eyes.

"Angel," Aurora said with a softer, gentler tone. "You are in good hands. Remember you can always call if you need anything. And Cici, the mind lock is a good idea. We may not live our lives the same way, but you are to be commended. I love you."

The rest of the family added their agreement and assurances. As if their loving words chipped away at the last of her attempts to keep everything inside, Cici slumped, and her shoulders shook with sobs.

"I remember being in your shoes," Adrian reminisced as Satchel rubbed Cici's back. "Damage-controlling this one." He spoke of Aurora. "Why do you think I lived as an octopus for so long afterward? It's not easy. But I am confident you can do it."

"Besides," Aurora added, "you both have wonderful mates, and they are there for you."

"Know that Mother is in no pain," Memnon said. "She is peaceful."

"We have slept," Menelik added, "and can promise you when she awakes, she will be stronger than before. Soon she will be with us again."

"She'll be with most of us, at least," Aurora said with a smile. "Who knows where, or what, Adrian will be when Mother awakes?"

Cici laughed between her tears, and even the twins looked relieved to see she was okay.

"I will be living as a dolphin soon," Adrian joked good-naturedly. "Anything to get away from you people." We all laughed before, one by one, the siblings signed off.

I walked around the room and turned off each monitor. The black displays seemed to add to the unspeakable emptiness in the house. The feeling of loneliness was unbearable.

"It's the house," Cici said as she finished making the bed. "The emptiness we feel comes from the house. It's infused with Dad's magic; it's a piece of him. It misses Mom, too."

The guys had left and we were alone in the room. With a last lingering look at the warm patterns and bright colors of the drapes, tapestries, and pillows about the India Room, I hit the light switch and closed the door behind us.

Mom was gone. Dad was gone. A hollow void of desolation threatened to engulf me.

"I'm here for you." Cici gave me a long hug. "Mom and Dad may be gone, but I'll never leave you."

"Neither will I," Sawyer said from behind us. I turned to see him carrying a tray of Mom's favorite cut crystal glasses, filled with blood. His biceps bulged through his long-sleeve tee as he worked to balance the heavy tray.

"Thanks, hun" was all I said before the glasses were drained.

Satchel presented a single glass of blood to Cici, from behind his back as if it were a bouquet of roses. "Hungry?" he asked with a smile.

Cici's head swiveled as she looked at the tray and back at the single glass meant for her. "Not as hungry as Angel," she exclaimed before we all burst out laughing.

CLOSE TO HOME

The plan was simple. I needed to be close to anything that reminded me of Mom. The obvious solution was to move back home and bring along a suitcase of all my clothes that'd found their way over to Sawyer's house over the past months.

Looking up from her paperwork, Cici raised her eyebrows as she watched me dump the suitcase onto the floor of the den.

"What?" I asked defensively. "It's not what you think. We haven't... You *know* we haven't."

"Why not?" she asked bluntly.

"You mean besides the fact that I'm a newborn and might lose control and kill him?"

"Angel, you really should go to The Nest. I get it, about not wanting to feed from Justin and have that...um...conflict, but you need fresh blood. Eventually you're going to get to a point where the stored stuff won't satisfy you."

The Nest was part of B.O.R.'s network and offered folks a cool place to hang out and grab a bite. To the public it was a trendy lounge/restaurant, but the other side of The Nest, inaccessible without immortal DNA, was an upscale place, featuring an extensive menu of willing blood donors.

But, the idea of returning to The Nest and getting another potentially blood-obsessed donor was an unattractive prospect. Blood Obsession—the condition a donor suffers when he lives only for the Shimshana—was what we all suspected Justin, my first and only donor, endured.

When we met, he was just a normal, mortal guy Mom had ordered for me at the Boston Nest. But when the archangel Bodiel breathed life back into him (I'd accidentally drained him dry at my Mahá), Justin became immortal. Blood Obsession and immortality were *so* not a good mix. Why would I want to go through that again?

Cici turned to her laptop. "Speaking of blood, I need to order some for the house. What types do you like?"

"O's good for a chaser," I said. "But A- and B-positive fill me up the most."

"How much do you need to order?"

"No idea. Mom took care of all the groceries. I'm not even sure where to get it from."

Briefly, I reminisced about the comforting sounds of plates clanging in the kitchen and the mortal food smells I used to enjoy as a child. How would the house ever be the same without Mom?

"Maybe I should call Aurora," Cici said.

"Yeah, if you want a lecture. She'd probably urge me to prowl the streets of Boston for my next meal." The thought of hunting people caused a shiver shimmy up my spine. Hmm…It wasn't necessarily a bad idea…

Sensing my dark thought, Cici flashed out of sight and returned a few seconds later with a pitcher half-full of blood. I downed it just as fast. "That's it?" I asked. "You can't be serious." I raced to the kitchen and looked in the fridge. Sure enough, the space that usually held several pitchers of blood was now empty. Just the idea of not having enough blood stoked my hunger.

"Cici!"

"I know!"

"Freezer," I said between dry swallows. "Check the freezer."

She did. There, among Dad's frozen steaks and fish, were a number of labeled blood bags. She grabbed some and popped them into the refrigerator, except for one. She then raced to the sink and filled a big pot with hot tap water.

"This will thaw the blood," she said, dropping the blood bag into the pot. "You shouldn't microwave it; it zaps all the nutrients."

"It'd be a lot quicker, though," I grumbled. My phone jingled from its spot in the living room near the grand piano. A text from Sawyer...

On my way with rest of stuff

Waiting for blood. Waiting for Sawyer. Was this my existence? No, I decided, I still had music.

I sat down at the grand and began to play an excerpt from *Madame Butterfly*. The opera had always been one of my favorites, but it wasn't until Sawyer taught me to seriously play the piano that I could revel in the gorgeous composition.

As my fingers traversed the keys, I thought of my girls, LaLa and Jules. We had to get together soon to work on our album. The tracks with Sawyer were pretty much in the can (at least as far as the writing was concerned) but there were other producers we were slated to work with. The music business seemed far away now, though, as I sat and poured my heart into the beautiful composition and imagined that Mom would call my name at any moment to ask me if I'd eaten.

Cici appeared in the living room with a pitcher full of blood. She placed it on the low coffee table. "It's warm, just like Mom used to make it." She poured some for both of us: a half-full glass for herself and full glass for me. As we sipped and savored the warmth, I thought how amazing it was that Mom, as busy as she was with her public-facing job as an attorney at B.O.R., found the time to do something like this that brought us so much comfort.

"You're not drinking as much as usual," Cici said.

"Yeah, guess you're right. I miss her."

Cici sighed. "Me, too. Being here, surrounded by her scent, helps."

There was a knock at the door. "Maybe we should give him a key," Cici said as she went to let Sawyer in. "Satchel has one, you know." Satchel had gone to the hardware store to grab some batteries, lightbulbs, and liquid drain cleaner. "I'll text him and tell him to get an extra key made."

I downed the rest of the blood while trying not to let the scent of him drive me wild as he made his way from the foyer to sit down next to me on the piano bench. It occurred to me most people spent the majority of their sitting time on chairs, couches, and the like, while we spent ours on hard piano benches. He smelled of grass, earth, and fruit...and love; soon he was the only thing on my mind.

"How are you?" he asked before pecking me on the cheek.

"Just ate," I said, loving the feeling of safety as he folded me into his arms.

"Good. Brought the rest of the stuff," he said. "I'll take it upstairs."

He was cool with my decision to spend more time at home and had packed up all my stuff and some of his own, too, including a portable keyboard so that he could write at my house. I wondered what it would mean for him to be away from his home studio. He was notorious for his work ethic—almost never left the studio—and sometimes went for days without being seen.

Another knock at the door. Cici immediately appeared in the living room.

"The scent's familiar, but I'm not sure why," she said.

We knew it was an immortal because mortals always rang the bell, while immortals knew our hearing could pick up a simple knock.

"I'll get it," I said. At the door was a lady with a pleasant demeanor and round face. Her skin was the color of a cup of caramel latte and her eyes were large, dark, and kind. She wore a black skirt, white shirt, and the type of shoes you'd see on nurses or other professionals who spend a lot of time on their feet. "May I help you?" I asked.

She smiled at me. "My name is Kiya." Her Egyptian accent was heavy. "I am your housekeeper. Your mother has retained me over the centuries to help with the households."

Not too long ago, I'd learned that our family owned a number of properties around the world, including a plantation property in Barbados that

Dad had gotten a great deal on during the island's slave uprisings. The newest property was my house, built for my Mahá, in Los Angeles. It made sense that there was someone to take care of all of this.

Cici's voice sounded behind me. "Kiya, it's a pleasure to meet you finally. Come in."

I saw her information in Mom's file and sent her an e-mail, Cici transmitted. *She came fast.*

I agreed. But one thing concerned me…

Now that Dad's gone, can we still communicate without other telepaths eavesdropping?

Don't worry; Dad's white-noise spell will keep our conversations private whether he's here or not.

I exhaled with relief.

Kiya came in reeking of practicality. Even her purse was sensible—the big, black Mary Poppins type, from which—I imagined—she would extract anything requested by the family members. Toys, Band-Aids. Blood…

"I'm Cici. This is my sister Angel. She's a newborn."

Kiya nodded her head as if she'd just heard the most important news on CNN. "Your mother loves you dearly. She talks about her children all the time. I am sorry for your loss, but she will be with you again someday." She looked around before running the tip of her finger over the foyer's French antique console table and inspecting the dust on her finger. "We will clean immediately. I will also take inventory of your stock: household items and, of course, blood for you." This she said with a wink at me that was probably meant to be friendly but struck me as super-annoying, as if she was mothering me. I stared blankly at her as she nodded, this time as if she knew the answer to every question ever posed by mankind.

"Now," she continued, turning to the big, black bag she'd placed on the floor. "Your mother prefers environmentally-friendly cleaning products. No harsh chemicals, biodegradable. Is that good for you, too?"

"Definitely," Cici answered as my head nodded in agreement.

Kiya reached into her black bag and pulled out a humongous quantity of bottles, rags, and sponges. She also pulled out mops, brooms, and two full-size vacuum cleaners.

Cici and I looked at each other in wide-eyed amazement. We'd expected her to be an everyday person with no particular abilities. *Whoa*, I transmitted. *D'you just see what I saw?* Cici nodded before her attention was snatched away by the housekeeper's loud clapping.

"Go, my lovelies!" Kiya said. The supplies literally rose and danced around in the air. "There!" She pointed to the foyer furniture as a couple of rags paused in midair while furniture polish bottles squirted onto them. The rags then started wiping along the furniture as if they were handheld.

"Incredible…" Cici sounded dumbstruck. The kid in me thought this was right up there with watching those old stop-action animated TV shows, or visiting Cinderella's castle at Disney World.

Kiya's hands moved like an orchestra conductor, and she spoke to the various objects as if they were small children. One duster got squirted with the appropriate cleaning liquid, and she directed it over our heads to the crystal chandelier, where it went to work on the intricate light fixture. Meanwhile, a large rag stretched itself to its full size and hovered underneath the chandelier so that the dust wouldn't fall on us.

"Come," she said, picking up her bag and walking down the hallway as the remaining supplies followed like loyal pets. Along the way she continued to direct, and soon we heard a vacuum going to work in the family room.

"Now I know why her scent seemed familiar," Cici said. "She's been with our family before we were even born. She was originally given to Mom by Grandma. In ancient Egypt, people got servants that stayed with them all their lives."

So why are we just meeting her?

Cici shrugged. *No idea.*

Satchel came in with the hardware store stuff. "What the heck?" he asked before laughing at the dancing rags that completed their task and went floating down the hall in search of Kiya and their next assignment.

"The housekeeper, Kiya," Cici said. "She's telekinetic."

"And obviously a Disney fan," Sawyer said. He wore a rare, small smile as he came down the stairs with his keyboard and laptop under his arm. I followed him into the living room.

He picked a corner of the room where he could work, and I located a stool and helped him with the power cords. Soon he was settled in and started to play Beethoven's "Für Elise" as a warm-up. I accompanied him on the grand, and we soon lost ourselves in the music, me with the lovely notes swirling in the air before me, and he closing his eyes every now and then, or watching me watch the music.

This was how we spent our time, lost in the sounds of all types of music and lost in each other. The beautiful music momentarily took the sadness of Mom and Dad's absence away. Eventually the song came to an end, and he made a notation on a pad of paper he'd set up near the keyboard.

"What's that for?" I asked. He usually made notes about songs we were creating, not old classical music.

"A note of the time you last ate." He opened the clock app on his cell phone. "This way when we lose track of the time, the alarm'll go off for the next time you need to eat."

When he was done setting the alarm, he put down his phone and started playing a melody line from a track I'd heard him working on a couple of days ago. It was a song he was working on with another artist. Soon he was deep in the process of working out the notes. I settled on the couch and suddenly, feeling exhausted, fell asleep.

# # #

In my dream I saw the stairwell. Memnon and Menelik were struggling to carry a large, golden coffin down the stairs. Like in most Beacon Hill homes, the stairwell was narrow but had a decorative niche in the wall that would help them to turn the coffin and get it down the stairs. As they attempted to rotate it, the coffin slipped out of Menelik's hands and shattered all over the first floor. Mom's body, mummified like Tutankhamun and covered in blood, spilled out of the broken coffin onto the floor. The Council members swooped in and started pecking at her body like crazed vultures.

I woke up screaming and crying. Sawyer knelt by the sofa, concern on his face as his long fingers gently rested on my arm. "You were talking in your sleep."

"Nightmare," I said, sitting up. The day was gone and, from the sound of it, so was Kiya and her cleaning-supply army. Cici and Satchel were in another part of the house watching TV. I stretched my arms overhead and noticed Sawyer's eyes on my breasts. Leaning toward him, I initiated the kiss that brought him down onto the couch with me. Soon I was breathless as his hands roamed the length of my body.

The cell phone alarm went off.

"Dinnertime," he said, jumping up and trotting to the kitchen. Straightening my clothes, I followed him before sitting at the polished, butcher-block kitchen table. I ran my hands along the hefty table, enjoying the smooth surface and aroma of beeswax oil from Dad's recent sanding and polishing session. Sawyer took a couple of pitchers out of the now fully stocked refrigerator.

"What're you having?" I asked. He shot me a spine-tingling glance that seemed to say "you" before turning back to the fridge.

"Kiya ordered stuff from a spot down the block. Home-style meals. Let's see..." He looked in the refrigerator as I surveyed the definition of his back muscles underneath his T-shirt. "Home fries, sliced steak, greens...a lot of stuff." He poured blood, placed a plate on the table and pushed me down gently when I tried to help. "Relax. You're going through a tough time right now. It's like your mom died. Let me take care of you."

At the mention of Mom, I felt a sudden rush of emotion and reached for a glass of blood. We consumed dinner silently, lost in our private thoughts. Afterward, we cleaned up, filled the dishwasher and dumped the trash before he turned to me with a critical eye.

"You look like you could use another nap," he said. He took me by the hand and led me up the stairs to my room. He was right. I fell on the bed and pulled him down with me. He settled on his back and after he made himself comfortable, pulled me closer so I could lay my head on his chest. We lay like that for a while as I listened to the beat of his heart, solid and steady against my ear, and his finger twirled a lock of my hair.

"You just picked at your food," I said.

"Not much appetite, I reckon." His pronounced Georgian accent signaled that he was completely relaxed.

"There's a lot of that going on in this house." I rolled to the side and lay on my back. "Mom and Dad being gone hurts, literally, right here." I placed his hand on my solar plexus, and his hand rose up and down with my breathing. "Like there's a hole in my stomach. As if I'm dying."

"That's grief, Angel. It's okay to feel that way. Normal."

"I'm sorry for being such a baby about all this."

His hand slowly stroked my shoulder. "I'm here for you." His eyes, as he bent over me, had that unfocused almost cross-eyed look that happens when faces are too close to each other. "There's nowhere I'd rather be than with you." His gaze, like his words, felt weighty enough to pin me to the mattress. "You're my reason for waking up in the morning."

"Even more than music?" The idea that my needs came before his passion for music blew my mind.

His head came down the rest of the way until he brushed my mouth with his firm lips. They were so light and fleeting, I thought it was my imagination until I felt the coolness of his breath.

"I love you, Angel. If I had to choose between you and music, I'd choose you. No doubt."

Our ballad started to play. The sound of a full orchestra assailed our senses. We not only heard it, we felt it.

Caught up in the music, I started to sing—a few improvised words but mostly the sound of *"ah"*— and temporarily lost myself in the beauty of the tune.

I remembered too late...my singing voice was having an effect on Sawyer. His brilliant-green eyes brimmed with tears as he held me tightly, staring almost thunderstruck at my lips as they formed the sounds.

"Unbelievable." His words were choked with emotion. "That I could feel more love than I did a couple minutes ago. All that…brought on by the sound of your voice. I could die, over and over again. Go to heaven, hell, or anywhere in between to be with you forever."

My singing, which had diminished into a throaty hum, stuck in my throat as the enormity of his words hit me.

"Forever." My tears flowed freely. "I'd give it up in a heartbeat to die by your side."

He kissed me then, and the force of it took my breath away. It was as if I was experiencing the depth of his love for the very first time.

Then I heard it. The rapid beating of his heart. He raised his head and his eyes grew desperate as he watched my face.

"No." His voice was low, tense. He panted with effort.

"Sawyer, what's happening?"

"I can't stop them. The tentacles."

The tentacles were an invisible, mysterious part of him. They were what he felt stretching and reaching out from his middle before the witchy incidents happened.

Our bodies, the mattress, and the entire bed started to vibrate.

I could do nothing except clutch his shoulder and watch him fight an internal battle to regain his self-regulation. Eventually the vibrating stopped and he lay there in a spent silence.

"The Magic Spark." My voice sounded tentative. "That's it, isn't it? The thing you can't control. The thing that sets off the tentacles."

"Yes." His voice rang with defeat.

An idea hit me.

"Sawyer, I don't think it's you. It's *me*. Remember? Large doses of me—my newborn presence—plus mortals equals…bad. I think that's what's going on here."

"No, Angel. I think it's because I feel so deeply for you. When you said…what you just said about dying with me, it made me feel something…something so intense I lost control."

The skin around his eyes grew tight as his fingers absently traced my collarbone. There was something else, something he wasn't telling me.

"Was this the first time it happened?" I asked.

"There've been other incidents, when you weren't with me." He didn't seem to be aware that he was pulling a long, unraveling thread that was sticking out of the pillowcase seam. "Little things happened, so little nobody else noticed."

Shocked, I sat up straight in bed. Of course! The floating blood jug and the drop in room temperature when we were making out earlier. Not only was he here playing nursemaid to me instead of working in the studio; my presence was eroding the control he'd worked so hard to maintain. The control that kept everybody around him safe.

I'd been too caught up in my own personal drama to recognize the warning signs in Mom, that she needed someone to take care of her. I wasn't going to repeat the same mistake with him.

"Sawyer." I said his name with great care, as if it were a nugget of gold in my mouth. "I feel bad about you not being in the studio."

"Don't. Seriously. We'll be back at my place soon, back in the studio. But right now, just take the time you need to be okay."

I kissed him with an air of acceptance and put my head on his chest, mainly because it was important for him to think what he'd said was okay with me.

But it wasn't okay with me. It was crucial to figure out a way to get through this and get him back in the studio, without me destroying what was left of his carefully constructed self-control.

I started to concoct a plan right before I fell asleep in his arms.

Ifè Oshun

DILEMMA

The same question I'd fallen asleep with was still on my mind next morning: what could be done to mitigate the damage my presence had on Sawyer's self-control? There was the obvious option, but the idea of shutting him out of my life was unbearable.

Sawyer reluctantly went home late last night after I'd reassured him I'd be okay. But now that there were no other heartbeats in the house, I felt a strange type of emptiness that had nothing to do with hunger.

The cell phone rang. Knowing it was him—outside of my family and music stuff, nobody else ever called me—I checked the screen. Sure enough, there was his pic in all his gorgeous glory, and those piercing eyes…I let it go to voice mail, rolled out of bed and stood there—staring at the missed-call alert. Should I call him back and tell him about my conflicted feelings? That I needed him badly, but also needed him to be who he was? I didn't know what to say to him, but knew any attempt to express my muddled state of mind would result in him telling me to just relax. Best approach: figure out a solution first, then have a logical conversation. Tossing the phone onto my pink beanbag chair, I whooshed through the floor to the kitchen.

The house felt gloomy despite the sunshine spilling through the plantation shutters. Impatient and craving comfort, I warmed up blood in the microwave. Cici was out jogging, and with a little effort, I could feel her exhilaration as she ran beside the Charles River. We were scheduled for tea later,

61

a Brown family tradition exclusively for the females. It'd be my first time taking part as an adult, and the first time Mom, who'd started the tradition with Aurora back in the 1700s, wouldn't be there to share it with us. I scarfed down the blood while simultaneously swallowing tears.

It was a little past eight o'clock. Sawyer promised to be back bright and early. He might assume I was still sleeping, that mourning Mom and missing Dad was still taking a toll on me, but it wouldn't be long before he returned. Our plan was for me to rest while he worked, until it was time for tea with Cici.

I decided to visit my old vocal coach, Mr. C., instead.

My feet quickly moved up the stairs. I grabbed the cell phone, punched in his number, and left a short inquiry with Mr. C.'s message service, asking if he had time to see me today. In the wake of Kat Trio's rising popularity, word made it through the industry grapevine and now his vocal lessons were in high demand. He could quite possibly be booked.

I quickly unbraided my hair and jumped into the shower. I hadn't seen Mr. C. for months—since our record deal party—but our vocal exercise sessions always helped me get through whatever was cloudy and whatever was scary. And it was a good way to get out of the house and stop moping about Mom and Dad.

Most of all, I didn't want to get in the way of Sawyer creating music, wanted to make sure my needs didn't eclipse his, and that our relationship was beneficial for both of us. I had a long list of benefits from being with Sawyer and could only hope his list was just as long.

The phone rang as I rinsed out conditioner. It was either Mr. C. or Sawyer. Quickly dressing in a short-sleeve tee and jeans, I then rapidly applied leave-in and gel to my hair before brushing it up and pinning it into a high bun.

The cell phone showed Mr. C. had called from his private number. I listened to his voicemail. "Of course, you may come over, dear. You are always welcome. How does ten o'clock work for you?"

That worked pretty darn well. Life just made more sense after an hour of no-nonsense vocal exercises. Plus, if I was at Mr. C.'s, Sawyer wouldn't be waiting on me hand and foot.

After confirming our appointment, I threw a few things into a backpack, ran downstairs, added a few thermoses of blood, put on my broken-in knee-high brown boots (even though it was warm outside) and was out the door before nine. I decided to walk to the studio, trying to enjoy moving at a mortal pace and reminding myself to wait for the pedestrian light before crossing the street.

Entering Mr. C.'s studio felt like a homecoming. He stood (I could hear the creak in his seventy-seven-year-old knees) and welcomed me with a warm grandpa hug. My maturation had caused him to be fearful of me, and it felt good that now, after some time had passed, he was giving me hugs again.

But something was…wrong. Mr. C. didn't smell the same.

His weird fortune-teller-like ability always helped clue him in when things were not going right in *my* world, but now the tables were reversed. It was clear something was wrong with *him*. I looked at the floor and tried to think of what I should say. He knew I wasn't "normal" but he had no idea what I was. I couldn't just blurt out that he smelled differently.

But I had to know.

"Are you okay, Mr. C.?"

The former international concert pianist who'd traveled the world and played to sold-out audiences for decades looked surprised.

"You may still be sixteen, but that, my dear, is just a number. You're no longer a child."

It wasn't an answer, so I continued to wait.

He sat down slowly, as if consciously allowing me to see that he was in pain. His fingers, soft on the keys, began to play Chopin's "Nocturne No. 2 in E-flat."

"I'm dying, Angel. I know this is an unusual way to break the news." His gaze took in the black-and-white keys as he continued to play. "But"—his fingers pounded an emotional crescendo—"we who live and breathe music are not usual, are we?"

I regained my ability to form words. "Is it the cancer? Did it come back?"

He nodded yes, and the nocturne's refrain petered out in an alarming way, as if he were dying right there in front of me.

Not too long ago, I'd watched him pass out; it'd happened right here in this studio, right over the keys. I was sure that if Mr. C. could choose a death location, it would be at a grand piano.

But he wasn't going to die anytime soon. I wasn't going to let him.

I'd healed my Uncle Set at my Mahá. Well, my voice made him joyful after he'd been morose for centuries. Could I really do the same for Mr. C.'s cancer—make it disappear and replace it with the opposite?

He picked up the notes where he'd left off in the piece; at the same time, I opened my mouth and directed a gentle, tangerine-tinted C note toward him. I imagined healing light entering his body, and soon, right before my eyes, his back straightened, and his skin grew vibrant. Everything about him— his posture, the way he played the nocturne—took on a certainty, an urgency that had been missing minutes before.

Mr. C. was stronger.

I walked to the other side of the grand, where I could see his face. His expression was joyous, and his eyes looked up at me with three parts disbelief, two parts wonder, and an ounce of fear. Mr. C. knew my voice had healing ability. I'd repaired a broken statue right in front of him before he himself taught me how to safely channel the power in my singing voice. Even before I'd matured, he'd suspected our regular sessions had caused the cancer to go away in the first place. I assumed the fear was due to the unknown, the info he didn't have—exactly what was I. I stopped singing.

"Angel...the pain. It's no more." The notes he played cascaded with the energy of rejoicing. The music was a boat, carrying me away. I gripped the edge of the piano and closed my eyes. I'd actually done it. My head felt as light as air, and my knees began to sway…

The difference in the way he stood, more fluid than I'd ever witnessed him move over the years I'd known him, spoke to the amount of pain he'd secretly borne.

His arms clasped me in a hardy embrace that reminded me of the haven I used to find in Dad's arms. After a while, Mr. C. pulled away and peered at me. "My dearest girl, are you okay?"

Why would he ask that? I'd just healed *him*. Perplexed, I nodded my head.

"Sit down," he said.

"No, I'm okay," I answered, slightly annoyed. I'd felt a little dizzy but it was only for a few seconds. Why was he babying me?

He continued to peer at me as if expecting me to fly away. "I think that what you have done for me…is…miraculous, and I thank you with everything I am and ever will be. But you should not do it again. It weakens you."

Looking up at him in surprise, I plopped down on the bench. He was right. I'd felt weaker right before he held me in his arms, but hadn't felt like that when I'd healed Uncle Set. Why feel weaker now and not before; what was the difference? The only thing I could think of was, when I'd healed Set, the room was full of Ancient Ones and archangels.

But the fact of the matter remained. Mr. C. was better. And if his body absorbed my intention the way I wanted, the cancer was obliterated and would never return again.

"I'd do it again," I told him. "I couldn't let you to die."

The thing about Mr. C. was he may not have known what I was, but that never stopped him from understanding me. No explanation was necessary. It was what it was.

"Being your mentor has been, and will always be, one of the great joys of my life." He turned his face and shifted his gaze to where the opposite wall met the floor, before clearing his throat, straightening his mint-green corduroy tie and adjusting his jacket with precision. "Now," he continued, "we attend to your needs. No need to stand."

He resumed his seat at the piano, and we immediately delved into scales, trills, and other vocal exercises as his knotted, nicotine-stained fingers glided across the keys. Music was always my medicine of choice; no matter how yucky I felt, it always made me feel good. When we were done with the warm-up, he played the intro to one of my favorite opera pieces and my heart lifted with joy. Our eyes met, and he winked at me before he threw his all into playing the music,.

# # #

I met up with Cici for Brown Girl Tea at the Randolph Room, Mom's favorite tea spot that we'd visited yearly since I was seven mortal years old. It was a classy place with a yummy menu of teas in so many flavors it could make your head spin; they even made awesome peanut-butter-and-jelly sandwiches and different flavors of hot chocolate—perfect for me when I was a mortal child. We had many memories of sipping, munching on scones and toast, and sharing "girl" talk. It was one of the rare times Mom and Cici ate, and enjoyed, mortal food, albeit in very small quantities. As a result of the years of this family tradition, I still liked the taste of tea despite turning Shimshana; as a singer it would always be my second-favorite beverage.

Cici was wearing a vibrant orange-and-lavender-print shift with platforms. She raised one eyebrow in surprise and then nodded with approval at my pencil skirt, silk blouse, and heels.

Look at you, all grown up, she transmitted as we were seated at our table.

You know this is one of the few places where I don't mind dressing up. It's for Mom.

Mom loved it when we wore dresses. Dad too. I figured it was due to their North African antiquity mentality, but had to admit wearing a cool dress always did make me feel special.

Cici laced her fingers through mine. "As you know, we get together every year, no boys or men allowed, to discuss anything we want. The only rule we have is that if someone asks a question, they must get an honest answer. As this is your first adult tea, you must be initiated into one very important part of this ritual…" She grinned and pulled a flask of stored blood from her purse. "Now you can sneak it in, too."

I'd guessed this was why Mom never let the waitstaff pour our tea like most patrons did, and the hunch was confirmed as Cici placed her point of view in my mind; it allowed me to see all the times Mom covered her cup with her hand and gave the waiter a polite "no, thank you."

"One step ahead of you." I laughed and pulled a flask from my purse.

Chuckling, she clapped her hands together. "So what we usually do is empty the original teapot and fill it with blood." Her teeth flashed brilliant white as she spoke in the rapid, immortal way that resembles a low hiss and is impossible for mortals to decipher. "Or if we just want a little, pour some into an empty teacup. I'm thinking the former is probably more up your alley. We'll rinse out all traces of blood with a little tea when we're done."

Earlier at home, after changing clothes I drank my fill of lunch. Sawyer had texted me several times asking my whereabouts and to let me know that he was going back to his studio to grab some backup drives. I'd managed to pop into the house, change and locate two stainless-steel flasks in the kitchen before he returned—all in less than five minutes. I was completely satisfied.

Our order arrived. Cici poured (as she was the oldest), and we clinked our teacups to signal the official start of Brown Girl Tea. I savored the lemony-mint blend and vegged out to the peaceful music strummed by the tearoom harpist.

"I heard from Dad," Cici said. Her tone caused me to open my eyes and focus on her. She tapped her temple to indicate that the communication had been telepathic.

"He's not coming back anytime soon, is he?" I could feel her resisting her initial response to my — sweep it under the rug, make everything seem okay. But she had to be truthful; that was the Brown Girl Tea rule.

"No, he's not." She sighed. "That area of Sudan is quite unstable due to mortal unrest—never-ending ethnic cleansing, even an increase in human trafficking. Dad needs to work more to help fortify Mom's resting place."

The horror from Mom's coffin dream returned. Cici quickly reached for my hand and gripped it across the table. "Angel, Mom is and will be okay. As long as Dad's there, along with all the others, nothing and no one will change that. I'll show you." She closed her eyes and placed an image in my mind. I saw Mom resting peacefully in a tomb that glowed with the blueish haze of Dad's high magic. The image brought a deep sense of relief, and I exhaled a long breath I wasn't aware of holding.

I remembered what Mom said before she fell asleep. "You think this is what she meant? She didn't want me to be afraid for her?"

I could almost see the wheels turning in Cici's mind as she considered the question. "It had to be," she finally answered. "Her way of saying when it comes to her safety, you have nothing to fear." We both took a long sip of tea.

"Unfortunately for you," she continued, "there'll be less damage control." She stirred her tea slowly. "Since Dad needs all his resources, it also means he won't be able to step in if there's…another incident."

Cici was referring to my newborn failings at controlling myself and my new abilities—the whole reason for the mind lock.

"So I might end up having a Trad experience after all—attacking somebody." I squashed a piece of red velvet mini-cupcake with my forefinger.

She set down her spoon, pushed her gold-leaf teacup and saucer away, leaned forward on her forearms and regarded me with an air of frankness. "Angel, the responsibility to make good choices still rests with you, whether you choose a Trad lifestyle or an Inc existence."

"Is it even real, the concept of the moral window? Or is it just something they made up to keep us in line?" According to our parents, the moral window was the length of time a newborn had when moral character was set by choices you made. It supposedly lasted for a year, and I was allegedly in the midst of it.

"Scientific fact," Cici answered confidently. "Similar to mortal kids and how the brain gets wired at a young, impressionable age."

We munched on finger sandwiches in a silence that lasted so long I almost imagined Mom sitting at the table, urging me to contribute to the conversation.

"Satchel's spending a lot of time here," I said, at a loss for a discussion topic.

Cici's face lit up. "Yes, he closed on his last property a couple weeks ago and now has put everything on hold to be with me. Don't tell anybody…We may be close to setting a date."

My face stretched into a delighted smile. Satch was perfect for her. Where she was fashion-oriented, he was practical, but wore Italian shoes. He was loyal, hard working, and the family liked him.

And it doesn't hurt that he's really, really, reeeaaally good in bed. Cici's smile was broad as she leaned down under the table and poured from the flask.

Totally TMI, Cici.

She sat back up and arranged her hair. It had grown out of the almost-bald Caesar cut she'd gotten back in the Fall, and now she styled it in a poufy, curly style that framed her face. "Why are you avoiding him?" she asked.

"Avoid Satchel? I have no idea what you're talking about."

"Sawyer. All day you've avoided him. Do you even know why?"

"Preposterous. Why would I avoid Sawyer?"

She leaned back in her chair, crossed her legs and looked at me as if I'd just exited an alien spacecraft. Brown Girl Tea rules demanded honesty…

"Okay. For one, my presence is affecting him. He's not able to control his magical abilities. Two, if he's with me and loses control, he'd never forgive himself. I think about how it'd feel if the situation were reversed—if I lost control—how angry I'd be at myself for subjecting him to danger. I won't put Sawyer through that." I could feel her concern emanating from across the table as she continued listening. "His life's falling apart because of me, Cici. He hasn't been in the studio for days. It's…not normal."

Sawyer outside of his home studio and not working was beyond abnormal; it shook me to the core. It made me feel that nothing was right with the world anymore.

"He's making a conscious decision to be there for you," she said. "Why not just let him take care of you?"

"Because I don't want to be the reason he loses control one day."

"Maybe it's not about him losing control." She said it lovingly, as if we were at an AA meeting and I was on the verge of admitting alcoholism. "Maybe *you* don't want to lose control."

# # #

Later, as I sat at the grand and tinkered with our ballad, I thought about what Cici said. She was right; I'd done a great job of ducking Sawyer all day. The texts he sent and the missed phone call from earlier this morning remained unanswered. My fingers glided over the piano keys as I savored the rhythm of a line of tender chord shifts. The resulting cascade of sound evoked feelings of joy and heartache all rolled into one. Was that our relationship? Joy and heartache simultaneously? We'd had plenty of joy over the past months, was it now time to pay the piper, to experience the heartache in order to balance everything on some cosmic lovers' scale?

My fingers repeatedly played the part of the song we'd heard last, seeking a way to connect it to the previous segments.

Maybe the solution to my dilemma *was* to spend less time with Sawyer. It would be easier once we went back to his place and picked up our old routine—attending to the constant flow of folks, recording, listening, building, dreaming of tracks— eating, breathing, and living music. I could take the opportunity to disappear more often, maybe spend more time on another floor, and if things didn't improve, maybe leave the building for longer periods of time. Sometimes he got so caught up in the music, he probably wouldn't notice if I was gone for an hour…or more. Eventually, my presence wouldn't have an effect on him, and then we could go back to the way things were.

But even then, his feelings for me could still cause the witchy incidents…

My laptop rang. A quick glance at the screen told me it was LaLa and Jules calling for our videoconference. I quickly pressed the Accept button.

"Hola, ladies," I said.

"Whassup?" asked LaLa, who, for once, wasn't wearing a baseball cap. Her new haircut was amazing—a short buzz cut on one side of her head and a chin-length, asymmetrical bob on the other.

"What's cooking, chica boom bap?" Julietta's smile was framed with glowing, orange lipstick.

Outside of Sawyer's studio with its assembly line of artists coming through for the last recording session (it wasn't the best place to catch up) and lunch at the school cafeteria a few times a week (which was always very quick because I never ate), we hadn't spent much time together for about three months. Not in person, at least; all of our writing sessions were done through videoconference.

My excuses for not seeing them in person were either being with Sawyer or doing stuff for Mom and Dad. But seeing them now made me feel homesick. I needed my girls. I needed music.

Nina soon joined us from her office and got straight to the point. "School's out, and it's time to work harder than you've ever worked." Her words matched her new minimalist eye makeup—no smoky eye shadow, just mascara. "Our agreement with your parents, putting all music obligations off until after the end of the school year, now puts the pressure on us to hustle. We have to not only squeeze out an entire album in the next three months, we also have two TV appearances to prepare for."

"The Cassidy and Steve Show!" Jules's excitement was infectious, and we all grinned, including Nina.

"Not to mention USAMA!" LaLa added.

My grin grew wider. One of my childhood dreams was performing on the USA Music Awards. "That totally eclipses everything we've done so far," I said. "Even our show at the Boston Garden."

"Angel," Jules said, "you sound like my mom, calling it the Boston Garden."

"Whatever. This is huge," LaLa said. "And we don't even know what we're going to sing."

"Why not just do 'Get Out of Here'?" I asked, referring to the underground hit that got us into House Quake.

"Too regional," Nina said. "Best thing to do would be "No. 8." It's still on the charts, and more fans know it."

"Will Little Wolf join us?" Jules's tone was hopeful.

"Doubt it," Nina answered. "The purpose is to shine the spotlight on you. For a song segment, we'll need to showcase your vocals. But then again, you never know what could happen at USAMA, so I'll leave it at that."

Little Wolf, one of the hottest rappers in the industry, was featured on the song's original version. He was also a werewolf and an old family friend—we'd played together as toddlers.

"Now," Nina continued. "Do you want to lip-synch for USAMA?"

We all looked at each other, puzzled. She'd never asked us to lip-synch before.

After a few moments of perplexed Kat Trio silence, Nina cleared her throat. "Here's the thing. The choreography will probably be energetic for the show, and you might get winded. If you lip-synch, you don't have to worry about losing your breath."

We all looked at each other. The girls considered the question as I waited, pretending to deliberate, to see what they would say.

"I don't want to," LaLa finally said. Jules and I agreed.

"We'll practice as much as we have to to make sure we get used to the moves, but we definitely want to sing live," I added as the girls nodded.

"Cool," Nina replied. "As for the album, you guys have a good head start on the material. You've finished up with Sawyer—" At this point everyone's eyes slid to look at me—Jules with a grin, LaLa with a you-better-tell-me-all-the-dirt glance, and Nina with her signature been-there-done-that-but-I'm-gonna-acknowledge-it-anyway nod of the head. "And now you have to build out tracks with the rest of the producers: Haz Bro, who's currently holed up in an old church in the UK; Lick A. Shot; EyeHeart Beatz; and William Wilson; all in L.A."

"What about some of the other producers, like Balls of Steel?" LaLa asked.

"Or Mo Mojo?" I asked.

"We'll see," Nina answered. "We're under no obligation to collaborate with them; we'll play them by ear. Bottom line: 'No. 8' performed well on the download chart, and now we've got to follow it up with a Top 10 hit on the traditional Billboard chart."

I mulled over her last statement as she wrapped up the meeting. Building up vocals for our performance. Following up with a Top 10. Three months wasn't a lot of time to do all the things we needed to do. There was no time to waste.

The album was slated for final mix at Sawyer's, and we'd decided that his studio would be the nexus of activity this summer, serve as *the* place where we could focus on nothing else but work. Being in a space dedicated to music was crucial in the writing and creation of more music. It was like a factory for the imagination and an engine for the musical soul. Being in that type of atmosphere this summer was essential to our success.

And it was essential to my success in getting though my grief.

But, there was another option, another place where we could write and prepare for our shows…There was my house in L.A.

I knew exactly what to do.

The question in my mind all day, how to make it work with Sawyer, was finally answered. It was simple. Clear. Obvious.

I had to leave him. Walk out of his life and never look back. I would no longer be Sawyer Creed's girlfriend. It really, truly, was for the best.

DEARG-DUE

"Cici, I'm breaking up with Sawyer."

It was the first time since making the decision that the words came out of my mouth. She dropped the huge bouquet she was carrying. It was a riotous burst of colorful wildflowers that reminded me of Sawyer's garden, and I caught it before it hit the floor.

"WHAT!" She followed me to the kitchen. "I knew you were considering it, but I didn't see this coming."

With immortal speed, I filled vases with water before distributing the flowers into them. "Maybe because I didn't even know myself—until just now."

"I'm staying out of your head," she said. "That way you can tell me, because I don't think this has been in your mind long enough to count as a real decision."

She followed me like a comet tail as I streaked from room to room, placing vases. Setting the last one down on the low wood-and-glass table in the family room, I turned to her. My lips pressed together. "What does it matter whether the decision was made one minute ago or one day ago?" I asked. "I gave this a lot of thought." Spent, I dropped into a deep, upholstered chair before sighing loudly and resigning myself to a long explanation.

Cici levitated and arranged herself the way people arrange themselves into seats before the start of an entertaining movie. She was gearing up to listen to my explanation, but she was also gearing

up to talk me out of my decision. It was no secret
that she loved Sawyer like a future brother-in-law.

But nothing was going to change my mind.

"I may still be a newborn, but our siblings are
right. I'm an adult and need to take responsibility
for my life. I've decided the best thing to do is
move to L.A. and live in my own house."

My "Mahá" house was actually a twenty-six
bedroom mansion that easily accommodated the
masses of people who came to witness my coming-
out and the accompanying rituals. I'd since installed
a studio (with Sawyer's help), and now it was the
perfect place to immerse ourselves in music.

"But if Sawyer came with me, it wouldn't
work. My being with him will continue to wear
down his self-control. Cici, don't you see? He's got
a lot of magic ability; even Dad agrees. What if it
all explodes finally? Who'll get hurt? Most
importantly, who will he blame? I can't let that
happen.

"The best thing is for me to leave him. The
work we need to do is the best cover. Soon he'll be
back to normal, focused on his music, and our
relationship would stop being a source of chaos in
his life."

Our relationship would just stop. Completely. I
felt like vomiting. Cici put her hand over mouth as
if she too felt the force of my nausea. Silence
reigned as I pushed down the queasiness.

"Give him a few months," she said. "By then
you'd no longer be a newborn and you can pick up
where you left off."

"True, I might not feel insane with bloodlust (couldn't imagine *not* being insane with bloodlust), but then what? My presence won't affect him negatively, but what about his feelings for me? It's the strong emotions that bring out the witchiness. He'd still have to constantly monitor himself."

Another long, thoughtful silence. Then…

"I'll call Kiya." Cici's tone was muted, resigned. "She can prepare the L.A. house for your arrival."

Now it was my turn to be shocked. "What, no argument?" I asked.

"Angel, you're right. You're responsible for your life. I'm here for you as your sister. I can't tell you what to do. I understand why you feel this way. The danger's real. But Sawyer's a good guy, and nothing good comes without a price."

She touched back down to the floor and stretched her back as if she'd just risen from a comfy lounge chair.

"We might as well close this house down." She pulled out her cell phone. "There's no reason for us to be here."

That made me immensely sad. After all, this was the only home I'd ever known. I'd spent only a week in the Mahá house, but this one was where I'd lived since I was born and reborn.

"I felt the same way when I left this place," she said, picking up on my feelings. "Believe me, you'll get over it soon. You'll love living there as much as I do. Remember, the reason I came back from L.A. was to help you through your Mahá and newborn period, so your moving there means I'm moving back home. Aaannd…" The corners of her lips turned up with delight. "…Satch and I can start looking for a house sooner." She smiled in a way that, for a second, made me wonder if I was making the right decision. Shouldn't I be smiling like that someday about Sawyer? Was I giving us a chance?

But the answer was clear. We'd had a chance; a really good chance. And I'd carry the memories of our time together into eternity.

"How are you going to break the news to him?" Cici asked as she finished texting Kiya and Satch. She popped into the kitchen and started warming and pouring blood.

"Oooooohhhh…" The word was a long, tortured exhale as I snuggled a little deeper into the comfy, cream-colored chair. "I don't know what to say, how to say it. But it's got to be a believable lie. If I tell him the truth, that I'm doing it for him, he won't accept it."

She re-entered the room, carrying a tray with glasses, which she placed next to the flowers. I poured a glass for her before pouring several for myself.

"Tell him there's another guy in the picture." She took a long sip of blood. I stared at her, surprised that she, my always-happy, social-butterfly sister could say something so bitchy and brutal.

"I know it sounds heartless," she continued. "But sometimes it's the best way to make a clean break. To ensure there won't be any loose ends."

She put down her glass and stared at her hands as if she was contemplating the existence of her fingernails. Whenever she did this, I knew she was about to reveal something juicy.

I immediately downed the rest of the contents of my glass and started to make a little nest to settle into and listen to what she had to share. The time it took to make the nest was part of an unspoken ritual we had. While the listener "got ready," the revealer had time to wrap her mind around the words she needed to say.

Without taking my eyes off of her, I grabbed a couple of throw pillows, arranged them around me within the confines of the comfy chair, straightened my T-shirt, pulled my knees up to my chin and tucked away a couple of loose locks of hair that had been hanging in my face. Then I sat completely still to show that I was ready when she was, and for her to get on with whatever the juicy secret was.

She sighed. "Don't judge me, Angelica."

Wow, it was going to be epic. "Get on with it already." I leaned forward.

"A while ago, back in 1872 when I was around five or six immortal months old, my bloodlust was so strong I could barely stop myself from tearing apart any mortal within five feet of me. Mom was sick of Reconstruction, and Dad wanted to take a break from the continual casting of white spells."

Well aware of how Dad used glamours to make the family appear as white people in order to live in safety here in the States, I nodded encouragement for her to continue.

"So we moved to the Barbados plantation house. We'd just bought it from a plantation owner who'd more or less taken his family and run when the slaves rebelled. We were treated like aristocracy. The younger folks had never seen blacks like us. But the older people—whether they were African, Carib Indian, or Irish—feared us. Our mystique led all kinds of people to our door looking for work, for adventure, and even death."

I settled further into my nest and sipped from a large goblet of blood, eagerly waiting for her to continue.

"One such person, one who sought death, came on a Tuesday. His name was Charles. He was what's known in Barbados as a Redleg—a descendant of Irish slaves in Barbados. He was seventeen and had an endless sense of hopelessness. Charles's ancestors had been brought to the island in the 1600s and were treated worse than the African slaves, who were considered more valuable.

"His family lived in a cave. He said they called the women in our family *Dearg-due*—after an Irish vampire legend. He'd walked through fields for days to arrive at our door and ask for a job. But his mind was an open book; he'd heard we drank blood, and he wanted to be drained.

"We took him in under the guise of a house servant, but Charles was my donor. Mom and Dad told me it was a mistake, but Aurora had a different view. At that point, she'd long been a Trad and saw the island as a great food source. She regularly went hunting and targeted criminals and other social misfits who added nothing to society. She thought Charles was perfect for me because he was not only a non-contributor to society, he also wanted to die.

"But Charles had a talent; he was a gifted mathematician. I started tutoring him and watched as his sense of self-worth began to take root. He became more attractive to me, and eventually we fell in love."

I nearly dropped my glass of blood. "You were in love with a mortal?" I realized I was yelling and lowered my voice. "What happened?"

"He suffered from Blood Obsession to the point where he couldn't bear to be away from me for more than a few hours. I told him to go away, even left him on the other side of the island. He kept coming back, and I kept taking him back. Mom told me it was heading for disaster, but it was too late. You see, Blood Obsession's a two-way street. While mortals become attached to us, we become connected too, and experience feelings of connection that can be mistaken for love.

"We knew that it couldn't end well for Charles. And it didn't. One day—it was a gorgeous Sunday, deep-blue sky, and we were at the beach enjoying the peaceful ocean—I could no longer contain my need to drain him. He met his end there. We buried him in the sand. To this day, I feel the guilt and the pain of his loss. If I'd made a truly clean break, perhaps he would have had a full life. But with the Blood Obsession, maybe that would have been impossible anyway."

She wiped away tears. I darted over to a box of tissues and brought it back to her.

"You're strong, Angel, a stronger newborn than I was. But you also eclipse almost every other immortal we know with the power of your abilities.

The road you have to walk isn't enviable." She blew her nose. "I support you and agree a clean break is for the best. Sawyer deserves a chance, and if you suspect he can't have that with you, trust your feelings. You'll get no argument from me."

Throwing away the bloodied tissues, I hugged my sister. "Cici, you're not a killer. You did the best you could. It was your nature that got the best of you, and the circumstances were beyond your control."

"I know," she said simply, sadly, before resting her forehead on mine. "You still haven't told me what you're going to say to him." And then she stopped as if something world-shaking had just occurred to her. She drew her face back to look me in my eye.

A problem never faced with Charles…What if Sawyer gets angry when you tell him and loses control?

Hadn't thought of that…How would that potential situation be diffused? My ability to stop time seemed to be malfunctioning or, at the worst, had disappeared. I couldn't use my voice to protect myself in the case of a witchy incident; that would kill him.

"If I tell him there's another guy, he'd automatically think it was Justin. That'd be cruel, seeing as he's spent the past few months making sure there was no need for Justin."

"Well you better figure it out quick," she said.

I heard it too…Sawyer's footsteps outside on the stone stoop and the jangle of his keys as he began to unlock the front door. No doubt the first thing he would ask me was why I'd been ignoring his phone calls and texts.

And then I'd have to tell him to walk out of my life forever.

WAIL

Cici and I listened to Sawyer turn the keys in the lock, and I steeled myself for what was about to happen.

"Of course," I said half-jokingly, "I could drain him dry and never have this problem again."

Frowning, she pointed at my remaining glasses of blood. "Drink up," she said before floating away to give us privacy. They were empty before he even opened the door.

"Angel?" His voice was soft as if he was in front of me.

Squaring my shoulders and wiping my mouth with the back of my hand, I joined him in the foyer. He looked at me, taking in my more-erect-than-usual posture.

"You okay?" The kink in his eyebrow revealed his puzzlement.

I swallowed hard and recalled a few months ago, at my Mahá, how the family thought the Council was going to destroy me. When it looked like it was the end for me, I looked my family members in the eyes and told them it was okay, to be strong. I drew from that strength now; this was much more difficult.

How to convince Sawyer it was over when all I wanted was him? I had to lie.

"I'm sorry I've been uncommunicative lately." My tone sounded dry even to my own ears.

"Uncommunicative? Angel, you're avoiding me. I told you not to worry about the witchy incidents."

"It's not about that," I lied. "The truth is, this isn't working anymore. I've had a revelation. My reaction to Mom's sleep has devastated me. I don't want to go through that kind of pain ever again."

My head rose with determination, and I looked him square in the eye. My next words had to be clear, convincing, because there would be no second chance. To strengthen my resolve, I refused to really look into his eyes, refused to connect with the confusion there—the pain I wanted to soothe—and instead focused on the color of his eye, viewing it in a detached way as if viewing the leaf of a plant.

Detached. Unemotional. This became my mantra.

I took a deep breath in order to support the words about to come out of my mouth. "I can't be with you, Sawyer, because you're mortal."

He took a step back, knees buckling as if he'd just been slapped in the face. His eyes took on a pained look and the color drained from his face.

"What? What are you saying?" His voice was strained. "What do you mean?"

"Our relationship's unnatural."

He looked down at the floor, and I would've given my legs to know what he was thinking. Would've given anything to tell him that this was all a lie, that I really loved him more than anything, more than anyone, but that this was for his own good. That this had to be, because I loved him, and there was no other way.

But instead, I added some truth to the lie.

"Cici and I have to go. Back to Los Angeles. I'm going to spend the summer there. Work on the rest of the album in my home studio."

His angled jaw looked tight enough to slice through anything, including my heart. He visibly struggled to maintain his self-control. He knew that it was about the witchy incidents, and having one right now would only prove my point. I stood there like a lifeless statue, staring at him, watching every emotion that crossed his beautiful face.

All the while his heartbeat remained steady. He was winning the fight. I simultaneously rejoiced in his victory while relinquishing my right to do so.

Finally he raised his eyes from the floor. "So this is why you avoided me all day. You've been rehearsing this speech. I don't believe you."

There was no question to answer, so I said nothing. He surveyed my face, and his eyes flicked over my body, taking in my frozen stance. I could only imagine how we'd look to another person— two people standing motionless, facing each other, and both in acute pain.

"You're saying you don't want me." Again there was no question. But the point needed to be driven home; the effort of making him believe couldn't be half-assed.

"I don't want you, Sawyer." The words ripped me in two. It was like a knife hacking my solar plexus. I was lying to him. I hated myself for hurting him, so much that the anger turned the room red.

And Sawyer interpreted the red to mean that I really, truly, didn't want him. He looked at me, and his face held no more emotion, as if it'd been removed by an invisible eraser.

He stepped toward me then, and somehow I managed to continue standing. He stood right in front of me and looked down into my eyes, into my soul.

"Okay," he said in a voice that matched mine. Dead and emotionless. "If that's what you want. Okay."

The scent of him filled me again, and I bit my tongue to stop from begging him to stay. My mouth watered and I swallowed repeatedly, fighting to retain my cold façade.

He hesitated and took all of me in with his gaze. "You're only six months old." It was the last thing he said before he left. He closed the door gently, but the click sounded loud in my ears. Final. The sound of his footfalls grew fainter and fainter. He must have planned to walk home. Made sense since parking was such a pain in the neck. Both of our neighborhoods made it hard for residents to park easily on the street...

I was mentally babbling. Babbling about parking when my soul mate just left my life because I'd kicked him out. I'd lost my mind.

And then it sunk in. I'd just told Sawyer Creed that I didn't really love him.

The tears came then. Then the sobs. Then the wails. Long, extended wails that seemed drawn from somewhere beyond myself as if I'd tapped into the sorrow of the universe. I fell to the hardwood floor and continued to wail helplessly, like an infant.

Soon Cici, weeping and wailing, trudged to my side. She clutched her stomach as if my pain and heartache was replicated inside of her.

My wails had intensified to the point where they resembled loud,guttural singing. The wails, combined with the mind lock, ensured that Cici felt everything I felt at the moment, on top of the grief she already felt for Mom.

I was emotionally torturing my sister.

Angel, please. Stop. Please.

She put her hands on my arms and struggled to use her mind influence to press her calming effect on me. We stayed like that, on the floor together, for a long time, until slowly, eventually my wailing subsided.

RIDE

The only thing that could keep my mind off missing Sawyer was leaving Sawyer, therefore, I threw myself into the process of relocating to Los Angeles.

First thing was first; I had to call the girls. It was crucial that Jules and LaLa be with me in Los Angeles, or my plan would fail.

Through the years of building Kat Trio, they—unlike me—always had the support of their parents. Jules's mom and LaLa's parents stood behind them for every gig, every contest, every singing competition, just as long as they continued to do well in school. The girls had a great relationship with my family (even though they had no idea we were immortals) and for years had come over to our house for writing sessions, sleep-overs, and everything in between. Now that it was summer, we had a ton of work to do, and we'd managed to maintain a collective *A*-minus average. Not to mention the USAMA and Cassidy and Steve show. I couldn't think of a reason why their parents wouldn't let them come to my house.

"You'll have to lie," Cici said as she packed her suitcase. "Their parents would want our parents to be there. You'll have to tell them that Mom and Dad will be with us."

"Or I can say *you'll* be with us and Mom and Dad will be returning after visiting family in Egypt." Dishing out white lies rubbed me the wrong way, but Cici was probably right. The mortal parents would want parental supervision for their teenage girls. In any case, I'd have to play my cards right because if the girls couldn't go, there would need to be a Plan B…and that didn't exist.

Cici sighed in exasperation. Her dislike of airlines' baggage fees and the luggage grab after arrival drove her to create a suitcase spell—similar to what Kiya had used—that allowed her to literally throw everything she owned into one small carry-on. She'd thrown at least ten pairs of shoes into the suitcase as if it were a bottomless pit. "Honestly, if I didn't have all this baggage, and you could take the speed, I'd forget about the plane and just fly."

"How about we charter a plane?" I asked. We looked at each other for a few seconds of consideration before shaking our heads. I'd never known we could even such a thing until recently because our parents raised me to be as average as possible. The idea of a plane all to ourselves seemed too la-di-da.

I dialed Jules.

"Eee-yes," she answered in her typical quirky way.

"Jules, listen up. I'm going to spend the summer in L.A., and my family's inviting you and LaLa to join us at our place out there. We can get all our work done there, plus be close to the list of producers we need to work with. Whadaya think?"

"The whole summer?" she asked.

It hadn't occurred to me that Jules and LaLa might not want to spend the summer in another city, away from home. I swallowed before pushing out a furtive yes.

"OMG, Angel! A summer away from my mom? Hell, yeah! Oh, but gotta get permission first. Let me call you back." She quickly hung up. One down, one to go...

Moments later, I had LaLa on the line.

"I dunno, Angel," she said into the phone. "My dad might not be down with that. He hates it that I'm dating Fearmonger."

Fearmonger was the street rapper LaLa started seeing when her personality became warped due to my presence. She'd stayed in love with him, even after she returned to normal.

"And what about Sawyer?" she asked. "Aren't we going to spend the summer at his new place?"

She'd freak when she found out we were no longer a couple. Luckily the other line rang. It was Jules.

"Hold on, LaLa." I was relieved to avoid her question, at least for now. "Jules is on the other line." I clicked over to find Jules was already talking. "Slow down, Jules," I said.

"Yes, yes, yes!" she screeched into the phone. "Mom said yes! She said it'd be good for us to get out of Boston and get a lot of writing done. She's all for it!"

"Cool," I said, calmly praying this plot would work. "LaLa's on the other line. Let's hope her dad's okay with it, too. I'm going to click to three-way. Call me right back in case the call drops."

But it didn't drop. We heard LaLa talking to someone on the other end.

"Mom, you think Dad'd be okay with it?" LaLa said.

Pause while we could plainly hear her mom say, "He'd love anything to get you away from those gang members."

"Mom, they're rappers, not gang members."

"Same difference."

"Dang," Jules whispered on the other line.

"I know!" I whispered back.

"So is that a yes?" LaLa asked her mom.

"Wait till he gets home."

LaLa grumbled a mutter into the phone.

"Don't worry, LaLa," Jules said mischievously. "If you can't come, we'll just have to split all the writing credits between the two of us."

"Screw you, Julietta," LaLa muttered before hanging up.

Well, that didn't go very well.

"She didn't mean it," I lied to Jules. "But it's good you've got the green light. Let's hope it works out for La." We hung up.

I ran to the kitchen for some blood and sucked it down. Strangely, somewhere beyond my digestive system, where my heart, solar plexus, and stomach converge, there was an emptiness, a gnawing that the blood could not reach. I was technically full, but still felt empty.

Was this the way I was destined to feel now that Sawyer was no longer in my life? The phone rang again. Jules.

"Wait a minute," she said. "What about Sawyer?"

Deep breath…"We're not seeing each other anymore."

"WHAAAAAAT?"

"Tell you everything soon. Gotta go."

"But—"

I hung up, unable to have that conversation. What would it take for me to ever be ready to have it? Maybe at my own house, I'd feel stronger, able to talk rationally about one of the most insane things I'd ever done: breaking up with Sawyer Creed.

I stared at my cell phone, was mesmerized by it, before opening the Facebook app. The only good thing about the situation was FB friends didn't know how many times you looked at their page. If Sawyer knew how often I'd checked, I'd look like a straight stalker. Alas, he wasn't into social media, and his page looked the same as it did the last time I checked it—a half hour ago...

Angel. Cici summoned me out of my daydream. *We've got to get a move on. Our plane's leaving in eleven hours. At the rate you're going, we'll be late.*

Ha, ha, very funny. You're hilarious...

But she was right. My decision to focus solely on the move was the only way to deal with the topic of Sawyer. I continued to pack my suitcase.

# # #

After a long, uneventful flight to L.A. and a slow trudge through traffic past perfectly manicured people and southern Californian sprawl, Cici and I climbed out of the cab in front of my "house." With its Victorian-style turrets, it was clear the word "house" barely described the multi-bedroom mansion in front of us. I wondered what Jules and

LaLa would make of it. LaLa's dad had finally given his okay; they were due to arrive tomorrow. As far as they knew, my house was the family's new "west coast getaway."

Cici had designed the house, but since my Mahá, I'd been continually putting more of my own touches on it; the next thing to change would be the front door—it needed to be red like our front door in Beacon Hill. A pang of homesickness for Mom and Dad took over momentarily.

My sister dragged her suitcase up the steps to the door. Her spell was great in getting all the stuff inside of the case, but it didn't address how heavy it was when she wasn't wheeling it around. My own suitcase was light, without a spell, since it contained the few jeans, T-shirts, and sandals I wore all the time now that the weather was warming up.

Unlike Cici, I was not a fashion plate.

She gave me a sticky smile in response to the cattiness of my train of thought and chucked the keys at my head with lightning speed. I caught them easily and commenced guessing which was for the front door. Wrong. Was it this one...?

A couple of minutes later, we stepped inside.

"Okay, I'm sorry for thinking you are an over packing fashion plate."

"Whatever," she said trying to hide the fact that she cared.

The place was just how I remembered it from my Mahá. Sunlight streamed through the foyer's large window and illuminated the grand double staircase and its winding wrought-iron bannister.

"I gave Kiya basic instructions to get the place ready for us. But that was pretty much it. The details will come from you. Oh, by the way, she's doing us a favor. Her contract only covers properties owned by Mom and Dad. She did make sure the sub-freezer is packed with blood, but soon you're going to have to get your own housekeeper."

Great, I grumbled inwardly. Like I knew where to find someone to do that.

"Easy," Cici said as she dragged the suitcase down the hallway to the small service elevator. "Just call the L.A. office of B.O.R. And by the way, you're going to have to learn how to drive."

All I wanted was to get into the studio portion of the house and listen to the work tracks we'd just received from William Wilson.

And blood. Cici did say the freezer was full of it.

I found myself standing in the kitchen, located on the other side of the house, down the great hall to the right. I sang the word *"Saucony"* in the key of F.

At the sound of my voice, a portal opened in the wall to my right to reveal another part of the kitchen. Dad had implemented the spell that opened this secret part of the kitchen where the blood supply was stashed. He'd let me choose the word and the specific musical key that would serve as a literal key, and I'd chosen *Saucony* simply because it was such a ridiculous word there was no way I'd ever sing, or even say, it otherwise.

Walking into the magic portion of the kitchen was like walking into any part of the kitchen; the décor was the same. Cream-colored granite countertops and dark-brown cabinets. Certain items were duplicated, such as the refrigerator, sink, etc., so it almost felt like a mini kitchen. Light streamed through the windows in the same way but it lacked the double island found in the main kitchen. The result was a warm, cozy feeling.

The chest freezer was located in the magic kitchen's huge pantry. It was packed with nothing but piles of blood bags labeled with donor names, blood type, collection date, and other details. Jetting over to the stainless-steel refrigerator, I extracted a couple of pitchers of type A from a donor named Justin.

I nearly choked on the air.

My Justin? Nose to the pitcher, took a deep whiff...No, it definitely was someone else with the same name. My heartbeat returned to its normal pace, but for those brief seconds, the idea of drinking blood directly from my first donor nearly sent me over the edge. Hurriedly pouring into glasses located in a cabinet, I drank thirstily before taking a look at the glasses. Didn't like the design...would have to order some that seemed less like Mom's and Cici's style.

Cici walked in, her eyebrows raised in a questioning arch. "You okay?" She grabbed a glass and helped herself. "Your heart picked up like you were falling off a cliff."

I pointed to the pitcher's label.

"Oh," she said. For a second there was nothing but the sound of me draining another glass. Then..."You know there's a Los Angeles Nest?"

"Ciciiii…"

"I'm just saying…"

The doorbell rang. The sound of it reverberated through the house like a chime. Very old-fashioned—would need to change that too.

It was Markus Seymour, the Top 10 rapper who'd guested on "No. 8" and went by the moniker of Little Wolf. He held a bouquet of flowers and smiled a big, wolfy smile that displayed his canines to perfection.

"Angel Brown, what's going down?" he said as I opened the door.

"Markus Seymour, pleased to see yer." We giggled like idiots as we walked through the grand hallway to the kitchen.

"There's a werewolf in the house," Cici said before giving Markus a hug. He'd always had a big-sis soft spot for her from back in the days of our toddler playdates.

"Nice flowers," I said, searching for a vase as he took them out of the plastic.

"Housewarming gift," he said.

"Love gladiolas," Cici said.

"Girl, me, too," he answered in his best "gay guy" voice. Besides our families, no one knew that Markus, one of the most masculine rappers on the charts, was gay.

I arranged the flowers in the vase and placed it on the kitchen table. "You're just in time. I leave in a couple of days to tour Europe and Japan," he said. "We're going to have to do a night out on the town."

"Count me out," said Cici. "Got a hot date with a realtor." She levitated, floated out of the kitchen and left us alone.

"I don't know," I said, finishing the last of my lunch and checking out his ensemble. He wore an all-black outfit: fitted T-shirt, skinny jeans, and black Nikes. A chunky silver chain hung from his belt loop. "We're already getting blasted with work. I should start listening to tracks."

As soon as Nina learned we'd be in L.A. for the summer, she shared the news with all the West Coast producers we were slated to collaborate with. As a result, we already had a bunch of files in the inbox, along with invitations to various meetings.

The massive amount of work and obligations was just what was needed to keep my mind off the fact that Sawyer's absence from my life seemed to eclipse even Mom and Dad being gone.

Markus didn't look convinced. "Plus we need to talk," he said. "What's up with your boy?"

He and Sawyer had become friends; that was the only way he'd know anything was going on. "Ugh, must we talk about this?" I asked before belting out *"Saucony."* We watched the portal close and disappear back into the main kitchen.

"Whoa," he said. I sang *"Saucony"* again, and he watched, transfixed, as the portal reopened. He sang the word in a comical, deep baritone, as if he was doing a parody of a male opera singer. Nothing happened.

"It only works with my voice; live, not recorded; the exact notes; and in the right key." I closed the portal again.

He scratched his head, backtracking to his previous train of thought. "It's the proximity thing, isn't it? You started to get to him, too?"

Months ago, Markus was the one to clue me in to the fact that newborn presence affects mortals who spend a lot of time in close proximity. He was the only other immortal I knew who worked so closely with mortals. Our role as undercover immortals in the music industry was another thing that bound us.

"Yeah, I was getting to him." Looking down at the ground, I fought the tears starting to prick the backs of my eyes. "On top of that, Mom's asleep. It's been a few days now."

"Damn, Angel." He closed his eyes and took in the news, putting his fist up to his forehead for a few seconds before folding me in his wiry arms. "Your world's kind of shitty right now."

"Plus, I have to learn how to drive."

"It's okay to forget the studio today," he said.

"Okay," I relented, in full self-pity mode.

I grabbed a number of flasks of blood and my backpack before he led me out of the house, into the side drive where a red-and-black Ducati awaited. It was exactly like the motorcycle he kept in Boston.

"They're even more strict about the helmet rules out here on the left coast." He handed me a helmet. "It's just easier to wear it."

I struggled to fit all my hair into the helmet but failed. "Who the heck do they make these things for?" I grumbled while undoing my two French twists. Markus leaned against the bike and started texting. Soon my hair fell about my shoulders in waves, and the helmet slipped easily over my head. "Okay, ready," I said.

We climbed onto the bike and took off at what felt like sixty miles per hour from the first second. The power of the bike's engine rumbled through my body. What if we crashed? I opened my mouth to shout at Markus to slow down, but then realized it didn't matter. We were immortal. Even if we crashed and got injured, broke a few bones, lost some skin, it didn't matter. We would heal. And nothing would change. Mom would still be asleep, and Sawyer would still be an eternal memory.

"Faster!" I roared.

Markus's diaphragm jerked in and out under my hands as he laughed. "That's the Angel I know!" He let out a howl and revved us forward faster until we were flying down winding roads through the canyon. The sun and wind danced on my skin as we raced along the edges of the road, sheer rock-face on one side, steep drop-off into lush, green canyons on the other side.

And I laughed and howled, too.

We eventually arrived at his house. "Welcome to my place." He said it proudly and even a little shyly. It was pretty amazing to see this side of him when his public persona was the tough rap guy. "Tour?"

It was a low-slung bungalow-style, spacious and dark with lots of wood—massive ceiling beams; intricate molding; rich, dark cabinets in the library, game room, even in the bathrooms—and ironwork, stone flooring, and gothic details in the chandeliers and vaulted ceilings in the hallways.

Also, apparently he had a thing for birds. They were everywhere: in paintings, living ones in birdcages, stuffed birds. There was even a sculpture of a peacock.

Eventually the tour brought us to his home studio. There were a few people in there: two guys, who looked like they were mixing, and a couple of girls, one who looked like she was working and one who looked me up and down like she wanted to rip my head off.

The studio was next to the game room, a massive room featuring a wooden pool table and a few old-school arcade video games along with a couple of huge flat-screens. One wall of the game room was glass and overlooked the pool where a couple of people were lounging on the deck. Beyond that was a breathtaking view of hills and the gorgeous sunny day. We went out on the deck where electronica pumped from hidden speakers.

"What up?" Markus asked one of the bikini-clad girls.

"You, dude," one girl answered while the other one laughed and splashed water on him before she jumped into the pool. The aroma of their skin, hot in the sun and slathered with coconut-scented tanning oil, eclipsed the stunning view. The edges of my vision turned red as my shimshana stirred. I froze and closed my eyes.

*Angel...*Cici felt the force of my urge. I held my breath to stop the olfactory assault and felt my temperature come down.

Whew. That was close. I was about to fly over there.

No need, Cici. I've got this under control.

Markus, eyes on me as if he knew what'd just happened, spoke quickly in introduction as if to cover the fact that I was standing there probably looking weird. "This is Angel. Angel, Samantha and Niana."

"What's up?" we all said to each other. Markus, giving me a look as if to make sure I wouldn't eat his lady friends, started taking off his clothes.

Niana, the one in the water, rolled her eyes. "There *are* bathing suits in the cabana." She pointed at a small guesthouse on the other side of the huge deck. "Join us."

"Sure," I answered, watching Markus, now butt-naked and doing laps as if he didn't have a care in the world.

"Show-off," Samantha mumbled. Her eyes narrowed as they flowed from him to observe me. "Aren't you the lead singer of Kat Trio?"

"Yeah," I said, slightly taken aback that someone recognized me.

Niana gave a little yip from where she clung to the side of the pool. "Love your song! 'Number 8,' right?"

Nodding yes, I blurted an awkward thanks before making my way to the cabana.

After checking the scent in the air to make sure no one else was there, I locked the door and quickly drank my way through the flasks to ensure my ability to be surrounded by baking mortal flesh without attacking someone.

There was a bathroom and a dressing room with a built-in wardrobe. Sure enough, inside there were all types and sizes of bathing suits, all with tags and stickers in the crotches to prove they'd never been worn.

I chose a one-piece and looked for the size. As suspected, it was too big. Looking through the others, it became clear that all the one-pieces were in larger sizes.

Exasperated, I finally picked a lime-green bikini and put it on. It wasn't my style, a little too revealing, but, after looking in the full-length mirror, I had to admit it looked good on me. The padded top gave my *A*-cups a roundness never seen there.

Wow. I felt sexy. Grown.

And again, with this feeling of being a woman, was the realization that the way my parents raised me didn't necessarily have to be the way I lived. I thought about the older siblings' Trad point of view and about making my own decisions. There was nothing wrong with this sexy look; Mom would have hated it, but it wasn't that bad. Would Sawyer like this suit on me? What was he doing right this moment? Was he in his studio? Was he thinking of me? Fighting the urge to locate my smartphone and check his Facebook profile, I rapidly downed the last flask, secured the empty flasks in my backpack's hidden compartment, and made my way back out to the deck.

"Nice suit," Samantha said. She reached a tattooed hand into a cooler. "Beer, wine coolers, anything you like, it's all in here."

I'd never had any more than a glass of wine and never in public. Sawyer didn't drink; he wouldn't compromise his self-control, so the only drinks at his house were usually brought by the guests.

I chose a peach-flavored wine cooler and placed it on a lounge chair before jumping into the pool to do a few laps. I swam like a mortal but really wanted to try my hand at jetting through the water to test my speed. It was the first time I'd gone swimming since The Change.

Eventually I climbed out and made my way back to the lounge chair. Markus lifted himself out of the pool and walked over to a chair, grabbed a towel and shook his tall afro like a dog shakes its tail. He wrapped the towel around himself, secured it, grabbed a beer and stretched out on the lounger next to me.

"I've got a couple tracks if you want to take a listen later and let me know what you think. Maybe drop a vocal if you want."

"Cool," I said, "but we'd have to make sure it's okay with everybody before it goes anywhere." There was nothing in our contract that said I couldn't do solo work, but I didn't want to do anything that could compromise Kat Trio, or our trust for each other.

"Cool," he said before popping up and going into the house.

"Rolling with us tonight?" Niana asked as she toweled off.

I'd no idea what she was referring to, but I definitely wasn't going back home to be alone. "You bet," I answered.

"Cool," Samantha said with a smile. Niana handed her a tube of sunscreen before kissing her full on the mouth. Not knowing what to make of their PDA, I shrugged and took a swig of my wine cooler.

Eventually I made my way to the studio, where Markus was listening to a track with the others.

"Everyone, this is Angel," he announced as they introduced themselves. The staring girl, a werewolf named Testa, toned down the glare she'd dressed me with earlier. No doubt Markus had clued her in to who I was.

Since my Mahá, I'd gained a reputation in the immortal world as a powerful Shimshana. Somewhere between my voice's ability to kill and my time-stopping ability, most people, including at one point my older siblings (except for Cici), gave me a wide berth.

Or maybe Testa didn't know Markus didn't like girls. Either way I chose to ignore her and focus on the music.

The hypnotic beat seethed under lyrics delivered with a punchy counter flow. Blue-and-grape-colored notes bounced before my eyes. Oh, this was easy; I already had a countermelody in my head, and a few lyrics started bubbling to the surface of my consciousness. Markus's head bobbed; his eyes were closed.

The spicy-smelling producer, whose name was RT, invited me to the sound booth. I dropped a tough, sexy, four-bar vocal heard clearly in my head as if it were being played out loud along with the track. Testa's territorial stare followed me as I hugged Markus.

"Ignore her," he whispered rapidly in my ear. "She's a new wolf. Not an immortal; just bitten and turned. She doesn't know yet that you can rip her to shreds without touching her, but I told her she'd better watch her back." He smiled wickedly.

We settled in and listened to the track as RT, smelling of curry and cinnamon, worked to mix in the vocal. The second guy, Nick, and other girl, Liz, offered feedback and provided assistance. We continued to work it, with me going back in to tweak and add vocal layers, and Markus adding adlibs inspired by my layers.

Samantha and Niana sauntered in from the pool and started tongue-kissing and dancing. Nick cracked a giant grin. "Little Wolf and Angel," Niana said with a smile. "Can't wait to hear it on the radio!"

I threw a look at Markus as if to say *remember*, and he nodded as if to say *don't worry, this track isn't going anywhere,* before turning to RT and whispering to him to put a lock on the file so that no one else could access it.

We started winding down then. A glance through the wood-framed windows in the next room told me it was already evening. We'd been in the studio for hours.

I pulled Markus to the side. "Who's for dinner?"

"Don't worry," he said, pulling me away from the others and down the hall toward the kitchen. "You're all set." He reached into the refrigerator and pulled out a few slim bottles. "There's more. They can go in your backpack too. For later. Grab what you want and come upstairs." He took me to one of the bedrooms, past its en suite bathroom and into its wood-trimmed, walk-in closet. "I got some gear for you, just in case you want to change or crash." He held up a sleek-looking outfit. "Black leather good?"

"Fine with me," I said between gulps of dinner. Usually I couldn't care less about my clothing, but it would be nice to change into something else. "What are we doing anyway?"

"Riding. What else?" he said before leaving the room.

# # #

After returning from sushi with Samantha and the others, Markus and I left his house at 7:30ish. Thirst sated, I wore the leather gear—comfortable pants, a cute top, and cropped jacket. He gave me sunglasses that matched his, even though the sun was about to go down—more for his benefit so that he wouldn't get mobbed by autograph hounds and paparazzi.

We rolled leisurely on his silver Ninja down through the hills until we got to Sunset Boulevard and he started to gun the engine a little. Traffic on the boulevard was typical L.A.; we relaxed and chatted while rolling from one red light to the next.

Soon we were in front of a burger place where at least twenty racing bikes were parked along with a group of bikers.

Markus whispered in my ear as we rolled to a stop. "All weres, most immortal Trads."

One girl eagle-eyed me before shepherding her mohawk-wearing boyfriend's gaze in my direction. In a husky Mexican accent, she introduced herself as Storm, from the all-female biker group Pink Mist, while her boyfriend and Markus slapped hands. I looked around at some of the other bikers and was met with more open stares. I asked Markus if they were Kat Trio fans. Storm answered my inquiry. "We don't care what you do in the mortal world. It's our world that counts. And we know who you are." Her smile was full of glistening teeth. "You're danger. You belong with us."

"Let's call her that," her boyfriend, Shank, said with a smile. "Danger." The bikers who stared nodded in agreement.

They were different from the majority of immortals I'd run into since my Mahá. Instead of cringing away from me, they welcomed me into their group. It was nice to be surrounded by people who were acquainted with me, but not afraid of me.

Markus handed me a clove cigarette. After a brief pause, I took it, and he lit it for me.

"You're a bad influence, Markus Seymour."

"Now that's what I want to hear." His grin stretched expansively between his ears. "Live a little, Beacon Hill princess."

He howled, and the biker crowd response-howled as smoke from various types of cigarettes rose up to waft and hover briefly above our heads before being dissipated by the breeze sweeping the twilight sky.

Bikes continued to line up along the curb until the gleam from their collective chrome rivaled the glare from the streetlights and illuminated storefronts. Leather was everywhere. Rap music blared from the bike of a Japanese werewolf named Black Mayhem, while rock flowed from another, and dubstep blasted from a third. Mortals wanting to be a part of the action rolled up on their bikes, too, while locals gingerly waded through the frenetic energy on their way to dinner. Tourists attempted to blend in, even as they stood gawking at the Hollywood wildlife.

A cop in a cruiser slowed down to observe us.

"Roll out!"

As soon as the words were uttered, people jumped on their bikes. The collective revving sent a thrill though me. Thrash and his girlfriend She Fiend led the way as we rolled twenty-six deep through the city streets. We rode until we were on the highway and out of traffic, somewhere past Malibu, and that's when all heck broke loose. Bikes pressed and broke the speed limit, leaving the last mortal biker far behind with only the sliver of the new moon for company.

"Where are we going?" I yelled.

"North, way up PCH to the beach," Markus answered. "Thrash is a teleporter. Don't blink!"

With that, we shot through a portal at hyperspeed and were soon racing along pitch-black stretches of highway.

"This is where we get wild," Markus yelled before whipping off his helmet. I took mine off, too, and the 135-miles-per-hour rush of air took my hair out behind me like a banner. Howls reverberated through the green-tinged black of night and mixed with the rumble of revving engines and waves crashing against nearby rocks. I let the pain of Sawyer's absence penetrate my heart before adding my voice to the werewolves' howls.

We continued to race along the black stretch of highway, through the wooded hills, following the smell of the sea until we stopped at a state beach.

Folks started unpacking their bikes, setting up small tents, spreading blankets and unfolding portable chairs. One immortal worked to gather firewood into the fire pit. He ran top speed, disappearing into the darkness of the dunes only to reappear a few seconds later with kindling and branches harvested in the wooded areas of the nearby state park. After he did this a few times, there was a gargantuan mound of kindling and dead branches. Another immortal extended her hands toward the mound, and it ignited into a bright bonfire. Someone else clicked on an old-school boom box, and soon people were dancing. Yet another person passed out glow sticks and blinkers. Beer and alcohol were extracted from coolers, and soon everyone was drinking and having fun.

Everyone except me. Sitting on a large rock, I watched the action below and wondered what Sawyer was doing at that precise moment. Probably sleeping, as we were three hours ahead on the time zone map, and it was now pretty late. The black hole inside of me longed to lose itself in the surrounding darkness.

Markus ended my morose reverie by leaping up to join me. "Look at it this way." He took a sip of beer. "In only seventy years or so, he'll be dead."

"That still seems like a long time to me. It's been a few days, and I can't think of anything else."

"Once you're no longer newborn, time will take on a new feeling; trust me. You're still on mortal time."

"How does that get me through the week? Tonight? This moment?"

He shrugged. "Remember when we were babies? You wanted a toy I had and you'd do everything to get it, sometimes wail at the top of your lungs until I had no choice but to give it to you." He chucked my chin with his forefinger. "Even then, you dropped that toy as soon as you found another one."

"NAKED!" Someone bellowed the word from among the group dancing around the bonfire. Immediately people tore off their clothes, leaving nothing on except flashing body jewelry.

"What is it with werewolves and nudity?" I said. "Seriously?"

"Try it. It'll get your mind off your boy." Markus began removing his T-shirt.

He was right; the darkness and my frame of mind colluded to take away any shyness, and I immediately started to strip. Soon, with nothing between us and the sea air, we ran with the others toward the ocean and jumped in, hooting and hollering like…well, like animals.

Mom so would have hated this. The thought made me laugh aloud as I floated in the water, my hair fanning out all around me.

A guy waded through the water until he stood in front of me. "Scorpio," he said, holding out his hand. He wore a flashing, spiked collar. His shoulders were incredibly broad, and a strip of hair ran from the middle of his chest to a point below the surface of the water.

My temperature rose, and the darkness around me took on a reddish tinge. His smile and gorgeous dark eyes drew me in.

But he wasn't Sawyer. And I so wanted him to be. An intense hunger rose from my core.

"The water's warmer right here, where you are," Scorpio said in a low voice. His musky scent filled my nostrils, and my mouth started to water. My senses locked on to the beat of his heart; it was wildly accelerated. My shimshana started to vibrate. He extended both hands toward me. "Swim with me, Danger."

The hunger now burned in my throat like fire. I imagined draining Scorpio and then every other werewolf around me until they were nothing but hollow shells floating in the ocean. The water around me started to boil. I closed my burning eyes.

Angel! You're thinking of killing over thirty people. Remember who you are!

Even if Cici tried to fly here to save these people, she wouldn't be fast enough to save them all. They'd be ripped apart before she hit the ground. And how could she then stand against me. I was too powerful for her. She could never stop me without Dad's magic.

My eyes opened and zeroed in on Scorpio "Run." The words fought their way through my clenched teeth. "Before I eat you."

He looked at the boiling water for half a second and followed my advice, running toward the shore, howling and morphing into a wolf as he hit the sand. The others followed suit, until there was no one else in the water.

I walked rapidly out of the water, past the remaining weres around the fire, who seemed frozen as they stared at me. Judging from their fearful expressions, my skin was probably flaming red. Leaping back to the top of the rock and swiftly draining the flasks, I wiped my mouth with my arm as a single gray wolf made its way toward me from beyond the fire. It stopped about five feet away, where it sniffed the air and started to whine. Its animal scent was slightly familiar...

"Markus...?"

The wolf almost seemed to nod and continued to walk toward me. Then he shifted midstride. It *was* Markus. He sat next to me and grabbed his beer with a shaky hand. "Damn, girl. I've never seen a pack of wolves run from anything like that. They knew what they were doing when they named you Danger. You good now?"

"I'm no longer hungry," I said through gritted teeth. But the emptiness was still there. What was going to fill the hole in my heart?

Markus exhaled in relief, howled and yipped into the air and was answered by several howls.

Soon folks started returning to their human form, and the party picked up again as if nothing had happened.

"I told them you were okay now. That you'd fed." He nodded at Scorpio, one hundred feet away from us, naked and dancing in the firelight. He smiled and lifted a beer bottle in my direction. And that was that.

"Welcome to Los Angeles," Markus said, also lifting his bottle to me. Frowning, I clinked his bottle with a flask and downed the rest of its contents.

It was my first twenty-four hours in L.A. and already I'd sent a pack of thrill-seeking werewolves running for their lives. What was next?

LAST VIRGIN

"It's like your thirst for blood is overshadowed by your longing for Sawyer." Cici made the observation the next morning as we sat around the breakfast nook. She poured me a seventh glass of blood.

"Can't get full no matter what." I wiped my mouth with the back of my hand before Cici pointedly handed me a napkin. "There's a never-ending, heart-wrenching, ultra-annoying emptiness."

Around us a few rags cleaned the kitchen. Kiya was elsewhere in the house. Fifteen minutes earlier, I'd woken up in my sun-filled grand master suite and spent a few minutes on the balcony enjoying the ocean view in the distance before making my way downstairs.

"What do you think's causing the emptiness?" Cici asked.

I knew she didn't expect me to answer, knew it was a segue into something else. "I saw an article online," she continued. She was about to drop internet advice, and it was all I could do to stop from rolling my eyes. She started scrolling her laptop screen. "Here it is." She lifted up and floated toward me, something she was doing a lot of now that we were living in a house with really high ceilings. She placed the laptop in front of me. The headline read: "Top Eight Ways to Deal with a Breakup When You're Still in Love."

I simultaneously hated and was fascinated by these types of unsatisfying lists, and was drawn to them again and again for the most ridiculous advice. Resigned, I started reading number eight, the least popular.

"It says to surround myself with friends and family."

My tears started before I finished the sentence. My family, except for Cici, was gone, and my friends didn't even know I was immortal. She pushed a box of facial tissue toward me, and I loudly blew my nose.

"Maybe they're right." She knew I was referring to our siblings. "Maybe a Trad outlook would make things easier?"

"Here's a better idea." She whisked away the laptop. "You can learn to drive today."

"With what?" I asked tearfully.

Cici looked at me with that special eyebrow-raised expression that meant there was a surprise for me.

"No!" I felt a glimmer of joy. "You didn't get me a car, did you?"

"Well, it wasn't me. It came from Mom and Dad. They were going to surprise you with it…eventually."

Immediately, we were both crying at the thought of the love that went into the gift. We hugged each other for a long time, each getting the other's T-shirt wet with bloody tears before finally pulling apart.

"Okay," she said while trying to smooth my hair, which had turned into a fluffy pouf after last night's ocean swim and return ride. "Why don't we see who can shower and dress the fastest, and meet in the entryway?"

I was already racing up the stairs, but Cici made my efforts look slow. I ran into my room's en suite bathroom, jumped in the shower, and applied conditioner to my tangled tresses. Immortal or not, I still hated detangling my hair, especially now that it fell past my waist. I reached for a wide-tooth comb and started humming the partial ballad.

Soon my hair was detangled and shampooed with some diluted castile soap.

Still in the shower? Cici transmitted in a mocking tone.

This isn't even fair. I countered. *I have five times the amount of hair you do*

I know. Ha, ha.

I rinsed my hair, showered the rest of me and got out. At immortal speed, I banged out my usual go-to hairstyle—two French braids.

By the time I was dried and dressed, Cici was outside in the circular drive. For a couple of seconds, I marveled at the sound of the L.A. sunshine—much keener and higher-pitched than the Boston sunshine at this time of year—before following my sister to the garage. She hit a clicker, and the garage doors rose to reveal a silver Mercedes.

"Holy flippin' hot dog! This is my car?"

"Yes!" She nodded happily. "They know you like speed, so of course Mom warned you about buckling your seatbelt."

"Safety first!" We said it in unison, imitating the way Mom had said the phrase for years as we'd climb into the car. We both relished the memory of her for a few seconds. Then…

"Get behind the wheel," Cici said, climbing in on the passenger side and buckling her seat belt.

"Okay, okay!" For some weird reason, I was nervous.

"No need to be nervous," she said. "It won't take long."

Sinking into the soft, pink, leather bucket seat, I inhaled the new-car smell and ran my hands over the steering wheel, black dash, and driveshaft. I recalled every time I'd ridden shotgun in Sawyer's Audi, and thought of the way his elegant hands rested on the wheel while waiting at a red light.

"Stick shift," I murmured, noticing the key was in the ignition. "What now?"

"We're going to practice this without the car moving, at first. Look at the floor. There are three pedals. The one on the far left is the clutch, the middle one's the brake, and then the gas/accelerator's on the far right."

"Clutch, brake, gas; got it."

"Left foot on clutch, right foot on gas."

I placed my feet accordingly. "Okay."

"Right hand on stick."

Did that, too.

"Play around with the stick. Put it in the middle, fiddle it around. That's Neutral."

"Neutral. Got it."

"Look at the diagram on the stick. Follow it with your hand, pushing the stick to match. R is reverse, 1 is first gear, 2 is second, etc., up to the sixth gear."

Rapidly, I did as she said.

"Again," she commanded. "And again."

Did it over and over, faster and faster until it felt like second nature.

"Now what?"

"Take the right foot and roll it ball to heel onto the brake and back to the gas, over and over again until—"

I repeated the motion hundreds of times until it felt like breathing. "Next?" This was kind of fun.

"Buckle up." I dramatically rolled my eyes. Cici was the most careful (and painfully slow) driver; she'd taken Mom's "safety first" message overboard and never even went above the speed limit. "I'll ignore that judgmental thought, Ms. Wannabe Speedy. Now do as I say the moment I say. Put the stick in neutral. Turn the engine on. Press the clutch, put the stick in first gear while pressing the gas to get a smooth rev and let's go."

I did everything she said at the exact time she said. The car jerked forward and came to a stop.

"Stalled," she commented. "Try it again. This time press the gas a little quicker and deeper."

This time the car moved forward. I was driving!

"Now shift to second, while pressing the clutch down."

Did it. The car went a little faster.

"Steer. Away from the big palm tree."

"Oops." I got back on the driveway.

"Follow the circular drive. Go round and round. Try it in reverse."

I felt her taking in the single-minded set of my jaw and my almost white-knuckled grip on the wheel.

"You know," she said, "it might be a good idea to visit the L.A. Nest. Take the edge off. You were pretty close last night." She pointed ahead. "It's okay to let the stick go and use both hands to steer."

I took her suggestion. "I don't want to be in another situation with a blood-obsessed donor." I smoothly made the turn with one hand.

"You're going through the fire, Angel. Take it from me, someone who's been there. Once you kill someone, or in your case a group of people, you can never take it back."

"But I didn't kill anyone, did I?"

"Think you're ready for the road?" she asked significantly.

"The moral window is still open, you know. You don't need to worry about me falling through the pane."

Driving was easy. For a moment, it felt *too* easy, like the car would explode or do something unexpected. Once on the road, I gradually picked up speed and soon we were traveling in fourth gear at the speed limit as I worked out the rhythm of simultaneously checking the rearview mirrors, checking my blind spot, shifting gears and monitoring the road ahead of me.

"Just be careful, okay?"

I looked at her from the corner of my eye. "You talking about the hunger or the driving?"

She gave me an enigmatic look and fell silent as we merged into traffic on the highway.

"How do mortals do this?" I asked. "I'm doing three to four things simultaneously at any given time."

"True," she answered. "But what takes them weeks, just took you less than a half hour to learn. You've got it all figured out." Another enigmatic look.

My phone rang. "Okay, how do I answer the phone and keep doing all this?"

"You don't. Some problems can't be solved by immortality." She looked at my phone. "It's Julietta."

I shifted down to get off the freeway and onto a side street.

"What's up, Julietta? It's Cici. Angel's driving."

She listened to whatever Jules had to say. "Cool. I'll let her know. See you soon." She hung up. "She and LaLa are on their way from the airport."

By the time we arrived back through the house's side door, the girls, surrounded by their luggage, were at the front door, their faces struck with awe as they gazed around the grounds.

We ran to hug each other—including Cici—before we all grabbed bags and suitcases and stumbled into the house.

"Oh my God!" Jules's widened eyes took in the entranceway. "Did you guys hit the lottery? This house is like *what*!"

"Whoa," LaLa said. "We've made a few bills so far but dang."

"It's so good to see you guys," I blurted, desperate to change the subject. "It feels like we haven't seen each other for so long."

"Not since the last session at Sawyer's," LaLa said before looking at me as if she wasn't sure she should have said that.

There was an uncomfortable silence. In the darkest place in my mind, I basked in the combined aroma of my best friends: Jules's cinnamon-y scent and LaLa's honey scent. They were fresh blood, here, right in front of me—

Cici grabbed my arm and squeezed hard enough to crack bone. *They're your girls! Get a grip!*

"Maybe we won't mention Sawyer just now." Cici's tone was diplomatic as she put a sisterly arm around me. "Wanna tour?"

"Yes!" LaLa shot me an apologetic look.

I swallowed what felt like a few tears starting to collect in the back of my throat. I'd just enjoyed a mental image of draining my two best friends dry. Maybe there was no hope for me. I'd fallen through the moral window. I'd let myself down and was a disappointment to my family...

Earth to Angel Brown! This is way too emo, even for you. Cici squeezed my arm harder.

"Let's start on this floor and work our way up," I said, mentally shaking myself. "Just leave your stuff here."

We passed Kiya in the hallway. She smiled at the girls and went along her way, pretending to be a humble housekeeper as she polished the furniture with a rag that, for once, was actually in her hand.

Jules and LaLa exchanged incredulous looks that seemed to say *They have a housekeeper?* as Cici and I exchanged our own look.

She's had centuries to pass as a regular housekeeper, Cici transmitted.

She's good at it, I countered.

We took them through the game room, through the east hall, through the gallery and into what used to be the drawing room and reception hall. The latter came in handy for the hundreds of Mahá, guests, but now the huge reception hall served as a listening area and dance floor, and the large drawing room had been converted into a studio complete with three sound booths, plenty of space for shelves, racks of vinyl albums, and comfortable chairs and couches. Soundproofed walls were covered in black and gave the room a hushed, almost sacred feeling.

"OMG!" Jules screeched. "This is the most amazing studio ever!" She scooped small instruments out of a large box labeled PERCUSSION and shook and rattled them while LaLa strolled around the live room, sat at the pink grand piano and drummed out beats on the various drums.

The studio doors opened into the former reception hall, with the wall in between the two rooms serving as a literal partition of sound. Speakers of various sizes—ranging from basic consumer speakers to dancehall-power subwoofers—were built into the wall, and hooked into a wireless surround. Sectional, white leather sofas resting on Persian rugs were strategically placed at the end of the hall nearest to the studio to allow for a primo listening experience.

The reception hall had been transformed so completely that I gave it a nickname: The Club.

The Club also featured hardwood flooring and a mirrored wall perfect for dancing and rehearsing choreography. The entire east wall was lined with large windows and French doors, which overlooked and opened onto the massive terrace, which in turn led to various spaces outside, including gardens and a pool.

On a clear day you could see for miles—over the landscaped gardens and pool and out to the Pacific Ocean. Even though today was such a day, the view within the studio—of monitors, instruments, and microphones—hypnotized us into forgetting about the rest of the tour. Cici excused herself as our conversation turned to industry speak and focused on the recording hardware and software.

"Moog, Yamaha, and Roland." LaLa's tone made me think of chocolate addicts talking about hot fudge. She shot me a look of admiration. "Good job, Angel."

We lounged on the studio's roomy red leather couches. "Steve Pile designed the space," I said. The couch's wide arm served as a pillow as I lay on my back, staring up at the soundproofed ceiling. Pile's name was known in the industry for designing home studio spaces for some of the industry's biggest names. "It's also set up for postproduction," I added.

"Very smart," LaLa said from her prone position on the opposite couch. "And you can rent this place out the way Sawyer rents his out."

Jules popped up from the third couch, turned onto her side to face me and rested her head on her fist. They both remained silent and motionless, waiting for me to fill the empty space with some sort of explanation.

And it was only right. There was no way we could talk business or just be normal without mentioning Sawyer's name. I couldn't possibly expect them to tiptoe around the subject, at least not without an explanation.

Still focusing my eyes on the ceiling, I let out a tortured sigh while steeling myself to say the unsayable.

"Snacks?" It was Cici entering the studio, carrying a tray full of snacks, water, and hot tea.

And it's time for blood for you. Drink a ton before you start explaining. There's a connection between your Sawyer thoughts and your I'm-going-to-kill-everybody-around-me thoughts.

The girls thanked her and, for a moment, it was like old times, back at our Beacon Hill home when they would come over for writing sessions. Mom, and sometimes Cici, would bring things for us to eat and drink as we worked so that we could stay in the flow of writing.

"Bathroom," I said, excusing myself before walking through the formal dining room and into the kitchen. Kiya was setting out multiple glasses for me, and I proceeded to drink them down, one after the other.

"You are very much your mother's daughter," she said to me in a fond tone. "I clearly remember her newborn period. You remind me of her."

"How?"

"You are both very strong."

Funny, I didn't feel very strong. I regarded her again. She'd known Mom for most of her life. Longer than any of us, even Dad. Now that I understood, I regretted thinking of her as annoying when she acted in a motherly way toward us earlier.

"Please stay with me," I said to her. "Stay here. There's plenty of room."

"I am bound to your mother's service by blood. I cannot serve another master. There are many properties to attend, so I travel near and far. But you are her youngest, and I will make sure your needs are fulfilled until you find permanent help. If I am not here, my assistant Sarah will be."

"Thank you, Kiya." I downed the last glass and dashed back to the dining room, where I began walking at a mortal pace back to the studio. I'd been gone for less than three minutes.

"So you were saying..." Jules prompted as soon as I sat back down.

LaLa's facial expression was expectant, too.

"Sawyer and I broke up." There; I said it. They both stared at me as if they wanted to hear more. "The music got in the way." An outright lie, but they knew nothing of my immortal world, so what else could I say?

Jules looked dumbfounded. "You two were...I don't know. Perfect."

I swallowed a lump and bit my inner lip to stop myself from screaming. How was I going to get through this conversation?

Maybe you need to have this conversation in order to move on, Cici transmitted. As usual, she was right.

"It's been a few days, and I can't stop thinking about him," I said. "I fight the urge to check his profile pages to see what he's doing and keep looking at my phone, hoping to see a text or call or something."

I stopped, not knowing how much more to say.

"I can relate," LaLa said. "I broke up with Fearmonger and went through the same thing. I ended up on Facebook, stalking him like I was mental."

Jules nodded her head in agreement before chiming in. "Oh, yeah. I found out a guy was cheating on his girlfriend with me when she tagged him on Facebook."

LaLa and I just stared at her, horrified.

"Has Sawyer called you?" LaLa asked me.

"Did you break it off?" Jules asked. "Are you seeing anyone else?"

"No," I said to LaLa. Turning to Jules, I said, "Yes. Seriously?"

"They just broke up," LaLa said to Jules in admonishment. "She's still going through the closure. They were in love."

"I'm just saying, sometimes the best way to get over a guy is to get a new one." Julietta crossed her legs. She was noticeably thinner, and I wondered what crazy diet she was on now. "That goes for you, too," she directed at LaLa.

"Oh, I'm good. Fearmonger and me are back together. And we did it."

"NO!" Shocked exclamations from both me and Jules.

Fearmonger was an eighteen-year-old rapper LaLa had met through Markus while we were recording "No. 8" months ago. He had a street-tough veneer, but LaLa said it was all an act. We'd never seen otherwise. But LaLa quickly went from never having a guy to being in a serious relationship.

"All the way!" I asked. My voice felt tight in my throat.

LaLa nodded with a little smile. "Yeah. At his place."

My mouth hung open. This news came as a shock, and I wasn't sure why; all I knew was that I was the last virgin.

"How was it?" I was dying to know.

"I thought with my first time, the sky would crack open or something earth-shattering like that. But the more we do it, the better it gets."

Jules's and my eyes met with looks of sheer amazement. There was a time when both of us thought LaLa didn't even like guys!

"Was Fearmonger a virgin, too?" Jules leaned forward, hanging on every word.

"No. He'd had one girlfriend before. They were together since they were both fifteen, and he thought they'd get married, but she left him for some actor dude right before I met him."

"What about Sawyer?" Jules asked, still leaning forward. "Was it good with him?"

"We um…never did it." My voice sounded flat as I tried not to think about the way it felt to be in his arms and the beautiful music that played in the air around us when our lips met.

LaLa and Jules looked at me as if I was developmentally disabled.

"My parents hate that I'm dating a rapper," LaLa eventually said, watching my face. "But they like the fact that he's been helping me with the 'Get Out Of Here' money. He's got investments, and he tells me the best thing to do with the money once it really starts rolling in is to put it away and then, when I get older, invest it."

"I've invested my money," Jules said, "in Jimmy Choo." She flashed her strappy, expensive sandals. "Well at least the money mom lets me spend," she admitted.

Jules had been on a shopping binge ever since royalties started rolling in. Not only was she thinner, but she was also manicured, pedicured and decked out in long hair extensions. Julietta was a good and loyal friend, but sometimes her insecurities got the best of her.

"You still talking to that label guy?" I asked.

"Yeah." She twirled an extension around her finger. "But he just bought a loft in Manhattan and spends a lot of time there working with new artists. Haven't seen him for a few weeks."

"Weren't you sleeping with him?" LaLa asked.

"Once, but then he got so busy with the New York business and whatnot."

LaLa and I could only stare at Jules. Neither one of us could say what we were thinking, that Jules had gotten dumped by a guy who just wanted sex. When was she going to learn?

"Whatever happened with Raj?" LaLa asked her. "He was really into you."

Raj was House Quake's A&R Director—a Londoner with a nose for talent and a love for 90s American hip-hop. They'd dated briefly before Jules dumped him when he got too serious.

"Nah," Jules said, scrunching up her face. "But I might go out with Robert Phillips. If we meet."

"The dude in the boy band?" I said incredulously. "You think he's hot?"

"Smo. King," Jules said, before we broke into giggles.

"Not as hot as Mister," LaLa said with a grin.

"Up in the club!" We all sang the words in a low register while striking poses, mocking his delivery of the line in his Top 10 rap song until we literally collapsed laughing.

"Angel," LaLa said once she'd regained her breath. "If you could be with anybody, any of these hot guys from music or TV or anything, who'd you be with?"

I thought about all the industry dudes, and my mind combed over every one we'd met over the past few months. But only one came to mind.

"Sawyer Creed."

LaLa and Jules looked at each other in confusion. "I thought you'd say Little Wolf," Jules said.

This caused us to all break into more gales of giggling.

And as I watched them peel with laughter, I marveled. I could actually say Sawyer's name now without boiling, raging, or weeping.

Cici was right. Now that my girls were here, it felt like a weight had lifted off of my chest. But the emptiness was still there. I'd just managed to shove it down enough to allow me to breathe.

"You've definitely gotten stranger, Angel." LaLa's giggles continued.

"Love you, too," I said before turning to the sound board.

BLANK CANVAS

It was time for Kat Trio to get to work. Once the girls threw their stuff into their rooms and made their way back downstairs, we started preparing to work on the producers' tracks.

The doorbell rang.

Let Kiya answer it. Smells like Markus. He's probably just ringing the bell for the benefit of the mortals in the house. I hadn't seen him since last night when he brought me home after the werewolf beach debacle.

"Damn, Angel." He prowled around minutes later, checking out the setup. "This studio's dope. Sweet Moog synth. You and your boy chose all this?"

I nodded mutely and looked down at the board from my seat at the console. Not only had Sawyer helped me decide on equipment and layout, he'd also started teaching me how to produce. Just watching him work was an education, and he'd taught me about the sounds and feelings certain types of equipment could evoke. I slid knobs up and down to hide the fact I was fighting back tears. At least I wasn't trying to kill anybody, I reasoned with self-pity. I was making emotional progress…

"Angel," Jules said. "Where's your mom and dad?"

Tongue-tied, I threw a surreptitious glance at Markus.

"They still visiting relatives?" he asked smoothly, covering for me.

"Yeah. In Egypt."

Jules and LaLa looked at each other momentarily.

"Everything okay?" LaLa asked.

"Someone's sick." I kept fiddling with the knobs. "In Mom's family." I hated lying to my friends.

"I'm sorry to hear that," Lala said, "but what should I tell my dad? If he knew your parents weren't here, he'd have me on the first plane home."

"They're coming back soon, right?" Jules asked.

"Not sure," I said. "In the meantime, they left Cici in charge since she's over twenty-one." At least that was the truth.

"Angel," Lala's tone was resolute, "you lied to your parents for over a year so we could do shows. Shows that eventually got us signed. It's my turn to cover for us. I'm supposed to call or Skype every day, but I won't say a word. Dad's not gonna know."

"Same here," Jules said, "although I think my mom would be cool as long as Cici's here."

We all exchanged a Kat Trio hug as Markus gave a thumbs-up.

"I'm so relieved," I said. "We've got a lot on our plate."

"Yeah," LaLa agreed. "We got a gig on the Cassidy and Steve Show."

"Stevidy," Markus said. "Sweet."

"We've gotta work out a routine," Jules added.

"It's gotta be simple, tight for the camera," I said.

"We can pare Redd's routine down," LaLa said, referring to our choreographer back in Boston. "Or maybe we should come up with something new?"

"I think we should focus on the song delivery and keep moves to a minimum," I said. "More about connecting with the audience and less about putting on a big show."

"True," Jules said. "It's the small screen; we should keep it simple."

"Agreed," LaLa said. "For USAMA, too. Something fresh."

"Yeah," Jules said, sipping tea and lemon. I assumed she was skipping the honey to save on calories. "We want to come in with a bang that's gonna help us stand out."

"Doing half a song between two big names?" Lala said. "We definitely need to bang."

"We should work with Redd on that ASAP," I said.

LaLa nodded. "They need to send him out here." We all nodded in agreement as I picked up my phone and opened the e-mail app.

"We also gotta work with wardrobe for USAMA," Jules said. "We need a look that'll blow people away. Hair, too." LaLa and I agreed. I compiled all our requests into an e-mail and sent it off to Nina.

"Okay," I said, putting the phone on vibrate and down on the console next to me where it could be seen flashing if I got a text or e-mail, but ignored if it started vibrating with a phone call. "So, we've got these tracks from Haz Bro, Lick A. Shot, EyeHeart Beatz, and William Wilson."

Jules and LaLa glanced at each other before simultaneously breaking out into a giggling fit.

"Producer names!" Lala fought for breath and slapped her thigh. "Sound stupider. All together."

She had a point, but I found it only slightly amusing. Jules took one look at my straight face and, between renewed howls of laughter, clutched her stomach with one hand and fanned herself with the other. Once they calmed down, I playfully rolled my eyes and continued.

"So…I've taken a listen and think we have some really interesting contrast with what we worked on with…um…Sawyer." I swallowed and moved on. "Ready to listen now?"

"Most definitely," LaLa said with a look that said she was proud of the fact I was able to handle saying Sawyer's name and stay on subject. "I think you're right. That William Wilson track's sick."

"The first Haz Bro track took a while for me to warm up to," Jules said, "but now it's my favorite."

"Really?" LaLa seemed amazed. "I fell asleep on that one."

"I wasn't crazy about it, either," I added, "but I'm interested in what you hear, Jules. Let's play that one first. Markus, tell us what you think."

He gave us a distracted thumbs up from the couch where he was texting.

Soon we were knee-deep in the track titled "Riot." Haz Bro was an eclectic guy whose background included punk and rock influences. As a result, his tracks had a jittery edge that was barely contained in a mainstream pop framework. As the track played, Jules sang some lyrics she'd come up with.

"Smooth," Markus said. "I hear what you mean." Jules visibly swelled.

"I like what you're doing, too," LaLa said, rolling her eyes at Jules's obvious crush on Markus. "But I don't hear anything coming up for me with this one."

"Same here," I agreed. "Just empty, blank canvas for me. Let's record the vocal, though, and incorporate it. If we think about it for a while, we might come up with something."

"Cool," Jules said before entering the sound booth.

I tested the sound of the mic through the sound board as she sang so I could establish sound levels. "Nice mic," she said, taking a deep whiff of it. "Smells like new microphone," she said in her over-the-top radio announcer voice. Amid the all-around laughter, I gave her the hand signal countdown before hitting the record button.

"Surprised you're not feeling that track more," LaLa said to me. She'd been scribbling a few lyrics as Jules sang but stopped as she, too, seemed to hit a wall. "It reminds me of you these days. Edgy, about to explode, but keeping it presentable."

"Got me all figured out, huh?" My tone was playful, but inside I was reeling. LaLa's insight was so on point it was like she'd read my mind. In fact, she'd put into words what I'd been feeling for the past few days. It did feel like I was about to pop. But with what, I didn't know.

We spent hours working. Listening to tracks from the various producers, reaching a consensus, throwing down vocal ideas, recording on the studio equipment and scribbling lyrics and/or singing into recording apps on our phones. Writing in the studio felt amazing. Every now and again, we'd exchange looks with one another, sharing the joy and happiness that comes from writing and creating. The fact that we could do this in my house was a bonus the girls didn't know about, but a friendly wink from Markus let me know he related to my sense of pride.

Eventually, he got up to leave. "Thanks for letting me sit in. I'm down to do some more work with you ladies."

He shot me a glance as if to remind me about the rough track we'd thrown together at his place. "Yeah, yeah, yeah," I said out loud, answering both his statement and unspoken reminder. I got up to walk him to the door.

"I've got a lot of running around to do before I leave tomorrow. See you when I get back?" he asked.

The girls exchanged glances with each other as we hugged him good-bye. Apparently they were convinced he was going to replace Sawyer, no matter how much I denied it.

He added fuel to the fire by putting his arm around my shoulders and whispering in my ear. "By the way, you'll need an assistant to run errands for you guys while you work. I suggest you get an immortal, someone who'll understand your needs."

"Good looking out." I made a mental note to contact my music attorney, Terry White.

"Keep writing," he said to me. "I'll see myself out."

I quickly texted Terry before running to the kitchen to chug some blood. On the way back to the studio, I heard my cell phone ring and automatically zoomed through the walls to answer it. Coming to my senses, I forced myself to walk and move like a mortal all the way back to the studio. By the time I'd gotten there, the call had gone to voice mail.

"Phone rang," LaLa said from where she was perched at the sound board, experimenting with a couple of features I'd shown them earlier.

The missed call was from Nina. I hit the Call Back button. "Hi, Angel," she said on pickup. "Put me on speakerphone, please."

"Nina," I announced before pressing the speaker button.

"Girls, I got your e-mail," Nina said. "I'll be sending Redd and Risa for prep." I nodded with secret satisfaction. A few months ago, I'd almost attacked Risa, the wardrobe stylist, when she tried to bite Sawyer at the Boston Nest. I forgave her because she didn't know I liked Sawyer, or that I was Shimshana. And since I didn't know she was a vampire, we were even. Nina continued. "And I have an assignment for you."

Assignment? The girls and I looked at each other with questioning eyebrows.

"Tonight," she continued, "there's a get-together in Studio City for Mo Mojo's upcoming album. There'll be a lot of record execs there, including James Hovena. Get to know as many of them as you can. Be sweet and all that."

"Um…why?" Jules asked.

"Backup. Everything's good with House Quake now, but you can never have enough friends in this industry. Things go wrong down the line, and you have someone else you can sign with. Look girl-next-door; sexy, not slutty."

I bit my lip, wondering if the last part of that instruction was geared toward Jules. She'd always had a tendency toward dressing a little provocatively, but lately she was looking like something out of a magazine—the ones that sell street clothes that somehow manage to look like lingerie.

"There'll be a car coming around to pick you up at nine o'clock p.m.," she continued. "Let me know if you have any issues."

She hung up and we all looked at each other. That was one of the weirdest conversations we'd ever had with Nina. The doorbell rang us out of our quandaries.

After a few minutes, Kiya led a guy about our age into the studio. "Ms. Brown," she said, keeping up the pretense of formality. "This young man says he was sent here by Terry White as an assistant."

"Yes, that's right. Thanks, Kiya," I said, pleased with the speed of the immortal world in general.

"Warren Miller," he said in a firm, quiet voice. He shook my hand. "I'm Terry's nephew."

He was unlike any of the other assistants we'd worked with in other studios, all hopefuls who wanted to be producers, writers, or music industry bigwigs. There was nothing bling-y about him. He wore open-toe sandals, glasses, and a tie-dye T-shirt. After intros, he immediately started taking notes as we got back into the swing of things.

Someone, either Terry or Kiya, must have told Warren I was a newborn Shimshana, because he quickly came up with a great way to make sure I could sip on blood without leaving the studio. He designated covered cups for all of us. Since the girls were both drinking tea, this worked. Simple, yet effective.

Soon the sun was setting, and the girls were hungry. We decided to call it a day, and they helped themselves to whatever mortal food Kiya had stocked in the fridge. Thanks to Warren, I was well fed.

"Want to go to the industry thing tonight?" I asked him. He was gathering his notes from our session and stacking them into a neat pile.

"No, thanks. I'm not really into the party scene," he said with a shy smile.

"What are you into, then?" I asked. Bold, but I wanted to get an idea of who he was.

"Not sure," he said. "I once thought I'd have my own label someday, but I hate the music industry. My Mahá was six years ago. Uncle Terry thinks I just need to figure things out. Anyway, tomorrow morning?"

"Yeah, come at nine."

He left, and I wandered up a back staircase to my room. For a few minutes I watched the last of the glorious sunset and marveled at the beauty of the sky flushed with glowing salmon and deep orange. I wished that Sawyer was there to witness it with me and, for the millionth time, wondered what he was doing. Squishing the urge to stalk his Twitter feed, I walked into the suite's gigantic walk-in closet. It'd been perfect for the frequent Mahá clothing changes but, since then, Mom had put the gowns and ceremonial outfits in storage. Nevertheless, many of the everyday clothes remained the way Cici had organized them, by color and function.

The closet had so much space—too much to be filled by my simple wardrobe needs—that I had a piano brought in. It was a cute 1950s baby grand, reconditioned and featuring rare ivory keys. Its light mahogany-stain finish complimented the wooden molding and carved details throughout the closet, particularly the floor-to-ceiling shoe rack. Along with the wall of shoes, the piano sat in the darkest part of the closet, farthest from the windows.

My immortal eyesight saw the piano clearly despite the growing darkness and, thinking of the ballad and how there were one or two parts still missing, I stared at it longingly. Maybe after this party, when I was alone in my room, I'd work it out on this grand. I smiled in anticipation before turning back to the matter at hand.

I drifted over to the dresses and allowed my fingers to caress the various fabrics. What to wear to this industry thing? I didn't know, but I was determined to figure it out on my own. All my life, Cici had made fashion decisions for me; now I

wanted to see if I could do it myself and pick an
outfit suited for an industry event.

My fingers paused on a silk dress that was a
dusty-pink color and my mind recalled picking the
fabric out with Mom for my Mahá. It was delicate
and shimmering with fine, gold threads throughout.
The style was Cute Cocktail—strappy and above
the knees. I pulled it out and hung it on a big hook
that extended from the wall.

Now I'd have to figure out shoes to go with it. I
turned a one eighty in order to walk back toward the
wall of shoes.

I nearly had a heart attack.

A woman sat on the piano bench and stared at
me. I didn't recognize her face, but I recalled her
unforgettable smile: a slanted opening that revealed
sparkling teeth and a signature abnormality—her
upper lip looked somehow partially stuck to her
front teeth.

Her strange smile stretched out fully as her
eyes met mine and glowed with a subtle, but warm
light that was unnaturally bright in the shadows at
the end of the closet.

Yes, I knew her. She was the fallen angel who
was the primogenitor of our family line. She was
our great mother.

I fell to my knees. "Star," I said in hushed awe.

SKY HIGH

"I am concerned." Star's voice resounded like holiday bells. She stood up and moved out of the darkness toward me. As she did, her body grew less transparent until it was completely opaque. The planes of her face continued to shift—sometimes she resembled known female family members and at other moments she looked like strangers who share various family features.

At one point she looked exactly like Mom.

That I would run into her in my closet, after all this time, was apropos. For my entire mortal life, she'd appeared to me as my own reflection, but only when I was alone. I had no idea she was an Ancient One until after The Change, when she revealed who she truly was. Nevertheless, there was a part of Star that would forever be part of my subconscious. Not even Cici knew of Star's presence in my life. Angels have the ability to cloak themselves so as not to be seen by telepaths. The only person who knew about my interaction with Star was Justin, whose immortality was a direct result of my run-in with the archangel Bodiel.

Aside from the initial shock of seeing her when I turned around, I was comfortable in her presence.

"You feel separation," she continued. "It is an illusion."

I was astonished by her remark. Didn't she know what was going on? "Mom's asleep. Dad's gone. And…Sawyer. I sent him away."

"They are not here, but they are not gone." She stood directly in front of me now, and my tears flowed. "There is no separation in love." Her voice now rang in my head, precisely between my ears and the middle of my forehead. "Focus on love."

Mr. C. told me something similar when he taught me how to sing without destroying things or killing people.

"Yes," she said, acknowledging my thought. "You know the sound of love. Sing it for me now."

I immediately opened my mouth to create the sound; it was a shimmery, pink note, which floated and bounced like a bubble. Star closed her eyes and sighed like I imagined a land-locked fish would upon being reintroduced to water.

As I sang, it occurred to me that the ballad would sound better with the introduction of this note.

"The song of love will be your light in the darkness," she said. "Remember."

And then she was gone. I stopped singing and blinked several times, feeling as if I'd just woken up from an intense dream. Again I looked longingly at the grand, both hoping for more time with Star and realizing I needed to work that pink note into the ballad as soon as possible.

I hurriedly showered and dressed before brushing my hair into an updo, twisted and pinned with many rhinestone-studded hairpins so that it formed a soft, elegant frame around my head. Kind of like a halo, I thought giddily, still reeling from the close proximity of Star. I chose a pair of shimmery shooties that echoed the effervescence of the dress, and found a clutch big enough for my smartphone.

But the clutch wasn't big enough for a thermos or flask. I zoomed down to the kitchen and downed a gallon of dinner. My stomach soon felt full, but there was that constant emptiness at the edge of it. I decided to follow Star's advice and imagined the ballad and the sound of love filling me. I felt a sweet sense of peace and smiled, ready to face whatever the night brought.

Cocking my head, I heard Cici and the girls talking in LaLa's room.

"This sucks," LaLa said, exasperated.

"What sucks?" I asked from the doorway. Everyone, including Cici, gawked at me as if I was a cartoon character come to life.

I always knew there was a fashionista being held prisoner inside of you, Cici transmitted with a proud smile. *Now she's free.*

Let's not get crazy now, I responded, smiling back at her.

Jules wore a turquoise-blue sheath that hugged her body like a glove. Jimmy Choo shoes and a cool Lucite clutch completed the ensemble. "Wow, you look amazing," she said. "Love, love, love that dress!"

LaLa pouted. "Angel, help. I have nothing to wear. Get me to look as good as you guys."

We all went through the suitcase and the clothes she'd hung up so far in the closet. She was right; she had absolutely nothing to wear. LaLa was taller than me and Jules, and would never fit into either of our clothes.

"I have an idea," Cici said as she ran at mortal speed to her suite down the hall. As we waited, and

I felt my sister's excitement of having at least one person to dress, we combed through LaLa's shoes. There was one pair of black high-heeled sandals, which Nina had made LaLa buy for business meetings and the like. Those would have to do.

"We're going to have to take you shopping," Jules told LaLa.

"I'm with Jules on this," I said. "This is sad." In retaliation, LaLa whip-snapped me on the shoulder with a bra.

Cici returned with an armful of clothes. She handed LaLa a pair of skinny, white jeans. LaLa was slim, too, but had a little more happening in the thigh area, so we all held our collective breath as she dipped into the guest bathroom and tried them on. Soon she walked out in what looked like painted-on jeans.

"So far, so good," Cici said. I nodded in approval. Cici and Jules rummaged through the tops and simultaneously chose the same one: a glimmering, white halter with lace and rhinestones.

We all exclaimed with approval when she exited the bathroom again. "Very sexy," Jules said, high-fiving us.

"How do you feel?" I asked LaLa.

She looked in the full-length mirror and surveyed the way the jeans fit like a second skin and how the top complimented her slim, athletic torso. A slow smile lit her face. "Not sure I can sit down, but I like it."

LaLa, the tomboy who collected baseball caps, stood before us now, looking like a superstar.

We hugged each other in congratulations and clicked selfies of the three of us as we oohed and aahed over our looks.

Don't stay out too late, Cici transmitted. *Too risky without backup food.* "I'd come, too," she said out loud as she handed LaLa a slim, black belt and patent-leather clutch to go with the black shoes, "but Satch and I have plans." She waved good-bye as the black car pulled out of our circular drive and made its way into the night.

Once we made it through the Valley's tangle of Saturday-night traffic along Ventura Boulevard, and drove up a dark, winding hill, we pulled into a long driveway that led to a huge house. The beautifully lit house was ultramodern—all angles, glass, and concrete—and we could see the partygoers through the floor-to-ceiling windows that wrapped around one entire side.

We looked at each other, all of us at a loss. We didn't know anybody here and were unsure what to do.

A woman exited the house and hurried toward us, or at least as fast as she could in her heels. She took careful steps in the knees-bent way of women wearing heels too high for them to actually walk in as she navigated her way across the gravel-covered driveway. Her many layers of makeup were applied so haphazardly I got the impression she'd started applying it sometime yesterday, fell asleep and resumed today in the last few minutes before the party. Her black leather dress had cutouts that left little to the imagination and accentuated the orange tint of her tan. Her face looked weird, as if the skin was somehow stretched over her facial bones wrong, and her big hair was an unnatural shade of blonde.

"You must be Kat Trio," she said when she finally reached us. We confirmed our identity and each shook her hand. "I'm Crystal, your chaperone for the night."

I'd always pictured chaperones as older adults who had an air of responsibility, but Crystal had none of that.

"She looks like she started partying back in the 80s," Jules whispered.

"That's not nice," LaLa said, stifling a chuckle.

Crystal led us into the house. "Jimmy's around here somewhere. He's so glad you're here." Our heads swiveled from left to right as she led us through the front room. People stood around with drinks in their hands, somehow managing to talk and thoroughly check us out simultaneously. Some nodded their heads in greeting, but most turned back to whatever conversation they were having that wasn't interesting enough to hold their attention in the first place.

She led us to another room, where there were more people sitting around on couches. The music was blasting. Black granite and frosted glass were everywhere. Actors we recognized lounged on the modern furniture.

We absorbed our surroundings in the way Nina had trained us: don't stare and don't approach anybody famous unless introduced to them, so you don't come off looking dorky.

"There he is," Crystal said with an extra big smile. A petite, round guy in black jeans and a white shirt got up from his perch on the edge of a leather couch and extended his arms to us.

"Kat Trio," he said with a big, friendly smile, hugging us briefly in turn as we gave him our names. "I'm Jimmy. I help run a little label called DCA."

The girls and I exchanged surprised glances. DCA was hardly a little label. It was a huge major, one of the largest, with a number of imprints.

"Ah, Angel." His voice was cool, but his heartbeat picked up a bit. "The voice of Kat Trio." I shot an uncomfortable look at my girls and decided to correct him.

"Actually, Jimmy, we're all the voice of Kat Trio."

"Of course. I meant you're the lead singer." Same big smile. Same accelerated heartbeat. He introduced us to the group of people on and around the couch—many of them execs at the label.

After a half hour of schmoozing, I had no idea where Jules, LaLa or Crystal were and I'd also had a couple drinks.

Eventually some people from Jimmy's original group invited us to hit a club with them, and I managed to locate Jules and LaLa before we all piled into a stretch hummer. The hummer stopped in front of a club just down the hill, where people with cameras and bright lights took pictures of some of us. Bouncers shooed them away and ushered our party inside.

The only reason I could remember anyone's name was because I was immortal. Other than that, everyone seemed so alike. There were a lot of weaves, too much makeup, and way too much Botox. The music was pumping, and I was pretty sure that if I were still mortal, I would be able to hear nothing said to me.

A bikini-clad server proffered a tray bearing wine glasses. I took one and kept chatting to a lady from DCA about some of the projects they'd recently completed with new artists. After a while I just nodded in all the appropriate places and eventually ended up talking to some artists about how great DCA is and how much money they were making, how many songs they were selling, how much access they had. After a couple more drinks, everything sounded like "Blah, blah, and more blah."

The electronica was banging and the lightning-colored notes beat like ephemeral heartbeats in the air around me. I found myself dancing with some guy from DCA. Or was it a friend of the guy from DCA? I had no idea and laughed loudly. I started singing along with the music, making up my own lyrics. Almost immediately, everyone within range of the sound of my voice started dancing and jumping around as if they were all drunk.

I was drunk! The realization made me laugh even more.

I reached for another drink and my hand went through the glass. I giggled. What would it be like to just go through a wall? Or a person? I tried both,

with the latter evoking a response from a girl who
was drunker than me.

"She went through me!" she squealed in
delight.

I marveled at the way the laser lights danced to
the rhythm of the music. So coooool…
*Stop it now, before someone becomes aware of
what you're doing. Drink some tea or coffee to
sober up before you kill somebody.*

Kill somebody? Oh, no, I couldn't possibly. I
was focused on *love*, just like Star said. In fact, I
was a walking vessel of love, love, love. I felt my
arms waving in the air around my head.

"Angel, what the heck?" It was LaLa, looking
at me like she didn't recognize me.

"Oh, just loosen up," I slurred. "You've got to
let go and let love."

"You're drunk," she stated.

"Yah-huh," I shouted.

"How many have you had?"

Hmmm, interesting question. I hunted for the
answer in my drunken immortal memory.

"Five," I said and held up some fingers, not
checking to see if the number of fingers actually
matched what I'd said.

"I'm going to get you some water or something
before you throw up. Have you seen Jules? I
haven't seen her for most of the night."

Come to think of it, I hadn't seen Jules, either.
LaLa wrapped her arms around herself and looked
around the club like a scared little girl. That shook
me up, and I stopped dancing. She led me over to
some lounge chairs.

"Sit here and wait until I get back," she said. I couldn't remember the last time I'd fed, but I didn't feel hungry. Did the alcohol take away the hunger? It seemed like only two seconds before she returned. She sat down next to me. "I got our car to pull up to the front. It's waiting for us right now." I took the hot drink she gave me, swallowed it and almost immediately felt more like myself. She gave me another one, and I drank that, too.

I strained my senses to see if I could pick up Jules's scent or voice anywhere in the club. The music seemed to grow louder, but eventually I heard her voice coming from what may have been a green room or some room in the back of the club. She was laughing hysterically. I rushed through the crowd, trying to remain mortal-looking, but at some point decided to just screw it and go through several intoxicated people. No one sober enough could tell what was going on with the flashing lights anyway.

I made it to the room where I'd heard Jules's laughter and saw a group of people around a table with powdery stuff all over it. Jules was leaning over the table and sniffing the white stuff up her nose. I felt my stomach flip with shock and nausea. I was pretty sheltered, but even I knew that was cocaine.

There was no way I was going to let my girl do that.

I literally dragged her out of the room. I may have done it a little too immortal-like, but everyone was high, so they didn't seem to notice the ease with which I did it.

"Hey," she squawked, "what you doing?"

"Jules, it's time to go. The car's waiting. We need to get LaLa." I guided her back to where LaLa sat. Not missing a beat, LaLa took her arm as I took the other arm. Jules's head snapped down as if it suddenly became too heavy for her neck. We walked her outside to the waiting car, picked her up, arranged her on the backseat and jumped in.

A few flashes went off, and it occurred to me that people were taking pictures of Jules completely smashed. This was so not good. If their parents saw the photos, it'd be over.

We tried to wake up Jules as our limo rolled through the streets. "What if she doesn't wake up?" LaLa said, voicing the same concern I had in my mind.

This was my fault. I'd behaved in a totally irresponsible way, not like an adult at all. Mortal teens were expected to make mistakes, but the bar for immortal "teens" was much higher.

If I weren't so sheltered, I wouldn't have gotten so wasted on a few drinks and would've handled myself better in the real world. And I probably could figure out what was wrong with Jules. From what I knew of cocaine, it wasn't a downer, and Jules was definitely going down.

"I saw her do cocaine. But it looks like she took something else, too."

"Oh my God." LaLa's tears flowed. "Maybe we should go the hospital?"

"I'm calling Nina." I started dialing. "She knows all about this stuff."

As a former pop star, Nina had done and seen it all. She, along with many of her friends and colleagues, had been in rehab for alcohol, cocaine, and/or prescription drugs. If anyone could tell us if Jules was okay, it would be Nina. She picked up the phone, and I quickly explained where we were and what was happening.

"She may have taken a combination of drugs," Nina said on speakerphone. "An upper and a downer. If it had just been cocaine, she wouldn't be passed out. Slap her face; get her to wake up. Hang up; call me back with video."

I called back while LaLa desperately slapped our best friend. Jules started muttering.

"She seems to be waking up a little," I told Nina. We were connected with the videoconference app. I turned on the car's interior light and held the phone up to Jules so Nina could see her.

"Good," Nina said. Her head was tied with a silk scarf, and her eyes were bleary as if she'd been fast asleep when we called. "Keep rousing her," she instructed. "Tell the driver to take you to the nearest hospital. Now think: you see any paparazzi tonight?"

"Yes," I answered. "They were taking pictures when we went in and when we left."

"Okay." I could almost see Nina's mental wheels turning. "Where was your chaperone? Did you check in with her before you left the club?"

"We hadn't seen her since Jimmy's house. We just left without telling anybody."

Jules sat up and vomited all over her pretty turquoise dress. LaLa gave her some water from the limo's fridge and tried to clean her up.

"She's awake," I said. "She's sitting up." I held the phone in front of Jules so Nina could see her face.

"Can you hear me?" Nina asked her.

Jules nodded. "Yes," LaLa confirmed. "She's nodding yes."

"Good," Nina said. She too sounded and looked relieved. "Ms. Julietta, how does your stomach feel now?"

"I'm hungry," Jules answered.

Well that was unexpected. "Is that good?" LaLa asked.

"Anytime there's a desire to eat food, that's a plus," Nina said. "Julietta, would you like to go to the hospital?"

"No!" Jules became agitated and started to cry. "Please don't take me to the hospital. Just take me home. Please!"

LaLa was already crying, and the only reason I wasn't was my bloody tears would have added to an already shocking situation. It hurt like hell to see Jules this way, and it hurt to know that I could've prevented it.

Angel, I've tracked where you are from looking from your vantage point out of the limo's windows. I'm on the corner roughly three blocks away. Have the driver stop.

"Before calling Nina, I texted Cici," I lied. "She just replied with her location. She happened to be close by." I instructed the driver where to pull over.

"Good," Nina said. "Julietta, when the car pulls over, I want you to get out and stand on the sidewalk. Angel and LaLa, if she can stand without falling, take her home and let her sleep it off. If she can do that, she'll be okay."

The car began cutting across the lanes of traffic in an effort to pull over at the designated curb. Cici stood there, her eyes on our car as we approached.

"I'm sorry I put you girls in this situation," Nina continued. She rubbed her face with her hand, and I realized she was crying, too. "No matter what generation, it's always the same scenario. The music industry eats its young. I should've been there with you to protect you from all this. I'll answer to your parents. This isn't your fault."

Outside the car, Jules was able to stand without assistance. Meeting my eyes, Cici nodded to me through the window and they all got back into the car.

"Take us home," I told the driver.

Let me be the adult, Cici transmitted.

"Nina," she said, "Julietta looks strong enough to return home. Our parents are out of town, but I'll take full responsibility for the girls until they return."

Nina nodded in acknowledgement. "Thank you, Cici. Girls, I have some contacts over at BNX, the gossip blog that more than likely took the pictures. Since I have a three-hour head start, I'm going to work to make sure they don't post those pictures."

"I'm sooorry, guuuys," Jules cried.

"What did you have?" LaLa asked her.

"Drank a few, tried coke...something else, had a girl's name..."

"Oh, no," Cici said. "You took Molly?"

"Yeah, that was it," Jules said. "They said the coke would straighten me out cuz Molly made me crazy."

"My cousin died doing what you did," LaLa said. "She was fifteen."

"You're lucky to be alive," Cici agreed.

I felt completely responsible. After all, I was the adult of the group. Instead of getting drunk, I should have been more accountable for what was going on with my girls. "From now on," I said, "we look out for each other. Agreed?"

Jules and LaLa nodded between tears. Nina got off the phone to attend to the potential publicity fallout.

And Cici and I made our own vow.

The alcohol does diminish the hunger, Angel. But soon you'll need to feed. Once it wears off, you'll want to kill everyone in this car. Promise me you won't use alcohol to control your hunger around your friends.

I nodded and quickly wiped away a tear before it made its way down my face.

Cici, I want to undo the mind lock. I want to live a Trad lifestyle.

You're still drunk, Angel.

"This will help sober you up," Cici said out loud to me as she pulled out a flask. "Old family recipe," she told a questioning LaLa. "It has a few supplements to help with her anemia." Affected by Cici's power of suggestion, LaLa nodded and backed off the subject, as I put the flask to my lips and quickly downed the contents.

Eventually, the car pulled into our driveway.

Cici was right. The flask of blood did sober me up. I was completely clear-headed.

And I still wanted to undo the mind lock. I was even clearer as to why: Storm and the other Trads were right; I was one of them. If I'd been living a Trad lifestyle, I wouldn't have gotten caught up in the alcohol so easily. I would've been more aware of my surroundings and alert to the danger that Jules was in instead of acting like a drunken child.

We carried Jules up the stairs, got her cleaned up and got her into bed. An exhausted LaLa volunteered to stay in Jules's room, just in case and we said goodnight.

I then followed Cici to her suite.

When Cici designed my house, she created a number of guest suites for family members, including herself. Her suite mirrored mine, except it was on the opposite end of the floor, and there was no Pacific Ocean view in the distance—just endless, peaceful canyon views. She closed and locked the door before turning to me. Her face was expressionless; not because she was trying to hide her emotions, but because she didn't know what to think.

"It wasn't your fault, Angel. Jules is going to do what she's going to do."

I sat down in a deep, upholstered chair. "I know, but let's face it: my life's been beyond sheltered. I'm in an industry where being naïve is dangerous. Everyone around me has done so much more than I have. I just feel like the Inc way isn't the best choice for me."

"I'm not going to talk you out of anything, Angel. But once we part, you're completely on your own. There'll be no one there for you...if something happens that you might regret down the line. You understand?"

"Completely. This is what I want."

She came to stand in front of me. I stood to face her, wondering what we needed to do to break the blood spell that'd formed the foundation of our lock. From what I knew of blood spells, they were difficult to break, maybe even impossible.

"No," Cici said before breathing out languidly as if she was savoring the last few moments of our connection. "It's easy if we're both in agreement."

"What do we need to do?" I asked.

She opened her arms and gathered me into her embrace before looking me in the eyes. "Do you agree to break the mind connection and release me?"

"Yes. I agree," I answered.

"Do you agree it is your own free will that leads you to this choice?"

"Yes. I agree."

"Now you repeat those two questions, and I'll repeat your answers."

I did as she said.

"And so it is," she said.

"And so it is," I said.

She closed her eyes. Immediately the white noise of Cici's thoughts and emotions was silenced. It felt like I'd lost a part of my hearing or a part of my overall senses, as if my sight had dimmed or I was missing a finger.

Instead of feeling emancipated, I felt desolate. And the love Star told me about seemed like a fantasy, a thing that existed in the same dimension as Santa Claus and the tooth fairy.

Again there was the feeling of unprecedented loneliness. It was happening so often now, I should've been used to it. But no. It still sucked.

"You okay?" Her lips turned down and her eyebrows scrunched together.

"I've no idea what I'm supposed to do," I said. The idea of curling up in bed was all I could focus on as my feet padded toward the door.

"It's normal to feel a little scattered, easily distracted, after a mind lock's dissolved, but the feeling will go away soon. In the meantime, call Aurora." Cici was taking off her sapphire earrings. "She can help."

I turned to her, feeling awkward in my solitude.

"Are *you* okay?" I asked.

She thought for a little bit, her hand paused midair, fingers centimeters away from the second earring, which flashed and glistened on her earlobe.

"We'll get through this," she finally answered in a tone seemingly intended to remind me she was the oldest. "It'll only be a few months before you'll no longer be a newborn." She glanced over and met my eyes. "You won't get into much trouble in that short period of time. Right, Angel?"

TRAD

"I wish I could say congratulations, sis, but it is no easy thing to be completely responsible for your own behavior when you have been raised otherwise." Aurora delivered this piece of information much like Dad would offer a scary diagnosis to one of his dying patients.

"Thanks," I answered dryly. I was in my room doing a videoconference with her on the computer. She was well into her day in Stockholm, where she lived with Roman and ran an antiques business, and was taking a break to school me in the ways of being a Trad newborn.

Despite the distance, our relationship had always been warm. She called Mom "Clee-Clee" and Dad "Abba," after having stopped calling them "Mom" and "Dad" long before Cici was born. As I looked at her face, it again amazed me how much she was like Mom. From the same touchy-feely vibe to the glowing eyes, it was like looking at Mom's twin, just taller and more jovial, like Dad.

Or at least like Dad *was* before the Council tried to steal Mom.

"Let's make sure I got everything straight," I continued, struggling not to think about Mom. "There are no rules. There's no reason to live with or have mortals in my life. They're little more than food, but if I choose to, I can have friendships with them. They're also susceptible to the Shimshana power of suggestion you showed me. Right so far?"

"You've got it. But also remember the Law of the Hunt: select your gaddis carefully and devour it without publicity."

"How do you go about picking gaddis?" I enunciated the second syllable of the ancient word that meant "prey" so it rhymed with please. A couple of months ago, the phrase "prey please" would have sent me into a giggling fit as soon as it popped into my head, but now it didn't seem funny, and my face remained smooth.

Aurora peered at me from the monitor as if I was capable of conquering the world. "Best way to do it is choose those who have few to no ties. No family, few friends. The more they are ingrained in everyday life, the more you want to leave them alone. Those types of mortals don't make good gaddis, partially because there are more consequences for devouring them."

I pondered this for a few moments. "What about The Nest?" I asked.

"The Nest, and other establishments like it, are a construct of Inc influences. You can still feed there but you have to utilize a technique called Sunan. It's specifically designed to circumvent the results of Blood Obsession and keep the gaddis alive."

If she hadn't already, she had my full attention now. I'd avoided The Nest because having one blood-obsessed donor—Justin—was complicated enough. I didn't want another one, but I sure wanted fresh blood.

"Tell me how the Sunan works," I demanded.

"Whoa, little sister, stay calm." Her smile was brilliant, and the intensity of the light in her eyes went up a few notches. "Sunan must be a mutual thing. The gaddis must agree to close themselves, close their minds as much as possible, as you drink from them. This minimizes the natural connection we make to human gaddis as we drink from them. You will keep that gaddis alive and never drink from him again. That is Sunan."

I became so obsessed with the idea of Sunan, I barely absorbed anything else Aurora said. After saying good-bye, I went back downstairs to the studio.

Warren had been there for a while. Jules, hungover and depressed from the alcohol and drugs, was doing vocal warm-up exercises with a recording. LaLa, the only one who hadn't drunk anything alcoholic the night before, was fine, dandy and ready to work. My mind automatically jumped to Sawyer, the only other mortal I knew who didn't drink. I put my head down, switched on the sound board and struggled to concentrate on the work at hand.

Warren literally ran nonstop getting water, tea, and blood, and restocking the small refrigerator as we worked on the tracks. At one point, he turned to me with a worried look on his face.

"Excuse me," he said. "Lala told me a little bit about last night. Is it okay that I invited my uncle Terry over? I should have asked you guys first, but I thought it would be okay since he represents you, Angel."

My mind went back to Sawyer and, for a second, I forgot what Warren's question was. Oh, yeah. Terry. He was asking if it was okay for him to come over. I shook my head, trying to clear the cobwebs. Maybe a visitor would be good.

"Sure," I said. "Why not. We might need a good lawyer after last night," I added in a joking tone.

"You got that right," Jules responded, obviously ticked off. "I screwed things up for us."

Earlier we'd combed the BNX website and search engines to see if any pics from last night came up and we saw nothing. Either Nina convinced the right people it wasn't news, or nobody cared enough to post it. Either way, we worried about whether the pictures would come out at a later time.

"Since we're on the subject of visitors," LaLa said, "I invited a yoga instructor over. Met him last night. Might be a good way to take a break later."

"Cool," I agreed. The idea of mortals being around reminded me of the times Sawyer and I would work surrounded by people at his studio. It appealed to me and was strangely comforting…like the white noise I was missing from the broken mind lock.

The doorbell rang. I barely recognized the scent and started flipping through my mental rolodex. By the time the visitors were escorted in by Kiya's assistant, Sarah, I knew who it was; Samantha and Niana, the lesbian couple I'd met at Markus's.

After introductions, they said they missed
Markus and hoped his good friend would be okay
with letting them help out.

"Whad'you do?" I asked.

"We give feedback," Samantha said. "We're
both writers and we help out with lyrics, too."

"Might be good to have extra ears," Jules said.

I hit the switch to play the current track.

"Cool!" Niana exclaimed, getting up to dance.
They wore clothes suited for sunbathing and lying
around the pool; I was dubious on how helpful
they'd be. But Jules was right about having fresh
ears, and since they hung out with Markus, we
could at least count on them to be confidential about
what we were working on.

Right…?

I quickly texted Markus with this question.
After a few minutes, he responded:

yeh, dont worry about them. they harmless.
japan rox.

We gave Samantha and Niana permission to
stay and continued working on tracks. Terry White,
the immortal entertainment attorney Mom
connected me with, came over with a couple of his
partners. After greeting us and clapping his nephew
on the back, he sat on a leather couch, hands
comfortably folded on his belly, and listened to our
story about what went down the previous night.
When we were done, he pushed his frameless
glasses a little higher on the bridge of his nose,

stroked his mustache and offered to help us if we ever needed it in the future.

His fingertips tapped and swished across the screen of his tablet as he spoke. "I'd also recommend that, as minors, you stay with someone over the age of twenty-one when out at industry events or anywhere alcohol is served."

Moments later, Terry pulled me to the side. "I'm sorry about your parents," he said in a rapid whisper. "From now on, take Warren with you whenever you go out. Always be with at least one reliable immortal at these industry events."

Made sense with my Trad lifestyle. Terry had been a close colleague of Mom's for centuries, and I trusted him completely. It also made sense to extend that trust to Warren.

He slipped me a card for an immortal-run PR company. "Contact them immediately," he said. "I just copied you in the e-mail I sent to them. Let them know what the situation is. They're expensive, but they'll clean up this mess in ways your manager can't."

"How?" I asked, pulling out my cell phone and opening the e-mail.

"They use magical computer operating systems, software and applications viruses to corrupt and/or delete all undesirable digital files."

I took his advice, and thirty minutes later, an e-mail confirmed that the situation had been taken care of. My eyebrows rose when I saw the invoice amount, and I forwarded it to Warren to take care of.

Later we had a yoga class on the terrace by the pool with the vistas of the hills, canyons, and ocean in the background. LaLa was right about it being a good way to take a break. Samantha and Niana joined the class, and it turned out they were experts who'd been taking yoga for years. We also learned they were in their late twenties. At first it was pretty weird; even as an immortal, I didn't hang out with many people that age who had lots of free time. Either way, they were fun and knowledgeable, and gave their opinions about our ordeal from last night. It seemed like drug overdoses and addictions were so common in L.A. that *everybody* had a problem, once had a problem, or knew someone with a problem.

Earlier that morning, before videoconferencing with Aurora, I'd told Cici it'd be okay if I never had another drink of alcohol again for eternity.

"I feel guilty for what happened to you guys last night," she'd said. "I'm going to give you all the information you need to deal with the jungle of a business you're working in."

It was the first time I felt like she was going to talk to me without self-censoring. I sat forward on the stool and gave her my total attention.

"The reality is, the immortal world, like the mortal world, has numerous problems including alcoholism and drug use. Shimshana sometimes use alcohol and other substances to dampen the thirst for blood. We don't get physically addicted, since our bodies' higher temperatures burn the substances more quickly. The danger lies in getting psychologically addicted."

I shuddered at the idea of being addicted to alcohol forever.

"Immortals also have a high rate of suicide. Mom and Dad didn't want to share this with you too soon, but I think you should know statistics show we kill ourselves more than mortals do. In fact, there are businesses that grant immortals their choice of destruction. It's a lucrative industry because we don't die easily, but if you pay someone to do it properly, you're guaranteed to stay dead and not revive in a few years like Maybe Dead Fred."

"Maybe Dead Fred?" I was still trying to absorb the dangers of addiction, but this sounded like another piece of information with the potential to throw me for a loop.

"Yes. Frederick's friend helped him commit suicide by chopping him into pieces only for the pieces to find their way back together over the course of a few decades, reconnect and, voila, Fred was alive again."

"No way!"

"Yes! I can't make this stuff up." We walked out of Saucony, and I closed it. "Fred now runs one of the most successful SA firms in the world," she said.

"SA?"

"Suicide assistance."

I was completely fascinated. "Why so much suicide?" She looked at me with a worried expression before answering.

"People get tired, Angel. Tired of all the ups and downs of life. In the case of Shimshana, we get tired of feeding on mortals to survive. As a matter of fact, the Inc movement started as a way to cut down the rate of suicide by giving immortals a solid life structure and parameters to operate within. Newborn rates are some of the highest; in fact, that's the time when most people are on suicide watch. The highest percentage of suicides, however, occur when a mortal mate dies."

She avoided looking at me as she delivered the last bit. Did she think I was suicidal over losing Sawyer? There was no way of knowing what she thought now that the lock was gone, and there was no way I'd ask her that question; one, because I definitely wasn't and two, I didn't want to know whether Cici would agree with me or not.

Each week of writing, listening and reworking merged into the next as people flowed in and out my front door. We went to William Wilson's and Haz Bro's respective studios, and EyeHeart Beatz came over several times. Warren coordinated all the session details, Redd traveled from Boston to work out dance routines, and Risa and the master stylist came to take measurements and update hair, makeup, and color palettes. Viewing the world through the Trad lens helped me deal with the business; I grew adept at handling the almost endless line of mortals like what they were—temporary.

The only ones I let myself feel anything for were Jules and LaLa; that would never change. As long as they were there with me, it helped to push away that niggling feeling of emptiness. Sawyer and I were no longer together, and my parents were gone, but the fact that I spent every day with my girls writing and living our dream made life blissful.

I should have known the happiness wouldn't last.

After a couple of weeks, it happened. My newborn presence was affecting them again—as it had after I'd first gone through The Change—and made them do and say things opposite of who they were. There was no way of knowing how extreme the effects could get, but according to Markus, there were instances of newborn overexposure that resulted in mortal death.

"He's right," Cici said. I'd spilled my worst fears as we sat in the Saucony kitchen one morning. "Maybe you can somehow use the other mortals who are hanging around."

By now, we had anywhere from ten to fifteen people in my house daily.

"I'll use them as a shield." I downed a gallon of blood and still felt the gnawing hunger. "Maybe if I spend more time with the other mortals and less with the girls, it'll lessen the effects."

"It's worth a try," she said, casting an apprehensive glance at the empty containers of blood surrounding me.

# # #

In order to put some distance between the girls and myself, I started going out in the evenings with Samantha and Niana, who seemed to know everybody in Hollywood. One night it was sushi here, the other night it was a reading of a new screenplay there. Soon paparazzi were taking pictures of me with various big-name celebrities and circulating them on the net. One blog posted a short article with the following title: "Who Is Angel and Why We Care."

"What the heck's all this crap?" LaLa said after reading the post on her laptop. It was the closest thing to a swear I'd ever heard her say. It was the end of the workday. Haz Bro had just cleared out of the studio, taking his eight-person crew with him.

"It quotes a 'reliable source,'" Jules read over LaLa's shoulder. "Says you're fed up with your, quote 'little group,' and you're pursuing a solo career and acting. What the fuck?"

LaLa, her tone beyond sarcastic, read the post word for word. ""'Let's just say Angel's done a lot of growing. She's recording stuff with Little Wolf. She's a real talent," the source connected with the "No. 8" artist tells us. "The others are just going to have to deal with it.""" They exchanged a deadly glare.

"Angel, Angel," Jules's voice was caustic. "It's Angel's world. We're just the fucking atmosphere on her planet."

I knew it was the chemical reaction to my newborn presence sparking this talk, but it hurt nonetheless. "Come on!" I said. "Didn't you learn anything from the biographies Nina made us read? They do this to all the girl groups and most of the guy groups. Divide and conquer. You know I'm not doing any of this stuff."

"Oh, yeah?" LaLa said. "Then you didn't really record anything with Little Wolf?"

"Yes," I admitted. "But it's not like that."

"So you backstabbing us like that?" Jules spat. "Hanging with the rich and famous. We not good enough for you?" She advanced toward me like she wanted to fight.

The corners of my peripheral vision turned pink. "I told you, it's not what you think."

"Look at this place." LaLa wasn't even listening. "You were always one of them. Miss Beacon Hill."

Samantha and Niana, wrapped in towels, came in through The Club from the pool. "What's going on?" Samantha asked.

"None of your goddamned business," LaLa's voice went down an octave and up a couple of notches in volume as she swore without a pause. "Why you even here?"

As Niana tugged Samantha by the arm and mumbled something about leaving, an idea started to form. But I'd have to act quickly for it to work.

"Don't talk to them like that." I rose to stand next to Samantha and Niana, exerting my power of suggestion the way Aurora had taught me. "I'm getting tired of you guys dissing me." I cranked up the emotion to make the next line have as much punch as possible. "At least I don't have to deal with insults from Samantha and Niana."

It worked. LaLa stood up. "I don't need this crap. I'm out."

"Me, too," echoed Jules. "I'm calling a car, grabbing my stuff and I'm ghost!"

My two best friends glared at me ugly and long before stomping out of the studio and up the stairs. Better to have them angry *at* me than sick, or worse, *because* of me. I wondered where they were going. They couldn't go far; we had shows coming up. As I listened to them pack their bags, Samantha and Niana took turns rubbing my back and offering canned condolences.

Warren, who'd probably heard the whole exchange from outside where he was taking a break, came in with my lidded cup. I woodenly chugged down blood as the logical part of my mind said it was a good time to do so in order to keep the people around me alive. "Go with them," I told him in a rapid whisper. "Make sure they each get a hotel room." He nodded and ran up the stairs.

The car pulled up outside, and I heard them dragging their bags down the stairs. The bags hit each stair audibly. *Thump, thump, thump.* With every thump my heart seemed to turn more into a strange, cold stone. They'd be all right, better off away from me. Safe, somewhere where they could get back to normal. By the time they'd loaded the car and driven away, I had no more heart. I just sat there as the emptiness engulfed me.

And I made a decision. There was no need to worry about anyone anymore. Not even myself.

"Thanks," I said to Samantha and Niana. "Sorry about that."

They looked at each other momentarily before Samantha said, "It wasn't your fault, Angel. They're totally jealous of you."

"Honestly, I don't know how you put up with their hateration for so long," Niana added.

"Let's go out," I said, jumping off the stool. I started turning off the various machines and closing down shop for the night. "Who else is here?"

Niana ran through a list of seven names of people who were hanging out in my house right at that moment.

"Great," I said. "Tell them dinner's on me."

"Cool," Samantha said in a neutral tone that bordered on indifferent. They both walked away at a casual pace, even though I heard their hearts race. I made my way to the Saucony kitchen.

As I guzzled my own dinner, I imagined what would happen if Cici was still in my head. She'd no doubt want to know what on earth I was doing. Or maybe she wouldn't ask; maybe she'd understand that I only needed to forget that the two people I loved the most outside of my family had just left in anger. Anger that my presence had created and my cunning had escalated.

I watched Niana through the window as she corralled people out of the pool and I listened to Samantha chattering into her cell phone in another room.

I drank extra blood, closed the kitchen and ran into Warren in the hallway.

"They're okay?" My voice sounded dead.

"They're not too far. Neither wanted to go back to Boston. They know they can stay at the hotel as long as they want." He awkwardly crossed his arms, as if trying to figure out what to say, before letting his hands drop to his sides and looking me in the eyes.

"I know you're not going to an industry event," he said. "But if you need me, I'll roll with you."

Cici was at Satch's place. But if she were here, I'd assure her I wouldn't drink alcohol. And if Star voiced any more concern about my bleak struggle with isolation, I'd respectfully remind her of my intention to focus on love. I had to make Warren understand I didn't need a babysitter.

"Unnecessary," I answered. Realizing I sounded like a defensive jerk, I softened my tone. "I'm okay. My plan for tonight's simple: stay out until exhaustion kicks in, come home and fall asleep."

Yep. That was the game plan, and I was going to stick to it even if it killed me.

DOWNFALL

Samantha and Niana not only knew everyone, they
also took the opportunity to call everybody they
knew. The three of us, along with everyone else
who'd been at the house (plus a few they'd invited),
went for dinner at yet another pricey sushi place. As
usual, no one noticed that I didn't eat anything.
Understandable; in L.A. it was uncommon to see
most girls my age eat much anyway.

After sushi, we walked down the block and
ducked into a hole-in-the-wall bar rumored to be a
favorite watering spot of Big Science, an
overweight pop/rapper who routinely ran around
doing comical things that fed the next day's gossip
blogs.

I wasn't surprised to see Big Science and his
crew there. And I wasn't surprised that Samantha
and Niana knew him.

He smelled like a steak.

"Another round of drinks," he told the group as
the waitress started taking orders. "Get whatever
you want," he told me. "My treat."

"They make an awesome appletini," Niana
offered.

I was tempted to drink. Being surrounded by
mortals, the majority of whom were inebriated—
and therefore vulnerable—brought an urge to attack
to the surface. I swallowed, took a deep breath and
whispered to the waitress, "Bring me grape juice in
a wine glass."

"So, Angel…" Big Science rested one massive arm along the back of my chair. "You think the president's doing a good job?"

"Come on, Big," Samantha said. She took a hit of a joint that was being passed around. "Angel doesn't talk politics."

"It's all the Illuminati, man." This came from Troy, a short, jumpy rapper whose eyes resembled slits. He took a long drag on the joint before continuing a hoarse, barely decipherable ramble. "The president, Congress, Big Pharma—all of them are in on it. Aliens, man. They the ones running things, and the government won't tell us, man."

Various people nodded their heads in agreement as he passed the joint to me.

"I'm good," I said, shaking my head no and remembering the drug-fueled fiasco with Jules.

While Big Science and his friends continued to wax poetic on the US government, various conspiracy theories, and the apocalypse, Samantha and Niana managed to notice every person who came into the bar. I'd gotten used to this constant checking-to-see-if-who-was-walking-in-the-room-was-famous tactic, but it was starting to really annoy me. The edges of my vision turned red, and I reminded myself to focus on love.

Focusing on love was getting hard.

Eventually the group voted to take me to the new, trendy club around the way. We piled into Big Science's minifleet of four limos to roll a couple of blocks west. Despite our casual dress, we were all immediately herded past the line of people waiting to get inside. Cameras clicked, lights flashed, and paparazzi called out for us to stop and pose.

A couple of the photographers called out to me. The abrasive sound of strangers yelling my name filled me with emotions I wasn't prepared for.

I'd always thought it would be cool to be a celebrity. To be the center of attention and get adoration from fans. But this felt like a million eyes leered at me and every part of my being was exposed for the world to see. I longed to crawl into a soft, quiet hole where I could be safe from prying eyes and probing questions.

Samantha and Niana seemed to like the attention, though. Although, no one asked them to, they posed arm-in-arm for the cameras and smiled like cheese was going out of style.

Inside, the club was a cool, dark refuge. We were led to the VIP section, where we settled onto couches, barstools, and swinging benches.

Samantha grabbed Niana's arm and blinked multiple times. "Isn't that Jennifer Watson?"

Even my head swiveled at the mention of the name. Jennifer Watson was one of *the* biggest box office actors on the planet. She was talking to someone with a recognizable face, but in her wake no one cared who he was.

Samantha and Niana were clearly at a loss. Here was one celeb they didn't know but wanted to so badly I could smell the desperation coming off of them. Their mouths dropped open when Jennifer Watson—followed by a ginormous bodyguard—waved and started walking toward our group.

"Cool J." Big Science greeted her with a hug and looked at her with fond relief, as if she were the only one he knew in the entire room. Their genuine friendship hit me like a whiff of fresh air and reminded me of my girls.

"It's been ages, Big Sci." She playfully punched his hefty upper arm with a delicate fist featuring glossy, manicured nails. "The only time I see you is in my news feed." They both laughed, as did Samantha, Niana, Troy, and a bunch of people who couldn't possibly have heard what was said to cause the laughter.

Jennifer Watson had one of the most delicious aromas my newborn senses had ever experienced. It was a bouquet of brown sugar, gardenia, chocolate, and some earthy fragrance I couldn't identify. As Big Science introduced us, it was all I could do to speak without drooling. Despite her fame, she was open and friendly. "Call me Jen," she requested. My shimshana stirred with pleasure as I inhaled and imagining drinking her.

Just then, out of the corner of my eye, a flash of something—I wasn't quite sure what—caught my attention. I turned to the left just in time to see the Council member Charleston move behind a guy standing by a bar less than fifty feet away. At least I thought it was Charleston. A flash of fear shot through my heart. Mom. But it didn't make sense for Charleston to be here in L.A. I walked over to the bar; the guy was still there, but there was nothing but an empty area behind him. A chill went down my spine. I whipped out my cell and dialed Cici.

Her answer was immediate. "What's going on?"

"Don't know. I'm at a club. Could've sworn I just saw Charleston." I relayed exactly what I saw.

There was a brief silence on the other line. "Angel…" Her tone had shifted from concern to bearer of bad news. "Another result of undoing the mind lock might be your feelings of anxiety about Mom escalating."

"You're telling me I just imagined seeing him?"

"I don't see why he would be here."

I hung up feeling foolish and annoyed. I'd been unaware of Cici's mental Valium, but it made sense; ever since we'd dissolved the mind lock, and despite reason, I'd felt increasingly nervous about Mom's safety. Skin crawling with anxiety, I left the club and went home.

# # #

"How was last night?" Warren asked. He placed a fresh, lidded cup of early brunch in front of me.

"Ton of people. Samantha and Niana." I downed the cup's contents. "Met Big Science through them. Met Jennifer Watson through him."

Warren stood up straighter as if he'd just been injected with a shot of alert. "Did you get their contact info?"

Nodding, I repeated the jotted-down cell phone numbers from memory as he wrote them down.

"Cool," he said. "I'll add this to your file of useful contacts." He poured more and replaced the lid.

"Good idea." I pushed the cup into the cup holder. "How long've you been building that file?"

"About two seconds," he said with a shy grin. "If it's okay with you, I'd like to roll with you to the social events, too, so whenever you meet someone this way, I can add them to our list."

Sounded like a plan to me.

As Warren implied, not many of my "houseguests" qualified as "useful" contacts. There were more visitors than the previous day; many of the new ones were people who Samantha and Niana met the night before. Two of them claimed to be witches, and another claimed to be a fairy; all of them were either actors or musicians who didn't have a lot going on at the moment for whatever reasons. Samantha and Niana entertained people at the pool, occasionally popping in to invite me to join them, while spurts of laughter and conversation emanated from the game room, where people played Wii and table tennis.

The background hum of mortality served as my emotional novocaine. The more strangers buzzed around me, the easier it was to distance myself from the fact that I'd never been so alone in all my life. Besides, there was still work to do. The girls may be mad at me but we could still work remotely the way we did the last time my presence affected them.

By noon, I'd hit a brick wall with the William Wilson track. I uploaded it for the girls before turning to the Yamaha keyboard. Soon I was immersed in finalizing a structure for the ballad's fragments.

Since I would never hear the rest of the ballad, would never kiss Sawyer again to hear more of its lovely notes, I decided to write the rest of the song using my imagination. I lost myself filling in the various places where there were no notes and summoning the emotions that had once led to hearing these beautiful mini-compositions within compositions. As if I was standing outside of my own mind, I marveled at how I could recall tender moments we'd shared without crying or even feeling sad.

As a matter of fact, I felt nothing but the desire to keep working, stay medicated with a steady supply of blood and remain surrounded by Hollywood's primo slacker population. The clock read 4:47 p.m. when Cici, who'd left early to view more properties with Satchel, walked into the studio.

"Who are all these people?"

"Friends," I answered. "Some are friends of friends. Most are just complete and utter strangers." She looked at me with her signature concerned-big-sister look. "And don't worry. I won't freak out over Mom anymore. I've turned that off, too."

"Angel, you're not a faucet. You just can't shut your emotions off and expect to be okay. The water's got to go somewhere."

My fingers paused above the keyboard. "Where then, since you have all the answers?" She pressed her lips together as if she was waiting for me to apologize. "Sorry, sis. I feel no regret for being a bitch to you now." My fingers pounded out the most passionate part of the ballad and ended in a defiant glissando to the top of the board as if to emphasize my point.

In the back of my mind there was a tug, almost like a nudge, to remember to embrace love. But love didn't play nice with the wasteland I was now cultivating inside my heart; in that desolate place, love withered away.

The next few days melted into one another in a bleak landscape of non-emotion. I worked during the day, and at night rolled with my personal entourage—now at about thirty people—on nightly excursions to squash the emptiness.

One night I decided to keep the party at home. One of Niana's friends, a DJ, brought a few crates of records over and The Club was transformed into…a club. Warren programmed The Club's lighting software so that the lights shifted between the colors red, purple, and blue. In less than a half hour, more people arrived and brought the total number of party people to one hundred and three. Eventually Big Science and Jennifer Watson showed up.

"Congrats, Angel!" Samantha put her arms around me. "This is one of the dopest parties ever."

She started to pull away, but my arms instinctively tightened around her. Funny, her somewhat nondescript scent wasn't appealing at all. Still…the idea of draining her dry, here in front of all these people, gave me chills.

But she misunderstood my tightening embrace. "Wow," she said. "You're strong. Wanna go upstairs? Don't want to hurt Niana, but I've liked you since that first day at Little Wolf's."

It took all my self-control not to send her flying across the room when I pushed her away from me. She fell backward onto the floor. Hearing her head hit the poured concrete made my shimshana shiver. She got up immediately and self-consciously arranged her hair before pretending it didn't happen.

It occurred to me then why I'd felt the emptiness despite being full. It wasn't what or how much I was drinking. It was *how* I was drinking. The realization was like a cloud shifting from its permanent place in front of the sun; the light appeared and I finally understood. The urge to attack needed follow-through. Drinking from glasses and flasks didn't excite my shimshana. It seemed that was key.

Warren came to stand by my side in the corner I'd retreated into.

"Jennifer Watson's about to come over here," he said. "Introduce us, okay?"

"You're telepathic?" I asked.

"No, I'm your typical guy; no special talents here." Indeed the majority of immortals had no special abilities; outside of the commonalities of healing much faster than mortals and heightened senses, most people were like Warren. "I heard her say she was looking for you," he continued. "I also noticed that you're red." He calmly guided me to an area of the room where the lighting was red and observed my face. "Better," he said.

Jennifer Watson and her glorious scent approached us. "Angel, thanks for having me in your home," she said. "It's breathtaking."

I thanked her through lips pressed together—so as not to let drool escape—and introduced Warren.

"Oh, you're Angel's assistant." She shook his hand. "Thanks so much for calling me. I'll be having a party at my place in a couple months."

"That sounds great," Warren responded. Smoothly covering up the fact that I continued to stand there swallowing, he gallantly thanked her and offered to show her the recording studio.

He may not have any special abilities, but he sure knew how to work a party. My gratitude for his people skills disappeared quickly, however, with the realization that he'd taken away the most appealing mortal in the room. I shivered with the desire to have her as my feet began to follow them. I was stopped in the middle of the dance floor by Jessie-Lynn, one of Samantha's cohorts and a self-proclaimed fairy who'd been hanging out at my house for days.

"Hi, Angel. Party's great. Need anything?"

I considered the question. There was definitely something I needed. I opened my mouth to answer, but she didn't stop talking. "Hey, I just wanted to thank you, I feel so welcomed here. Like I belong."

I didn't care. Tuning her out, my hearing honed in on the sound of Jennifer's heartbeat as she and Warren lingered in the studio. But Jennifer didn't fit the description of acceptable gaddis; everyone would know the minute she disappeared.

A drunken guy jostled me, and I swore inwardly. Jessie-Lynn was still talking. Struggling to forget how much I wanted to drain Jennifer Watson, I focused on Jessie-Lynn's drone in order to distract me from what I couldn't have.

"I get the feeling you know what I mean, Angel." She put a hand on my arm. "I sometimes think you're a fairy, too."

There was nothing insulting about her weird hypothesis, nothing that should have indicated that it would serve as the touchstone for my downfall. But it did. Her hand was on my arm, but both looked very far away. My head grew hot. I knew what I was about to do, but I didn't know why. Maybe the idea that anyone could feel a connection to me, or claim to understand what the heck was going on in my tangled, red brain drove me to have a fit. I didn't know why I fell off the moral cliff, but all I could see was red. Jessie-Lynn was little more to me than a walking blood bag. And the massive 808 bass beat of the rap banging out of the speakers echoed the rhythm of the veins pounding within her like multiple universes of sustenance.

I. Was. Hungry.

It was hunger beyond anything I'd ever known. It was the longing to hunt, to capture gaddis and drain it completely into myself. Not because I needed to, but because I can.

It was the instinct to hunt human beings.

The power of suggestion Aurora showed me came in handy before, and I would use it again. Looking them in the eye while impressing a thought is all that it takes, but I wanted to try something different. Put my personal spin on it, so to speak.

"Come with me."

I sang the words, in a charming soprano, into Jessie-Lynn's ear, forming the last word in an extended note that trilled into a seductive run. And it worked. Completely entranced by my voice, she had no choice but to do what I'd sang.

Like a blood-driven pied piper, I led her past the dancing bodies on The Club floor, through the people talking, laughing and saying hello in the hallway, up a minor staircase to a bathroom on the second floor. A guy was in there.

"Leave and forget you saw us."

I sang this command, too, and with a blank expression, he left me to my bloody devices.

I immobilized Jessie-Lynn by wrapping her long, blonde extensions around my right fist and drawing her face close to mine. My shimshana started to unravel and begin its journey up from my intestine, through my esophagus and into the back of my mouth.

Aurora would be proud of my choice of gaddis. Nobody would miss this fake fairy. I had to breathe a different way and stop my mouth from automatically closing in between improvised lyrics, but despite my unraveled shimshana, I managed to sing in order to keep her quiet. A flood of red clouded my vision. The anticipation of penetrating her neck caused my entire body to throb. For a few seconds, I was so blinded by red that sound and scent were the only means I had to hone in on the vein in her neck that would deliver her to me.

She was quieted by my voice, but her eyes bulged as she stared at me, horrified, as if she wanted to scream and couldn't. For a second I felt empathy for her situation, but it was quickly swept away by the desire to drain her.

I licked her neck slowly, languidly. The tang of skin on my tongue, the warm scent filling my senses, caused my mouth to open with a small, ecstatic cry as my shimshana, led by its proboscis, stretched out of my mouth past my lips. I bent her back and aimed—right at the vein in her neck. While doing so, I caught a glimpse of myself in the mirror.

No, that couldn't be…the planes and contours of my face were shifting. The exact way Star's did. I was looking at someone I barely recognized. Someone made of the same stuff as all those who came before me.

I was Angelica Brown, daughter of my ancestors.

Then someone pulled my gaddis out of my hands. The roar that I would have emitted traveled back down my throat as my eyes focused on the perpetrator.

"No, Angel." His voice was forceful, yet quiet. "Take me instead."

For the second time in a span of less than a minute, my eyes seemed to deceive me.

But it wasn't an illusion. Right in front of me, challenging me, offering himself to me, stood my eternal blood donor, Justin Diego McCarthy.

PRECIPICE

"Take me, Angel," Justin repeated. "You want me." He unzipped his black hoodie. My insane hunger honed in on the familiarity of his blood. "Tell her to go away and forget what's happened."

With my proboscis still protruding from my mouth, I sang the command to her, and as soon as she complied, Justin turned and ran out of the bathroom. That action reduced me to pure instinct, and I chased him like an animal. Zipping at a speed I didn't even know he was capable of, he ran down the hall to my suite.

Once I entered the room, he was behind me in a flash, closing the door.

Locking the door.

He hadn't run away from me. He'd led me. He wanted us to come here to my room.

I swung around to find him standing before me, his eyes boring into mine. His dark, almost black hair was tousled, a little longer than his usual clean cut…and where there used to be a friendly twinkle in his eyes, there was now a steeliness so intense it excited me down to my bones.

He'd changed, as if he had been rewired somehow and was now simmering with secrets. But despite the mystery and the newness, it was the familiarity of him, of his blood, that excited me the most.

My heart raced as I inhaled his scent, warm and dominated by jasmine. He stood perfectly still as if allowing me, inviting me, to explore the newness and familiarity of him. There was no struggle here, and the part of my brain that needed to hunt switched off.

He extended his hand toward me. That was the Justin I knew. Romantic and wanting to do sweet things like hold hands. I took his hand, my fingertips pressed along his sinewy wrist as our palms flattened against each other, pressing firm, and his fingers closed around my wrist.

Then, surprisingly, he pushed my opposite shoulder with his other hand, causing me to pivot outward and away from him. Simultaneously he took a step to the right, which brought him behind me, his hand still folded over mine. The result was that my hand was pinned behind me—the elbow bent comfortably but firmly—and nestled between the small of my back and his stomach.

His heart beat rapidly against my back, the warmth of him engulfed me, and his breath tickled my ear.

With his other hand, he gently turned my chin to the side as he leaned forward a little to look me in the eye. As if to see if I was okay with this new side of him. If I liked what he was doing.

I felt my lips part with the proximity of his mouth to mine and I closed my eyes as a jumble of sensations flooded my senses.

As if that was a green light, his free hand traveled down from my chin to grasp my other hand and gently fold my arm so that both hands were now behind my back, between the two of us, and my weight leaned back into his chest and torso.

Again he turned my chin to the side as he leaned forward to look me in the eye. The effect of this eye contact tilted my head back, into a posture of surrender, and I felt like I was falling. Backward over a precipice. I closed my eyes.

The predator was now the prey, and I reveled in the feeling of offering something to him. I wasn't sure what I was offering, but I knew, without a doubt, in that moment he could have whatever it was I had to give.

I opened my eyes, and he was still leaning into me, face close to mine. He leaned his head closer and brought his lips to within a fraction of a centimeter of mine. So close I could taste his breath. He stopped there and continued to watch me, taking in my reaction, absorbing the facts: my rapid heartbeat, my accelerated breathing, the red tinge that swept through the space, and the heat that continued to intensify.

I wanted him. And he knew it.

His mouth drew closer; a tiny bit more and the smell of everything he was, everything he wore, commanded my attention. He was so close, I imagined I could taste his thoughts.

He was torturing me. And I liked it.

I don't know how long we stood like that, with me held a willing captive in his dominating embrace. I lost track of the time. My mind registered the sounds of the ravers throughout the house.

"We're missing the party," I whispered in a voice so guttural I didn't even recognize it as mine.

Swiftly, he repositioned his body so that he was now standing in front of me. My arms were still pinned behind my back, and my breasts were flattened against his chest. Caught off guard, I looked up into his face and watched his eyes observe me as he leaned in and down, his lips slowly closing in on mine, until finally…he kissed me on the chin.

The anticipation of the kiss had caused my temperature to rise substantially, and the fact that he kissed me on the chin instead of the mouth made me want him more.

My shimshana shivered in my belly, and I felt a rush of heat. A glance in the full-length mirror confirmed my suspicions: my skin and eyes were glowing a violent, deep red.

And he could take the heat. He wasn't affected by it at all.

I pulled my arms out of their pinned position and stood before him in all my red, Shimshana glory. His face registered pleased surprise. Splaying my fingers and extending my hands in front of me, I connected them to his massive chest and pushed. He moved backward, rapidly, until he fell backward onto the bed.

Justin was no stranger to my bed. We had fed there many times during my Mahá. But never like this. The room was red, and his skin reflected the red glow as if red lightbulbs were turned on. As his back hit the fluffy, white comforter, he reached up and pulled me down so that my back was now sunk into the softness of the covers.

He flipped himself up to kneel next to me, and I propped myself on my elbows, curious to see what he was doing. He took one of my braids and started unraveling it, smiling and managing to look deadly serious at the same time. Soon my hair fell around my back and shoulders in fat, black waves. He let himself fall backward again on the bed while clasping his hands around my waist so that I fell partially on top of him, my leg thrown over his thighs, and the majority of my body weight on the mattress.

Running his hands through my hair until his fingers got lost in it, he closed his eyes. His heart beat as wildly as mine. He gently tugged on the roots of my hair.

I fought the urge to take him right then and decided to prolong the inevitable. I nibbled his neck as payback for the torture he'd put me through with the chin kiss.

He brought my head down to his neck and moaned. Begged for it.

There was no more reason to wait. No reason to show any self-control. I leaned in to take what he was offering.

Then he spoke.

"Take me how you want." His voice was deep, commanding. "I can take it."

I fell off the precipice and responded in true Shimshana form. Forcefully. With a surge of strength, I quickly pinned him to the bed, letting my full weight crush him down onto the mattress. My instinct to immobilize kicked in and I pinned his hands above his head.

I leaned in and penetrated his neck.

It felt like my entire body exploded into a million pieces of glory. The familiar taste of him shot through me like lightning as I sucked stronger and stronger with each pull.

His moans and urgent whispers urged me on.

I didn't have to worry about killing Justin. He'd been reborn for me, and I could never kill him again. He, and only he, had the ability to feed me forever.

The warmth that comes from connecting with human gaddis swept through me, and his consciousness started to open to me. He started to unbutton my top. I didn't stop him. I didn't care. I wanted it all. To merge on every level. To erase the emptiness, the void that had taken over my heart. I wanted to *feel* again. To pulse and throb like an individual ray of light leaning toward an infinite sun.

It was like a colossal wave had picked me up and now carried me helpless toward a distant shore, a place I had only heard of and never visited. I was helpless but willing. Powerless yet determined.

I drank him in more as his hands began to unhook my bra. His fingertips pressed into the small of my back while his thumbs massaged my lower belly.

And then I saw into his consciousness. He was angry with me.

I sucked harder, faster. It was too good to stop.

But, eventually, I did stop. Passed out beneath me, Justin's skin was pale and his body looked pounds lighter. I'd literally sucked him dry.

I was confident he was okay. At least physically. But the emotion of anger was so strong it caused me to wonder if he really was all right as we lay there on the bed, him completely knocked out and me curled up along his side with my head on his chest. I drifted to sleep a cloud of blood satiation.

GRAY AREAS

The next morning, I stretched myself awake as brilliant sunlight cascaded through the windows. I paused in disbelief, recalling the events of last night. That didn't really happen...did it?

I looked under the covers and down at my clothes. I wore the same thing from yesterday, which was highly unusual for me because sleeping in street clothes was uncomfortable and kind of gross.

I sat up in bed as every tiny detail flooded my head. My face grew hot with embarrassment as I recalled the way our bodies moved together and burned with shame when I recalled that I'd completely drained him without a shred of concern.

Guilt soon joined the shame and embarrassment when I thought of the intimate way we'd stared into each other's eyes. Even though I'd formally broken it off with Sawyer, a part of me felt like what we had shared was sacred and that I'd crossed the line with Justin.

But Sawyer was gone.

Where was Justin?

My eyes quickly scanned the room and came to rest on my flashing cell phone. I zipped over to it and scrolled through text messages. There were a number of texts from people I didn't know, asking where the party was. I made a mental note to get a new phone number—for family and friends only. There were more texts, including a couple from Samantha and Niana, asking me where I was and could they crash. Toward the bottom was a text from Justin. I looked at his name on the screen for a few seconds, absorbing the fact that it hadn't been in my call log for a while. Now that it was there in front of me, I felt alive again, free in a way I'd taken for granted before.

His text was short:

> Going to get groceries. Took your car. Be back soon.

He was recharging his energy and fueling up for the next feeding.

I stretched and yawned and looked out the window at the position of the sun. That didn't seem right...I looked at the cell phone again to check the time.

Was it really that late? I felt...the way I did after the night I got drunk. It was so long since I'd had fresh blood, it was like I was hungover.

I took a shower, and let the hot water invigorate me, before I rebraided my damp hair and got dressed in jeans and a T-shirt.

By the time I was done, I heard Justin in the kitchen. I didn't hear any other heartbeats in the house, so I made my way through the walls and floors until I was sitting at the breakfast nook.

He was at the stove, cooking bacon. The vent was turned on high and rock music blasted from his iPod on the dock. A bag of Yum Yum donut holes sat on the counter next to the stove. He popped a couple powdered ones into his mouth before throwing some bread in the toaster oven.

"You were knocked out like a light." He turned toward me with a wicked smile. "Exhausted."

"Hardly," I said, easily falling back into our old pattern of banter. "But it had been a long time since I had fresh blood. It's affected me, I suppose."

For the first time in a long time, I didn't wake up starving. That too was an effect of having fresh blood. It was like the organic oatmeal Mom used to make for breakfast—all natural and it made you feel fuller for longer.

"There were a lot of people here," he said, turning back to flip the bacon. "I took care of it for you."

"What do you mean?"

"I asked them to leave." He placed the spatula on the counter and turned back to me. "Angel, there were at least twenty people here after the party. A few of them looked like they were moving in, complete with small suitcases and overnight bags." He looked into my eyes with concern. "Why are you surrounded by people but seem so...lonely?"

I inhaled shocked gushes of air—first in surprise and then in self-pity—as the tears started to flow. I told him everything that had happened: Mom's sleep-death (he held me in his arms as I relayed the story), Dad's leaving, Sawyer and I breaking up, scaring a pack of werewolves (he seemed especially interested in that story), fighting with the girls, and dissolving the mind lock. It all came out in an emotion-filled, lengthy monologue that he listened to intently while eating bacon, eggs, toast, fruit, cheese, and a large salad.

As I spoke, the fact that Justin knew me in ways nobody, not even my family, knew me hit me once again. I could talk to him about anything; I couldn't even say that about Cici. He was the only one who knew about my relationship with the angels, and the fact that he was immortal—and more importantly, *why* he was immortal—was a secret we would carry through eternity. Although his consciousness opened itself to me in the usual way of gaddis, the transference of our emotions to each other was unique. It was easy for him to pick up on the way I felt, in a way no one else could.

We were bound by blood.

"So," he said between bites of scrambled eggs, "being surrounded by strangers and wannabes are a way for you to not have to focus on the fact that you feel alone. But you aren't alone. I'll stay with you as long as you need me. Forever, if necessary."

"Justin, I don't want you to get the wrong idea. Just because we were…affectionate…last night doesn't mean you have to do all that."

"I know I don't *have* to do anything." He placed his fork down, crossed his arms and looked at me with a somewhat stern look. It was the up-and-coming cop stance; he may've been just a Boston Police Department intern, but as the son of the Superintendent he had stern down to a science. "You were about to kill somebody last night, Angel. Why?"

"Besides the obvious fact that I was starved for fresh blood?" I instantly regretted my sarcastic tone. "I'm sorry, Justin. You see, in my world, immortals have different ways of living their lives. It's not illegal to eat people, just morally questionable given today's options." I went on to explain Trads and Incs, and how I'd made a decision to live as a Trad, and how that tied to the mind lock dissolution.

"You're not the same girl I knew a few months ago, Angel." He picked up the empty dishes and started washing them. "That girl would rather kill herself than kill another human being. You've grown into a woman who understands that nothing is cut and dried, that life is full of gray areas. It's your instinct that drives you to hunt. But your nature is love. I'd think no matter what way you decide to live your life, you'll make decisions that will affect you for the rest of your life."

The truth of his words hit me. He understood the dichotomy, the tightrope I was walking.

On one hand, I needed to be true to who I am, but who was that? At my Mahá, it had been determined that I wasn't too dangerous for the Council to allow me to live, but it was also established that I wasn't an ordinary immortal. There was no benchmark for me. No set definition as to what Angel Brown was even supposed to be about.

And there was my legacy. The last immortal to be so powerful was my half brother Tunde. At one point, even some of my own family members were afraid I'd turn out like him: evil and destructive.

Was I just a girl—or according to Justin, a *woman*—making my way in life, trying to figure it out as I went along? Or was there something more to my existence? Was there something that I could do that no one else could do, something important that I was supposed to contribute to the world?

How long would it take me to figure this stuff out?

Justin finished washing dishes and wiped his hands on one of the blue dish towels hanging on a stainless-steel rack on the side of the granite island that served as my breakfast nook. He sat on the stool next to me and took my hands in his. It wasn't my imagination. He'd grown more muscular since the last time I'd seen him. Even his hands were bigger. At the age of eighteen, he was still growing.

"I'm ready for you," he said.

It was my turn to cross my arms and look stern. "You're angry at me, Justin. Why?"

"Am I?" He looked down as if he was turning his awareness within. After a minute, he looked back up and nodded. "Yes, I guess I was. For letting it get to the point where you would kill someone. But now that I understand, that's no longer an issue."

I almost believed him, but there was something too tidy about that explanation.

He got up, swept me off the stool and threw me over his shoulder. "You're getting hungry."

"Put me down. I'm not hungry."

"You will be by the time we get upstairs."

He was right. Just the fact that he was there, ready and willing, made my mouth water.

Afterward, I made my way downstairs while he slept. I saw Cici outside on the grounds. It looked like she was coming back from the tennis court. I swished through the walls and raced across the grass until I was beside her. She practically pounced on me the moment I fell into step beside her.

"I can smell Justin all over the house." She stared at me for a long, silent moment as if that would give her information that talking couldn't. "Angel, did you mate with him? Tell me what's going on!"

Poor Cici; she was having a hard time adjusting to having to ask for information now that she was no longer in my head. I held my face up to the sun as we walked along, loving the way the warmth caressed my skin. "First of all, no I didn't mate with him."

Staring at me expectantly, Cici raised her eyebrows as if to say *And...?*

"But I think we almost did...It."

"No!"

"Yes!"

We came to one of the garden benches. She pulled me down to sit in the little nook surrounded by tall hedges drenched in fragrant jasmine. The scent made me think of Justin. Matter of fact, the spot where I'd accidentally killed him was only twenty yards away.

Cici sat in a normal mortal position and fussed with her tank top, shorts, and tennis shoes. I sat trying to formulate my words before finally folding my hands to signal my readiness to talk. She exhaled in anticipation of hot-off-the-press news and became perfectly still.

"Well...I was about to eat somebody, here at the house party, and he showed up." Her mouth dropped open slightly before she snapped her lips shut. She obviously didn't want to do anything that would stop the flow of my storytelling.

I continued to tell her everything, including the feeling of wanting him in every way.

"Weird timing on his part," she said almost to herself. "To show up at the precise time you were about to eat someone."

No one knew that, as a result of Bodiel's resuscitation, Justin was seemingly wired to respond to my hunger no matter what. It was better to let her think it was a coincidence, so I said nothing. There was a short, comfortable silence as she continued to process my story.

"Are you over Sawyer?"

"I don't think I'll ever be over Sawyer. But he's not here. He's better off living his life away from me."

"Do you think the feelings you shared last night were due to the Blood Obsession?"

"Justin says he's not obsessed."

"The blood-obsessed are the last to know they are, so that doesn't mean that he's not. And it doesn't mean you're immune to the intensity of his feeling. The blood tie, once established, is a force to be reckoned with, almost impossible to break."

"I was so hot wanting him," I said.

"Ewww, too much information." She wrinkled her nose.

"You never said that about Sawyer."

"Well," she changed the subject. "It's not like before your Mahá. Back then, Justin was mortal; you hadn't turned him into a vampire yet."

The general belief was that Justin was a vampire, since Shimshana are responsible for accidentally creating the vampire race. Nobody knows why, but eons ago, random mortals probed by Shimshana died and resurrected as the blood-sucking creatures now known as vampires. There are many varieties of them, but the main difference between us and them is that we're alive and they're subject to us. So even though it's a rare event, the fact that Justin was now immortal and seemingly ruled by my hunger fit that explanation.

"So," Cici continued, "with Justin, the stigma of mating with a mortal is gone. He can be with you forever, albeit still your blood-obsessed vampire slave, but at least you wouldn't have to experience his death. Is that what you prefer?"

"I don't know. I just know I feel so much better now. More grounded. Less kill-happy."

Cici nodded in agreement. "It helps that there aren't a million people here anymore. A couple of them were pretty ridiculous. Actually had the nerve to try and order Kiya around."

"They did *not* mess with Kiya!"

"Oh, yes. They did." Her smile was devious. "But she taught them a lesson. Apparently, objects mysteriously appeared in front of their feet as they walked down the stairs. A few bumps and bruises, nothing serious."

"Better they didn't end up as my dinner," I said.

"Speaking of dinner, why's Justin eating food? I can tell by his scent that he was in the kitchen cooking."

Even if I could answer that question truthfully, that Justin wasn't a vampire but a recipient of angel's breath, I'm not sure she would understand. But I couldn't answer. I literally couldn't open my mouth to form any type of answer, whether truthful or not. Bodiel and Knowledge, the angels responsible for bringing him back to life, made it impossible for me to reveal anything. All I could do was shrug and widen my eyes in helpless silence.

"Very strange," she muttered. "Anyway, I've got to admit, he takes good care of you. Sawyer did too, but Justin's way is different." She looked at her watch. "Oh, no. I have an appointment to see a house with Satchel. I'll be late." We raced toward the house and were back inside in less than ten seconds, with me arriving a few seconds after she did. She flew up the stairs and returned a couple of minutes later in a simple sundress, shoes and purse in hand. She could fly to make up lost time, but hated doing so in a dress or when she didn't want the wind to mess up her clothes and hair.

"I can't wait to see this house." Her eyes sparkled as she bent down to put on her sandals. "None of the others seemed right, but this one might be the perfect one." We shared excited smiles and a warm hug before she left.

Still smiling, I grabbed a blanket from one of the linen closets and, deciding to become more acquainted with my own backyard, wandered back outside.

And I wanted to test something…

It bugged me that my time-stopping ability had disappeared. Even though this type of thing happened with newborn abilities all the time, I still wanted to see what would happen if I really concentrated—hard, without distractions.

During my Mahá, I'd had a few moments to check out the grounds, but honestly I was so wound up from the drama and the guests, I'd had no time to enjoy it and just chill. I basked in it now, luxuriated in the riotous colors and combined fragrances of grass, dahlia blooms, and trees, along with the ocean breeze coming in from the coast a couple of miles away. I made a mental note to send a thank you note to whomever was responsible for the grounds upkeep; it felt like my own, private slice of heaven.

I rambled down the white, stone steps that led to the pool, loving the feeling of the hot sun as it caressed my skin. I'd always loved warm weather but now, as a full-grown Shimshana, I appreciated it even more. It seemed as if my body was a sponge that soaked sunshine in and processed it as energy, even fuel. Shimshana love sunshine. Ironic since our spawn, vampires, were for the most part inherently averse to sunlight.

Once past the pool, I stopped along a crushed-stone footpath and let the rays bathe one side of my face before slowly turning my head to the other side. The heat warmed, and then slightly burned my cheek as my shimshana quivered delightfully.

Banking a right at the jasmine nook, I meandered across the emerald-green lawn (the color of Sawyer's eyes), through the formal rose garden with its pink roses, and past manicured hedges, before a small path led me to a clearing featuring a koi pond. My lips parted in surprise as my eyes took in the man-made waterfall; I'd heard the water from the house, but had never seen it. The music of the graceful, cascading water, blended with the symphony of insects and birds, as I watched the dazzling koi fish swish along. I unfolded my blanket on the surrounding grass. It was the perfect place to figure out what could still be done in the time-stopping department, as the only way to gauge what was going on was to observe living things for signs of movement.

Sitting down on the blanket, I took a deep breath and searched for the "button," a depression in the air molecules around me that when mentally clicked would begin the process of the time freeze.

Try as I might, I couldn't locate it.

My exasperation grew in spite of the tranquility surrounding me. "Stay calm," I told myself. Although my time-stopping ability had originally been activated at times of duress, I'd learned how to initiate it while calm, thanks to Bodiel and Knowledge. Still, no matter how much I concentrated, nothing happened.

Finally I located the button and focused on pressing it with my mind. I peeked at the koi. They still swam. Frustrated, I tried again. Located the button and depressed it. This was it, it felt like something had happened. I looked at the fish again. But to my horror, they were still moving—not swimming as before, but stopping and going belly-up. I felt dizzy, as if my head was swimming like the koi used to.

212

"Angel, you okay?" Justin's voice came from a few feet away down the path as he walked, and then ran, toward me. My head pitched toward the blanket. In a flash he was by my side, just in time to catch me as I fainted into his arms.

COLLABORATION

I woke up on my back, the feeling of the blanket and cushy grass beneath me. Justin relaxed next to me, his bleeding wrist in my mouth. The last thing I remembered was the dying koi.

"You passed out." His voice was low. "How do you feel?"

I turned my head and saw concern on his face. He was propped up on an elbow while his arm, the one attached to the wrist that was feeding me, rested gently on my chest.

I recalled the feeling I'd had after seeing the fish die and finally realized what'd happened. But I couldn't understand *why* it happened.

"You came just in time." My voice, as my lips moved against his wrist, was slightly hoarse.

"I felt something wrong with you," he answered. "When I saw you, it looked like you were concentrating on something. What happened?"

I told him what I'd been trying to do. His facial expression went from a frown to looking disturbed to looking confused. "Do you know why you passed out?"

"No idea." It was an admission and a frustrated exclamation all at once, and his wrist now rested somewhere near my throat. "Poor, sweet fish." I felt tears well up as I recalled the rapid way their bodies turned forty-five degrees in the water to expose their bellies and profiles. "They didn't deserve that."

He withdrew the wrist and quickly proceeded to straddle me, blocking out the sunshine so that the only thing in my line of sight was his broad chest straining within its Red Sox T-shirt. Alarmed, I glared at him. "What the heck are you doing?" I demanded.

"Changing the subject." His tone was matter-of-fact. "Besides, you need to feed. I can feel it."

As soon as he said it, my stomach growled, and my shimshana started to unravel. Darn it, why did he have to be so in tune with me?

He bent his head down next to my forehead so that his neck was in line with my mouth. All I had to do was lift my head a few centimeters. He gently placed a hand under the back of my head so I didn't even have to do that. I parted my lips and took him in.

The more alert I became, the more aware I became. Aware of Justin. He'd come to my rescue again. And now covered me with his body and his strength. I felt protected here in this garden. Cared for. And I knew that he felt protective toward me.

Was I...falling in love with Justin...?

"I can give you everything that you need," he whispered as if in answer to my unspoken question. The fragrant air, sunshine, and birdsong served as a backdrop to the urgency in his voice.

Without breaking our connection, he rolled over, taking me with him, so that I lay on top of him. He held my hips down so that I had no choice but to feel the length of him pressed against me. My breath caught with the sensation of pleasure his unexpected move caused.

"Everything," he repeated in a ragged whisper.

I closed my eyes and kept my body still. I couldn't afford a repeat of last night's nosedive off of the emotional edge. Sunshine burned the space between my shoulder blades as I steadied my breath.

He said he could give me everything. I could definitely feel the intensity of his emotion. But was it really everything? Or was it just a distraction from the truth: that there was no getting over Sawyer. I pondered these questions before drifting off, there on the blanket and on top of his chest, to join Justin in sleep.

# # #

A couple of hours later, I was in the studio, working on the ballad track. Since it was the weekend, Warren wasn't around. It felt strange, but good to be alone. From the ballad segments, I'd created a track of the piano solo and was adding a rough vocal when the doorbell rang.

A quick sniff told me who was at the door: Jules and LaLa. It was all I could do not to jump for joy and jet to the door. But I had to play the role of the one who wanted them gone. I took my time opening the door.

I looked at them, they looked at me, and we all began talking at the same time: "I'm so sorry." / "Why were we even fighting?" / "What the heck happened to us?"

I was relieved that they seemed like their old selves and vowed they'd never know what'd really happened. My newborn phase would soon be over,

216

and this weird effect would be a thing of the past; until then, I'd find ways to take frequent, small breaks for their sake. "I'm sorry whatever happened happened," I said, "and hope it doesn't happen again." I picked up a couple of their bags, and they came inside.

We hugged in the foyer while the California sun streamed through the oversize windows. The sweet smell of my best friends filled my heart, my soul, and my nostrils. Thank goodness my stomach was completely full. In no time, we were back in the studio and back in our groove.

"What made you guys come back today?" I asked Jules during LaLa's pee break. The massive tea drinking was taking a toll.

"Nina."

LaLa returned. "Yeah, she told us the only reason we were here was to make an album, and if we weren't doing that, then we were just wasting time."

"Working remotely slowed us down," I said in agreement as Jules made her way out of the studio to the bathroom.

LaLa continued. "This morning I called J and was like, 'What are we doing? We've got all this stuff to do,' and she was like 'Yeah, this is stupid; let's go back.' I hadn't even unpacked. I was like so out of there."

"It sucked not having you guys here."

"Yeah," she agreed. "I finally bought some new clothes, though."

"Thank goodness," I said playfully as she hit my arm.

Her smile melted away. "But I felt strange, too." Her voice lowered as if she expected someone to overhear. "I slept a lot when I wasn't writing or working on the tracks you uploaded. It was weird."

Only if you don't know your body was healing from your best friend's immortal newborn influence. "That *is* weird," I agreed before hurriedly changing the subject.

We rehearsed "No. 8" and reviewed Redd's choreography in front of The Club's floor-to-ceiling mirrors. When we were happy with how the moves looked, we took the rehearsal to the Sound Room— an auditorium-like space that had great acoustics, a ministage, and room for a couple hundred seats. We set up our wireless microphones and got to work.

After a few run-throughs, Justin walked in. I'd heard him earlier, foraging and cooking in the kitchen. "Need help?" he asked, throwing his voice from the doorway to the stage. LaLa and Jules stared at him like he was a Martian, and we all stopped dancing.

"Yeah," I answered, making an effort to keep my face expressionless and my voice even, despite what I could only imagine was going through their minds. "We could use a videographer. Stand where the camera is." I pointed to where my cell phone was positioned. "Jules, LaLa, you remember Justin, don'cha?"

"Weren't you at our record release party back in the winter?" Jules asked, barely hiding her confusion.

His smile was scintillating as he said "Yeah" and walked over to my cell phone. "This good?" he asked.

"Perfect," I said, taking great care to tone down the intensity that had taken up residence in even our most benign conversations.

I could almost feel four eyes boring into the back of my head as I stood slightly in front of my girls and picked up the routine where we'd left off. I'd be hit with twenty-one questions later, but, for now, I decided to ignore their looks.

We repeated the routine a number of times, with Justin changing positions to record different viewpoints; he even got video footage of our feet as we worked the routine.

"We need an audience," Jules said, jumping down from the ministage and panting from exertion.

"Yeah," LaLa agreed, toweling off her forehead. "The video will be very helpful"—this she said with a grateful nod at Justin—"but we still need people's responses while rocking the song."

"Agreed," I said. I turned off all the electrical devices and lights before closing the room's doors and leading everyone down the hall to the kitchen. Night had fallen, and the sliver of the new moon was visible through one of the skylights.

Justin and the girls immediately started rummaging around; Jules grabbed fruit and more tea, while LaLa and Justin started collaborating on different types of sandwiches with all the fixings they discovered, including a whole roast chicken, hummus, and grilled veggies.

"The good thing is," LaLa said between bites, "there aren't a ton of people here hanging out."

"Definitely not missing the Bobbsey Twins," Jules added while slicing an apple.

"Thank Justin for that." I took a sip of tea. "He kicked everybody out."

LaLa high-fived him. "Yes!" she said. "You so rock."

"Gotta have law and order," he said in a light tone.

"I agree we had a lot of people around," Jules said with a daintier high-five to Justin. "But it was good to get feedback from people."

We all agreed. I started tapping an e-mail on my cell. "Maybe Nina can recommend something. E-mailing her now." I pressed Send and put the phone down, purposely ignoring the double digits on my text notification icon. "In the meantime, we can make a list of people who were actually helpful and invite them back," I said.

"It'll be a short list," LaLa said. Jules snorted, and we all laughed.

Justin shot me a brief but significant look before heading out of the room. By the time I was done laughing, I felt it too. Hunger…

It was time to lie.

"I'm exhausted," I said in a casual tone. "Was up all night." At least the last part wasn't a lie. I started backing toward one of the minor staircases. "Time for bed."

Jules threw a side-eye at Justin's partially eaten sandwich. Her lips pursed as she stared at his now empty chair and then looked at me as if to say *you better tell me what's going on.* But all she said was, "Completely understand." She grinned widely and exchanged a long, significant look with LaLa, who simply winked at me and said "Sweet dreams, Angel."

FEEDBACK

The next morning, the sun had yet to rise as I made my way to the studio. The girls were playing the ballad track, Justin was in the kitchen again and I felt amazing, like I could go on indefinitely. My body was satisfied, the emptiness was gone, my girls were back, and life was good.

But the track's raw emotion crept into my head, and by the time I stepped into the studio, the melancholy within the chord structure had found its way into my heart.

"It's about Sawyer, isn't it?" LaLa asked me as she lowered the volume. I nodded.

"It's beautiful." Jules's voice was awed.

I started singing the rough vocals. Soon the sadness in my voice had the girls close to tears.

"I don't understand," Jules cried. "Why are you with—*ow!*" LaLa punched her in the arm as if to say *shut up*, and I tucked the ballad away in my head where it could vegetate more.

For what seemed like the millionth time, my cell phone vibrated with another text, so finally I decided to go through them. Just as I thought, there were more texts from people I didn't know, or Samantha and Niana asking if everything was okay. A quick scroll through the remaining texts told me Markus's tour was on its last leg, and Demeter was looking for work. Demeter was a makeup apprentice at my Mahá, and also a big fan of Kat Trio. She'd started a fan club for us that was pretty popular on the social media circuit.

And there was a text from Nina.

"Nina's coming to L.A. tomorrow to check on us," I said, reading the brief text before putting the phone down. "She also asked Cici to take us to a party tonight."

"A party?" LaLa asked. "On a Sunday night?"

"Where?" Jules asked.

I texted Cici with a single question mark. We worked on tracks until my phone vibrated again. It was Cici:

> Nina says u guys nd a chaperone. Said I wld. Tell u mre whn I get back. 2 hrs.

We continued to work. I briefly wondered what Sawyer was up to, but I pushed the thought to the back of my mind where the ballad was and focused doggedly on the music.

Soon—well, it felt like soon, but it had really been hours of being lost in music—Cici walked in and expressed surprise to see the girls back, even though she'd surely smelled them the minute she walked in the door. It blew my mind how our lives with mortals were so deeply rooted in lies and illusion.

"So, we're going to Mystery Perkins's house," Cici said as she sat crossed-legged on one of the couches.

"The guy who produces that vampire show?" LaLa asked. Cici nodded, and Jules, Lala, and I exchanged wide-eyed glances.

The show *I Need Your Blood* was very popular. It was one of those vampires-in-high-school shows with really cute guys, cute girls, and cute parents.

"That show is always looking for music from up-and-comers," I said.

"Maybe that's what this is about," LaLa added. "Maybe they want to feature our music on the show." We all considered the possibility for a few seconds.

"Nina's sending a car," Cici said. She sipped out of a lidded container. A quick whiff told me it was A-positive. "She said it's Mystery's third wife's birthday," she continued. "So, little-black-dress it up, with makeup."

Cici used to hound me about hating makeup. While I still thought it was a waste of time, I resigned myself to having to pay attention to it for industry stuff—like tonight's party at Mystery's house. If wearing makeup was key to making a good impression on folks, then it was part of the job of being what Mom called me: Ms. Pop Star.

I texted Demeter back, asking her if she was available to help me tonight. Almost immediately she texted back:

YES!!!!!!!!!!!!!!!!!!

Well, that was easy.

We worked until the sun started to set and the layered vocals on the EyeHeart Beatz track were sounding like perfection. It was time to turn our attention to dressing for the party.

"What on earth are we going to wear?" Jules asked as if she'd never asked the question before.

We were developing a routine based on Cici's help in the past. Dubbed the Fashion Train, we'd each run to our rooms and pull out clothing items. Then we formed a "train" that stopped at everyone's room, where we'd help each other put together a complete outfit until everyone knew exactly what she would wear and how it related (or didn't relate) to what the other two were wearing. The routine was usually accompanied by a lot of hooting, giggling, screaming, and general silliness. Justin popped his head into my room when the Fashion Train came to the Angel stop.

"What's going on?" he asked in a tone that said he was afraid to ask what was going on.

"C'mon in," Jules said between giggles. "We're trying to sexy Angel up. What do you think of this?" She held up a little black dress, which she'd pulled out of the clothes from my Mahá.

Justin's eyes took in the dress, and his face clearly showed he was imagining it on me. My face burned with embarrassment.

"Very nice," he said after a long moment.

The girls agreed. We quickly picked out shoes and accessories, and then it was time to go to LaLa's room. The train pulled out, but my car got held back by Justin's hand on my arm.

"You need me there or will you pack your lunch?"

He had a point. The little dress wouldn't work with a backpack of blood.

"Sure," I said. "You can be my date."

It would definitely help get Sawyer off my mind. All night I dreamt that I was tiptoeing around his studio as he and his assistant, the dearly-departed Heist, worked on a track.

After admiring LaLa's new clothes, the train finished its rounds, the girls started getting ready, and I went back to my room. I heard Demeter arrive and join Justin in the kitchen where he was, no doubt, fueling up for our next session. His entire life now revolved around me and my newborn needs.

I ran an extra-hot shower and scrubbed my skin as if trying to wash the ballad and all thoughts of Sawyer Creed from my mind. I had no idea how to style my hair in a way that would go with the classy, little black dress. After several failed attempts at twists, and a horrid French braid, I decided to wear bantu knots. I divided my hair into four even sections and then, at immortal speed, gelled, brushed, twisted and pinned them into perfectly coiled, large twists.

"Demeter, I'm ready now," I said in a conversational tone. While I waited for her to come up the stairs, I added a few rhinestone hairpins that Cici would approve of.

Demeter appeared in the doorway with her makeup box. She looked like the same super-awkward seventeen-year-old from my Mahá, but her style was more goth—loads of black eyeliner, lipstick, and false eyelashes. She looked great.

"Hi, Angel!" Her enthusiasm hadn't changed. "Your hair looks amazing! I know the exact way I'm going to make you up for the house party. I love *I Need Your Blood*. It's very dark, so that look will really fit with the theme: dark and dramatic. It'll look great!"

She was good at what she did, and I felt free to let my mind wander as she worked. I thought of

Sawyer again. He'd never seen this particular hairstyle on me. Would he like it? He always enjoyed playing with my hair. My mind went over the last time we'd made out in my room. How we talked about being together forever...

Demeter was finished. I looked in the mirror, and my jaw dropped nearly to the floor. Looking back at me was the most beautiful, mysterious Shimshana chick on the face of the earth. Was that really me? My eyes looked so dark and mysterious they didn't look like mine.

Surely this was beyond mere everyday-beautician capacity. I turned to Demeter. "What are you?"

She wore a small smile. "I have a gift for illusion." Her smile melted into a worried expression. "Did I go too far?"

"Well, I'm shocked, but it's probably because I don't wear makeup a lot." I surveyed my face. True it was dramatic, but other people might think it was just a professional makeup job. I backpedaled so that she didn't feel bad. "It looks so good, I was completely bowled over. Will you be my makeup artist from now on?"

Her face broke into another big smile. "Of course! I do hair, too!" She hugged me quickly, awkwardly. At my Mahá she'd grown terrified of me, despite her fandom, but time seemed to have taken that fear away. She quickly cleaned and stored her tools, before following me down the stairs. "Oh, by the way. I helped Justin with his clothes for tonight," she said. "A date wearing the wrong thing can bring your look down. Hope that was okay."

He stood at the bottom of the stairs. The way he watched me descend the stairs took my breath away, and then I realized I was experiencing *his* feelings of breathlessness as he watched me.

"You look beautiful." He didn't even try *not* to stare.

He didn't look so bad himself. Demeter had somehow come up with a great outfit that accentuated his broad shoulders. She also trimmed his hair and styled it so that it looked like he just rolled out of bed.

The doorbell rang and Cici, in a hot pink minidress with platform sandals, opened the door. It was Satchel carrying another cluster of flowers—orchids this time—for Cici. Jules and LaLa came down, and we all complimented each other, especially LaLa's new clothes.

Clearly uncomfortable with the fashion-focused attention she was getting, LaLa quickly turned the spotlight on me. "Angel, you look like a sexy vampire."

I passed the compliment ball to cover my shock. "Jules, you look like a hot R&B megastar."

We all laughed as the other immortals and I exchanged super-quick glances, too fast for mortals to notice, in a purposely delayed reaction to LaLa's vampire remark.

Shimshana hate—absolutely *loathe*—being referred to as vampires.

We continued to make small talk until the limo arrived. As we climbed in, Justin held out his hand to help steady me as I sat down next to him, and then whispered in my ear, "Since you're officially the sexy bloodsucker, I guess that makes me the sexy, and very willing, bloodsuckee."

"Now that's the old Justin starting to shine through," I answered. "Majorly corny."

Mystery Perkins's house was ginormous. He'd recently married Tara Hennigan, the famous actress who played mom to the vampire witch on *I Need Your Blood*. She was more beautiful in real life and welcomed us, and a hundred other "specially invited" guests, into the Encino mansion they'd just renovated for themselves and their blended family of three kids and five dogs. None of the latter were anywhere in sight. The house had extensive grounds, including two tennis courts, a small golf course, and a second two-story bungalow, which served as Mystery's office, where he sometimes holed himself up to write for days—this according to Tara, who was down to earth in a way I hadn't seen much of in L.A.

We chatted with Mystery and some of the other *I Want Your Blood* writer/producers and made the rounds the way Nina had taught us: be friendly to everyone, no matter how weird they seem, because you never know who your next business partner may be; never ogle the really famous people; talk for a little while but never stay too long with anyone—just keep it moving; and, no matter what you do, absolutely don't be surprised when other people know who you are.

"This working-the-room crap is killing my feet," LaLa said after an hour of schmoozing.

"Seriously," Jules replied as she threw a little wave and a smile to someone across the room. "I'm about to take these things off and kick it barefoot. Angel, you have the freakishly good memory. Have we hit everybody on the talk-to list?"

"Think so," I said, recalling Nina's e-mail containing detailed instructions on who to talk to and exactly what to say to exactly whom. I pulled out my phone and pretended to review the e-mail.

"I want a drink," Jules said.

"You guys are too young to drink," Justin said with a lightning-quick wink at me. He put a protective hand under my elbow and, annoyed, I shook it off.

"And you're not?" I shot back defensively. Who did he think he was?

Cici ignored the tense little exchange between me and Justin. "I promised Nina that I'd take good care of you tonight. So don't make me look bad."

"Can we go home now?" LaLa begged.

"No," I answered, still pretending to scroll through the e-mail. I repeated the request from Nina. "After making sure we personally touch base with all the folks on the list, we're to hang out and be seen by as many people as possible for one whole hour."

"Time to dance," Cici said as she and Satchel headed to the dance floor. They were followed by Jules, who became the life of the party after taking off her shoes. Soon a number of female celebrities and a couple of guys followed suit and formed a barefooted circle around Jules. LaLa and I watched from the sidelines until a well-known TV actor asked her to dance.

Justin and I stood there, alone and together. I could feel the weird energy between us. For some reason, and at that precise moment, I found him highly annoying.

Or maybe I was just annoyed at myself for calling him my date, annoyed at having him at my elbow as if he were my boyfriend, and annoyed at myself for not being sure whether he was or not.

The outer corners of my vision clouded with a red tinge.

"Come on," he said in my ear. "I saw a place."

He led me by the hand out to the house's extensive grounds. The backyard—more like the back *football field*—was terraced, and its massive trees were lit from lights in the ground beneath them, which made it feel like we were walking through a magical land. He kept a firm grip on my hand, and I followed him blindly, thinking of only one thing.

We walked over a charming footbridge that led to a cleared circular area where people dressed in leather and wearing fake fangs walked around posing for and taking pictures with the guests. Surrounded by trees, the clearing featured stone flooring, small bistro tables with candles, and soft Dracula-ish music piped from speakers hidden around the perimeter.

It was like every Shimshana's nightmare.

"Welcome to The Grotto," one of the fake-fanged dudes said. "Picture?"

"No, thanks," Justin quickly answered.

Another dude carrying a tray approached us as Justin pulled me off the path and toward the trees. "How about some blood?" dude asked, dramatically baring the fake fangs and proffering red wine.

"Yes, I'll take some." I said it sweetly and took a step toward him, ready to suck someone dry.

Justin's grip on my arm tightened and he clamped the other hand around my waist. "No, thanks, man," he said quickly. He literally dragged me away. My heels dug into the grass, and I stumbled. Justin picked me up midstride and quickened his pace.

I hissed with disappointment. "Party pooper. That guy was type B."

Soon we were deep in the woods, away from the house's grounds, and away from the sound of human heartbeats. He finally put me down.

"I'm Type J," he said. "And I'm the only one you'll have tonight."

# # #

The next morning, Nina arrived shortly after Jules and LaLa's caffeine had kicked in. We talked about business, including the fact that Demeter would be my personal expense, not Kat Trio's.

While we listened to tracks, Justin came and sat in. Jules and LaLa continued to *not* pepper me with questions about him, but they'd gone gaga after seeing us walking out of the woods disheveled and brushing dirt off our clothes the night before. Nina, after being introduced to him, didn't even blink at what may have been perceived as a Sawyer replacement. She was in the business for so long, it was doubtful anything shocked her.

Despite an early morning feeding with Justin, I still felt annoyed. Wouldn't he be a good choice for me? He was immortal, and I'd never go hungry; what could be better than that? But on the other hand, one day I'd stop being a blood-hungry newborn. On that day, would I look at him and realize I'd made a mistake? And what about the continual question: was he blood obsessed? Were his intense feelings for me really love or were they just a chemical reaction?

My eyes slid in his direction at the same time that he took a glance at me. Yes, we were going to figure out the answers to these questions. But for now, I had to focus on the music.

Today was a huge day. Nina scheduled listening sessions for a number of handpicked tracks, including two of Sawyer's. Heeding our plea for feedback, she'd also arranged for a steady stream of people to come through during the day. Both Kiya and Sarah were on hand. Warren was nonstop. Nina critiqued the video footage of our Stevidy/USAMA dance routine and then watched as we performed live on the ministage. Even with not having a lot of time *and* Kat Trio taking time away from each other, the general feedback was that we'd made excellent progress.

By the end of the day, everyone, mortal and immortal, was beat. Unlike the days when I looked for some evening diversion, now I wanted nothing more than to go to bed. Jules and LaLa were still excited by the positive feedback and decided to celebrate by going to the movies. Nina had a meeting with House Quake the next day and congratulated us before making her way to the airport. I said good night to Kiya, Sarah, and Warren before heading to my room, where Justin was waiting for me.

We began immediately. Not even a hello, just a tumble to the floor and the intense feeling of becoming one. Afterward, as we lay there, he started doing something he'd never done before—kissing my neck.

I didn't stop him.

Soon he pulled himself up on one elbow and ran his hand lightly up and down my stomach until it started to quiver.

"I can stay with you tonight."

If I mated with Justin, what would it mean? Was the way I was raised—one guy forever—the way I should proceed? Or did the Trad way—take what you get as long as it feels good and doesn't hurt anyone, and then move on when/if it isn't good anymore—apply to my relationships now?

Taking my silence as a yes, he continued to caress my stomach and started to slowly bend his head toward mine. My breathing stopped. Remembering we were alone in the house, I rolled away and zipped through the wall to the pool, where I immediately stripped and plunged in. The water boiled slightly on first contact, but it brought my temperature down.

Why did I run from him? I didn't have an answer, and for some reason, I was okay with that...at least for tonight. I listened for the sounds of him returning to his own room, and when the coast was clear, I casually walked back to bed.

ELECTRIC BLUE

The next day we flew to New York to prepare for our Cassidy and Steve show appearance. We spent the rest of the day doing a basic sound check, getting acquainted with the stage we'd be performing on, and other things to get ready for the next morning's live broadcast.

Rolling with us were my personal entourage: Warren, Demeter, and Justin. Not once did any of the mortals ask why Justin was there: my girls avoided the topic of his perpetual presence as much as possible, while Nina and every other industry person assumed he was my boyfriend.

But a dark cloud hung over Justin's head. He wasn't happy with the way I'd run away from him the night before.

"I just couldn't," I told him. We were all making our way from a lunch meeting at the House Quake New York office. He hadn't said anything to me, wasn't even looking at me when I said it, but he knew exactly what I meant.

"You ran away," he retorted under his breath. "A simple no would have been enough, don't you think?"

I felt like crap, because he felt like crap. "I'm sorry." I put my hand on his arm, and we stopped walking.

I didn't realize we were staring at each other until Nina yelled from the limo. "Angel, Justin, we're late. Let's move."

After we'd finished with our appointments, we were free to do what we wanted as long as we stayed with Nina, our official NYC chaperone. This pretty much killed any motivation to go anywhere, so we just stayed in the hotel and went to bed super early.

The next morning before sunrise, our limo dropped us off at the studio where the Cassidy and Steve show was taped. Outside was dark, but inside the building was a hive of activity. I called Cici back in L.A. to make sure she and Satchel were awake and in front of the TV. Lala and Jules did the same, calling family back in Boston to make sure they were tuned in. We met Redd, Risa, and the House Quake makeup people.

Stevidy, already dressed and in full makeup, came by to say hello. They were friendly, but the complete opposite of what they portrayed. On Cassidy's breath, the smell of wine competed aggressively with the scent of mouthwash and coffee. Meanwhile, Steve looked at Justin a couple of times as if he wanted to invite him to the prom. Stevidy seemed way too hyper, but that was to be expected, seeing as their job was to help wake up America. They placed their coffee cups down and gave us welcoming hugs before being rushed away to connect with the show's other guests. The girls and I exchanged raised eyebrows in the wake of their departure.

There was time for a quick sound check before we were herded to our dressing rooms.

"Individual dressing rooms!" Jules exclaimed.

"We're moving on up," LaLa said.

"Like the Jeffersons," I said, finishing the joke as we broke into giggles.

"Time to get cracking, ladies," Nina, from her spot against the wall with the phone up to her ear. Justin—still somewhat tired from last night's feeding, but in a slightly better mood—hung back in the hallway as Demeter and I entered my dressing room. I quickly put on the outfit, and ten minutes later, my hair was up in a high ponytail, cascading around my shoulders and framing my face, while my makeup was perfect girl-next-door—the public image House Quake's marketing team was shooting for.

I met up with Jules and LaLa in the hallway, clicked selfies for social media and reviewed the choreography with Redd in order to get used to dancing in the clothes and shoes. He liked what he saw but gave us an adjustment, which we rehearsed a few times to commit to memory.

"Dang it," LaLa said. "Wardrobe has to put some traction on the bottom of these heels. I nearly busted my butt with that half turn." She went in search of the wardrobe stylist just as the stage manager gave us a half-hour call.

I found Justin, led him into my dressing room and locked the door. "You're still mad at me," I said. Feeding from a ticked-off Justin wasn't that enjoyable. He'd warmed up a little after last night, but there was still residual resentment. I gently pushed him down until he was seated on one of the high-back chairs. "I told you I'm sorry," I said coaxingly, in a sweet, teasing voice. I straddled him, sitting in his lap, facing him and pressing my torso against him. "Now get over it, or I'll let Steve have his way with you." That got him to smile a little.

"You're a bad girl, Angel," he said. He placed a hand on my waist and ran the other up my thigh.

"Not bad. Just hungry," I said before penetrating his neck.

By the five-minute call, I was energized and ready to take on the stage, the world, and anything that came my way. Jules, LaLa, and I huddled in a tight circle for a quick prayer and affirmations.

We were led to a part of the stage that was off camera. The band was already there, and we got into position while stagehands did hurried last-minute tweaks before high-tailing it out. Stevidy sat about twenty feet away from us and excitedly introduced us as "a group to watch." A wall of glass behind us revealed a large crowd of people on the sidewalk watching us set up and cheering us on while the studio audience quietly sat until they were encouraged by the audience handlers to applaud and look excited.

The music started, and it felt like a surge of electricity shot from my solar plexus through my entire body. After executing a couple of the tight, sexy moves, I opened my mouth to deliver the first note. I watched the electric-blue notes fly from my lips to the furthest reaches of the back wall and knew the audience would respond to the energy in my voice in a matter of seconds.

And they did. We harmonized on the next few notes, and everybody from Stevidy to the stage crew to the outside audience who listened to the music piped from the outdoor sound system seemed to let out an excited sigh. The electric-blue notes ricocheted back to us, and I wondered if this wave

of excitement that my voice generated also affected
the at-home TV-viewing audience.

When I hit the highest and most prolonged note
in the song, someone in the back of the studio
started hollering along to the music. Soon a few
audience members were hopping up and down as
handlers tried to get them to sit. The monitor
streaming the live telecast showed that the camera
was, indeed, trained on the audience member who
was dancing *on* her seat.

Both Cassidy and Steve were dancing,
something they rarely did when a guest performed.
A quick look over my shoulder confirmed that the
girls and the smiling band members were all totally
hyped and caught up in the music. Feeling like I'd
gone to heaven, I closed my eyes and lost myself in
the circling energy of excitement as the electric blue
pulsed behind my eyelids.

We ended the song on the usual anticlimactic
note, and the crowd—both inside and outside—
went wild with applause. We bowed as the sound of
the crowd's appreciation washed over us like an
awesome crashing wave. Stevidy, even more hyper
than before, came over to pump our hands before
commercial break.

Giddy, we exited the stage as congratulatory
words abounded, more pics were clicked, and Nina
gave notes. Moments later, the silence in my
dressing room was a welcome haven as I changed
into my own clothes. I'd just sat down to take off
my makeup when Justin knocked on the door.

"How're you feeling?" he asked. He noticed
me looking at the way his arms were tightly crossed

in front of him. "If my arms were doing what I want them to do," he said, "you might run away again."

One part of me wanted him to hold me, one part was relieved that he'd made that decision. "Fair enough," I said before turning back to the mirror and dragging a makeup remover pad across my cheek. "You're the only one I can say this to...For a moment, I was afraid the audience was getting too wild. And I'd be responsible if people got hurt."

His eyes met mine in the mirror. "D'you notice the two security guards they called out?"

I went back in my memory to search for the guards and saw them standing closer to the stage as if protecting us from a potential stage rush.

"In fact," Justin continued, "I'm wondering how they're planning on getting you guys safely out of here without having to deal with a mob."

He was right. Fifteen minutes later, as we tried to leave, we were confronted by an excited crowd, firmly rooted between us and our limousine. LaLa's expression said it all: pleased, frightened, and shocked. After we signed a number of T-shirts and even faces, Justin and the studio's security guards formed a human barrier that allowed us to walk to the limo and get in. Once inside, the driver could barely roll out as the guards worked to get people out of the street.

In direct contrast to the screaming that met us outside of the studio, the silence within the limo was almost too loud to bear.

"I can't believe that just happened," I said.

"I'm exhausted," Jules said.

"Me, too," LaLa said. "I feel like we just dropped from a twenty-thousand-foot skydive."

"I'm making sure we get bodyguards from here on out," Nina said. The only one who seemed ready for more was Demeter; she wore a big smile as she uploaded pics of the crazed fans.

Back at the hotel, after I threw the last of my things into the suitcase, Justin took my hand.

"I won't be coming back to L.A. with you today," he said.

His words caused the strangest sensations. First, there was numb surprise and the urge to ask him to repeat himself as if I'd heard him incorrectly. Then there was confusion over how he could ever *not* be with me, followed by relief that he wouldn't be with me all the time the way he'd been over the past week. But finally there was just sadness.

I missed him already.

"Look at it this way." He took me in his arms. "Your entourage travel expenses will shrink. I'm driving back to Boston with Nina."

His lips brushed against my hairline, and I knew he was trying his best not to make me feel uncomfortable with the intensity of his feelings.

"Of course, you have a life." I fought tears as I spoke into his chest. "Your dad's probably wondering where you are."

"I stored my blood for you at the L.A. Nest. I was able to get expedited service since your mom's a Council member. That means I was able to go in without an appointment, and it'll be ready for you whenever you want. They have a special way to keep it fresh. They say it's just like drinking live."

I doubted it could be that good. I took a deep breath and filled my lungs with his scent.

"I don't want to go," he said. His voice was hushed as if we were in a church.

I looked into his eyes. "Thank you for waiting to tell me." If he'd told me of his plans before the show, it would've affected my performance. I could feel how hard it was for him not to kiss me, could actually feel him keeping his hands and lips to himself as he struggled to follow unspoken rules. "I appreciate you," I said before gently letting him go. He stepped back and looked at me with large eyes that seemed to hold all the longing in the world.

"I'll be back with you as soon as I can," he said before stepping out the hotel room door and out of my life.

The trip back to L.A. was torturous. After Demeter made a comment about someone being missing, and I growled at her to mind her business, no one asked me anything about Justin. I fell asleep for the rest of the flight back to L.A.

Cici met us at the airport and drove us home. More than a few times, she shot me a concerned look but she wisely kept the conversation light.

Back at the house, the girls dragged themselves upstairs, and I dragged myself toward the kitchen at Cici's insistence.

"Why do you want me in the kitchen?" I was beyond frustrated.

"I've got a surprise." Her tone and smile were equally mischievous.

I kept walking forward, but I didn't want a surprise. I wanted to go to bed and curl up into the fetal position. As we walked into the kitchen, her steps started resembling skips. "Cici, what the heck…?"

She pointed to the breakfast nook. "Look."

I did. And saw the back of his head…Was it really?…Yes! "DAD!"

DADDY'S HOME

I ran to Dad, momentarily forgetting my status as an adult and a newborn Trad Shimshana. I'd always been a daddy's girl and, in that moment, I still was.

Cici laughed and clapped her hands. "It was my idea for him to mask his scent," she said. "You were totally clueless that he was here!"

Dad's smile flashed brilliantly against his dark skin as he picked me up in a big bear hug, the way he used to do when I was little; for a few seconds, it once again felt like all was safe in the world.

"Angel Brown, I do believe you got a little taller." His deep voice boomed in the spacious kitchen.

"You were gone for so long," I said. "Is Mom okay?"

Cici and Dad exchanged a look.

"I was gone for what was the blink of an eye to me, but that is only because of my age. For you, a couple of months is a long time. And yes, your mother is fine."

He paused and gestured to us to sit down, positioning his stool so that he could face both of us.

"Angel, I understand you have struggled with worrying about her safety. Your fears were not unfounded. They pursued us. But many influential people supported us in our quest to keep her with family. There was much back and forth. But in the end, the Council had no legitimate grounds for taking her. You have nothing to worry about now. That is why I have returned."

245

I inadvertently released a long sigh of relief, as if I'd been holding my breath for months. Dad gave me another hug, this one tender as if he was holding a baby. A tear made its way down my face. Cici handed me a tissue.

His eyes took us both in as he continued. "Now, I must tell you I have taken a professional sabbatical and will be on leave from the hospital for an indefinite period of time. I will stay here in Los Angeles with you, if that is okay, Angel, until it is time for you to return to Boston for school."

"I get it; it's my house and up to me who stays here." Obviously, he'd been talking to Cici about my Slackerville houseguests. "Of course you can stay here, Dad."

He nodded. "Second, I must apologize to you both." He turned to Cici. "Leaving you alone with a newborn as powerful as your sister was a mighty task for you to accomplish. I am proud of the job you did, but I take responsibility for putting you in this situation." He gave Cici a kiss on the cheek and held her close before turning to me.

"Now that I am back, we can restore the mind lock to its former strength."

Right then and there, daddy's girl left the building.

"No. I don't want the mind lock to return. I've been monitored all my adult life, by everyone, it seems. No more. I need to do this thing on my own."

"I understand the choices you have made," Dad said, "about the mind lock and the Trad way of life.

I respect your decision to live your life as you see fit."

I was so used to having to fight Dad and Mom for what I wanted that his statement left me speechless. I stared at him blankly, wanting to express something but not quite sure what it was or how to say it.

Jules and LaLa were debating whether to do some writing in the studio and were looking for me. We heard them coming long before they reached the kitchen.

"Dr. Brown!" they exclaimed simultaneously. They were so desperate to see a parent, any parent, they bobbed around like joyous little birds.

As I watched my friends act their mortal age, it became clear that even though I was sixteen in mortal years, and LaLa and Jules were both now seventeen, the fact that I was a newborn Shimshana afforded me a layer of maturity they had yet to reach. I felt no need to have parents around as much as I did even when Dad had first left.

"Where's Mrs. Brown?" Jules asked Dad.

"Mom's still in Egypt with the family," I said quickly, not sure if Dad was briefed on the running untruths we were disseminating among the mortals.

"Yes she is, but it is good to see you girls again," Dad said, easily falling back into the role of everybody's favorite dad. I exchanged a glance with Cici and assumed she was thinking the same thing I was. That this Dad was a long way from the scary sorcerer Dad who could make houses breathe. "And we have a surprise," he continued. "We'll have a family USAMA viewing party here while you're on stage." You could always tell when Dad was trying to "hang" with the kids; he used contractions. "Julietta and LaLa, you'll be happy to know your parents will be joining us."

The girls started jumping again, and I joined them.

"I knew my dad sounded too happy on the phone this morning!" LaLa said.

Jules's face beamed. "I can't *wait* to see Mom."

I was happy for my girls. It'd been hard for them to cover the fact that my parents weren't here with us. I exchanged a smile with Cici, knowing that she was the mastermind behind all of this.

"Maybe you can convince them to stay with us," Cici said. "It'll only be for the night, but they insist on staying in a hotel."

"Yep, sounds like my mom," LaLa said. "She never wants to impose."

"Mine, too," Jules said.

"Well, our door is always open." Dad gave me a wink. "Now, I don't know about you," he continued, "but I'm hungry." He walked over to the refrigerator and pulled out a fat loaf of sourdough bread. "I was just about to make some grilled cheese sandwiches. Who's with me?"

Unfortunately, Dad didn't know that our love affair with comfort food ended almost a year ago when we all became obsessed with looking skinny for the fans. With the USA Music Awards coming up, it was a wonder that Jules, especially, ate anything at all.

"Um, no thanks, Dr. Brown," she said, pouring herself a glass of water and savoring it as if it were soup.

"No, thank you," LaLa said, grabbing an apple and shooting him an apologetic smile.

"Too fattening, Dad," I explained. "You'll have to enjoy them without us."

"The more for me," he said with a dazzling smile that didn't quite, at least in my mind, hide a hint of sadness in his eyes.

His mate, Mom, was gone. His little girl was no longer a little girl. It occurred to me that Dad was suffering, and I had an opportunity to take care of him—the way I should have for Mom when she was going through her stuff.

"Dad, it's been a while since I made a grilled cheese." I located a spatula and held it up in the air to emphasize my intention. "May I make it for you? After all, I learned from the best."

He couldn't resist when I put it like that. As I proceeded to make him the best grilled cheese in the history of the universe, I hummed a nameless tune and purposely infused it with all the feelings of love and appreciation I had for him. By the time I was done, the kitchen felt like a loving space, where everyone, including Dad, was happy.

As Dad enjoyed the sandwiches, LaLa, Jules, and I agreed to take a break from holing ourselves up in the studio. They were struggling with jet lag and the physical repercussions of this morning's draining performance and mob scene.

"I'm taking a nap," LaLa said. After the show, she'd realized she'd tweaked her ankle while we were on stage. Now she was limping. Jules, who I hadn't seen eat anything all day, was probably running on fumes. I considered taking a nap later, too—after all, the USAMA were tomorrow night.

But first I needed to take care of something...

"I have to go to The Nest," I whispered to Cici after the girls had gone. "Justin stored blood there, and I need to get it."

She rubbed her hands together with excitement. "Let's go. You'll love the L.A. Nest. We can bring Dad." A few minutes later, we piled into Dad's rented SUV, and she punched The Nest's address into the GPS.

"Angel knows how to drive now," she told Dad. He nodded in approval as he navigated through the entry gate.

"Thanks for the Benz," I said from the back. "Pink seats are a nice touch."

"Your mother was responsible for that. She knew you would love it." We lapsed into a short silence as we thought about Mom. Then...

"Your sister has told me what has been happening with your..."—he cleared his throat and swallowed loudly—"your love life."

"Dad!" I was über-embarrassed, not to mention slightly annoyed.

"I know that Justin has returned to the role of being your donor," he said. "But why did he store his blood?"

I briefly explained what was going on and why he had to go.

"Well, Angel," Dad said, "there is the answer to a question we have all had. Whether or not Justin is blood-obsessed. The answer is an emphatic no. If he were, he would be incapable of making the decision to leave you for any period of time and travel back to the East Coast. Biologically, that would be impossible, as the hormones released in blood-obsessed individuals signal to the brain that the subject cannot be away from their Shimshana unless commanded to do so."

"So he's just in love with her?" Cici asked.

"It would seem so," Dad muttered.

The SUV's interior became a deep shade of pink, and I crossed my arms. "Really, must we talk about this like we're talking about the weather?"

"Justin's done nothing but wait on her hand and foot," Cici continued as if she hadn't heard me. "Now it's clear that was his own choice." She turned to me. "Food for thought, huh?"

Despite my defensive reaction, I had to admit the news was intriguing. Blood Obsession, or at least the question of it, was until now, my reason for not considering him as a potential mate. That last barrier between us was now gone.

So what was keeping me from claiming him? He'd already showed me that was what he wanted. What was my hang-up?

The answer was clear—I was still in love with Sawyer. But was I in love with Justin, too, just in a different way? I wasn't sure what my feelings were…but I sure wasn't going to figure it out with Dad.

After a long silence, Dad changed the subject. "What is going on with the grocery list? I saw what

Kiya wrote down. The girls are not eating all that food."

"That would be Justin, too." Cici threw a dubious glance in my direction. "He eats enough food to feed Rhode Island."

In the rearview mirror, the space between Dad's eyebrows squished up. "Justin eats food?" His eyes rested on mine in the mirror for a long moment, as if he didn't need to look at the road. "Angel"—he spoke in that extreme "dad" tone he used whenever I'd gotten into (or was suspected of getting into) shenanigans—"why is Justin eating mortal food?"

And again, just like the last time, when Cici had asked me this question, all I could do was shrug. I couldn't even open my mouth to lie and say I don't know. The look that Dad gave me would have been humorous if he didn't obviously find the topic disturbing. He redirected his gaze to the road and continued to follow the GPS instructions.

The Los Angeles location of The Nest was in the historic downtown area known as the Arts District. Like the original Nest in Boston, the space had a public and an immortals-only section. Unlike the Boston location, the public part was full of super-trendy, ultrahip patrons, edgy art, cool installations, and was just in general way cooler than anything I'd ever seen.

They served mortal food which, according to the posted copies of recent restaurant reviews, was rated five stars. Further into the large loftlike space, there were pool tables, flat screens, several bars, and a general sense of happening, happening,

happening. The look on my face must have said it all.

"See," Cici said under her breath. "Told you it was cool."

"Yeah, but you didn't tell me it makes the Boston spot look like a graveyard!"

A number of patrons turned toward me as we entered. Some, probably the mortals, openly stared, and some looked away quickly as if trying to hide the fact that they'd turned to stare in the first place. Some whispered, and one even pointed.

"Angel's become a star," Cici told Dad. As we got situated in a booth, I told them about the Cassidy and Steve show and the madness that had followed. Dad's brow took on a worried bend.

"You should start wearing sunglasses like Markus," Cici said.

"Yeah, I'll grab some after we leave here."

"Here you go," Dad said, holding out his large, open hand. A pair of sunglasses sat in his palm.

I tried them on, checking the way they looked in a mirror way across the room. The lenses were reflective and made me feel mysterious. "Thanks, Dad."

Cici whispered rapidly, "You can order blood here, but there's a code." Her eyes focused on the table where we sat. "If you look carefully, you'll see a few grooves on the edge."

I scanned the edges of the thick table and saw a couple of grooves roughly the size and shape of a silver dollar. "Yeah, I see two."

"There are probably four at this table," she said. "All you do is this." She surreptitiously licked the tip of her finger. "And place that finger on the groove. Try it but don't be obvious about it."

I licked my fingertip and placed it in the groove closest to me.

"You just sent a signal to the kitchen. Your DNA has been identified as immortal by the technology inside the table. When they come to take our order, you'll order a type of soda that is code for a type of blood. For example, root beer is code for type A. Then you just touch the tip of your nose."

"Wicked cool," I said, thoroughly impressed. Between the code and the black sunglasses, I felt like I was in a James Bond movie. From behind my dark frames, I observed the people around me. I saw a couple of recognizable faces, but then there was one I actually knew…I took off the shades.

"Isn't that Tara Hennigan over there?" I asked Cici. We both looked and, sure enough, it was. Tara was dressed down—way down—in jeans and a tank top, no makeup, and her hair pulled back in a ponytail. As if she sensed someone's eyes on her, she looked in our direction, squinted as if she was trying to figure out who we were, and then upon recognition waved at us with a bright smile.

Soon she was at our table and chatting up a storm. We introduced her to Dad, and she accepted our invitation to join us. When the waitress arrived, we casually ordered a bunch of mortal food for Dad, and Cici ordered two root beers before touching the tip of her nose.

Once the waitress was gone, Tara turned to me. "I saw you on Stevidy. That audience never acts like that. Look at this." She gave me her smartphone. There was a CNN.com article about the uproar on the show, along with a video clip of our performance. Kat Trio was mentioned on a major news site; how unbelievable was that? I showed it to Cici and Dad.

"We might have to get a bodyguard for you girls." Dad's tone was light, but I could tell he wasn't joking.

"They'll forget all about it by tomorrow," Cici said. "That's how these things work."

"Not if I have any say in it," Tara replied. "I've told Mystery that Kat Trio music absolutely must be featured on the show. You'll be hearing from our people." She stood then and took her leave with a sincere smile.

"Wow," Cici said. "You really are becoming a pop star."

I wasn't sure how much of this pop-star attention I was comfortable with. Now the stares we got when we first walked in made sense. I anxiously looked around The Nest again. "Don't worry," Cici whispered. "The L.A. Nest is notorious for being protected by magic. It keeps the paparazzi away and allows even superstars some breathing space."

Later, after leaving The Nest with what looked like large takeout bags but were really Justin's stored blood in a special container, we shopped for a few pairs of real sunglasses—although Dad's magic glasses were hard to beat. And we went to Home Depot to get tools for the workshop Dad wanted to make at my house—similar to the one at the Beacon Hill house. He loved making furniture, had even worked as a master craftsman centuries ago in Asia. "I will need to stay busy somehow," he said, winking at us as he placed a circular saw in the shopping cart.

I squeezed Cici's hand as we smiled at each other. "It's good to have you back home, Dad—I mean, in L.A."

"You were correct the first time, Angel." He put his long arms around our shoulders. "Where my family is, that is my home."

Later, I found myself back at the closet piano, playing the ballad melody. Despite the sense of normalcy Dad's return brought, my mind reeled with thoughts of Sawyer as I closed my eyes and let my fingers travel up and down the keys.

Mom and Dad once told me that an important part of being an immortal was the ability to adapt and change with the times. It was the only way to thrive through the centuries and it was, it seemed, the only way to get through my so-called love life.

Sawyer, in all his beautiful glory, was the past. I'd cut him down, cut us down, with my own hand. The ballad was the only thing left of our love. I needed to move on.

That was it! One of the missing parts of the song needed the feeling of moving on. What would that sound like? I experimented with chords until I hit a few that felt like moving on—light, breezy. Free. Starting from the beginning of the ballad, this time incorporating the new "moving on" chords, I played it repeatedly. There were still some missing pieces, but the song sounded better. *I* felt better.

Was Sawyer working on the song as well? I hoped so, because as much as I loved him, I knew he needed to move forward, too. This song that symbolized our love, and grew out of our time together, was now likely the soundtrack of our efforts to deal with our failed relationship.

And no matter how many times I repeated the moving-on chords, the question still remained: where was I moving to, and was Justin the logical destination?

BLING

The next day felt like Magic USAMA Day from
the moment my eyes opened. Sun streamed through
the windows, birds sang, there were excited texts
(on my new phone number, yay) and e-mails from
Nina, who'd forwarded much of the press covering
the Stevidy gig. Warren forwarded my new number
to everyone we worked with and set up a handy
system of organizing my contacts by indicating
their projects and what we collaborated on. To top it
all off, LaLa's limp was gone, and I witnessed Jules
actually putting food into her mouth during brunch
with all of our parents.

Well…almost all of our parents. Seeing Ms.
Hernandez and Mrs. Lee made me cry. I had to
excuse myself from the table to get rid of the tears
on my face and push down the ache for Mom in my
heart.

We were scheduled to rehearse our routine on
the USAMA stage where we'd be performing later.
By the time we'd left the house to go to rehearsal,
we were prepared for the possibility of more public
scrutiny. All of us wore sunglasses and purposefully
dressed down the way Tara Hennigan did, although
honestly that was way too easy for me and LaLa.
Warren rolled with us.

At the theater, we met up with Nina, Redd,
Demeter, the wardrobe folks, and a couple of House
Quake NYC folks, including Raj, our A&R guy. It
was obvious he was still hung up on Jules, but she
tried her best to be polite and act as uninterested as
possible. Although I'd thought their pairing was odd

at first—he's way older than her, at least twenty—it turned out that Raj was a decent guy. Too bad that wasn't what Jules was into. Dorito Jones, the multiplatinum singer whose act we were scheduled to follow was exchanging googly eyes with her as we waited. LaLa and I exchanged here-we-go-again eye rolls.

Our technical rehearsal was scheduled down to the millisecond, and we saw every other artist scheduled to perform just before and just after us. We all waited to go up on the stage to allow the crew to perfect the light transitions, set changes, etc. During the downtime, we rehearsed choreography with Redd. Also, the wardrobe stylist handed out a stack of tablets, showed us pics of what we were going to be wearing, and did last-minute measurements. LaLa made sure there was traction on the shoe bottoms, and Jules needed her dress taken in again.

There'd be three wardrobe changes for the show. The arrival dresses were super classy, red-carpet wear. The onstage wardrobe was down-to-earth girls next door, and then there were the after-party donations from various designers like Mokiu Smith, who offered a super cute purple sequined dress with hot-pink crystals.

"After yesterday's show, we received triple the amount of designers sending dresses," Nina told us. "The Internet went nuts, and your cache went up."

We each went about bookmarking dresses as she also told us we'd heard from Mystery's people and negotiations were starting for featuring Kat Trio music on *I Need Your Blood*.

Jules's mouth formed a large *O* as she looked up from her tablet. "Get out!"

"Seriously?" LaLa asked.

I had to admit, even though I'd gotten the heads-up from Tara, I still had trouble believing our music was going to be on an actual TV show. We all fought to contain our excitement and focus on the task at hand. I handed back my tablet with my bookmarked dresses.

"Next step," Nina said as she perused our choices on our individual tablets before handing them to the stylist, "is to try on your wardrobe choices and decide what works."

Demeter made notes on what I was wearing and started sketching hair ideas. "Maybe I'll buy some extensions," she said.

"Like I don't have enough hair?" I asked.

"You can *never* have enough hair for the USAMA," she replied before high-fiving Shay, the House Quake hair/makeup stylist whose own hair and makeup was flawless (plus she had a delectable vanilla-and-berries scent).

Finally it was our turn to hop onstage. Compared to the hour we waited, the actual rehearsal took less than fifteen minutes. Nina shot video to review later.

After we were done with tech, Dorito was still hanging around the edge of the stage. Jules went over to him, they pulled out their cell phones, and I got a bad feeling. Dorito was in the news almost every day with some new exploit, usually some stupid, illegal thing that he did while traveling all over the world on tour, or racing his various cars through the streets of Los Angeles, drunk, high or over the speed limit.

Poor Raj finished up his business and made his way out. Seemed like I wasn't the only one having a hard time moving on.

Next we tried on all the dresses we'd bookmarked and made final decisions. Nina blew a strand of hair out of her eye. "The last piece is jewelry," she said. We hopped into an SUV big enough to accommodate everybody and rolled over to the jeweler's. There we met up with Raj again and tried on pieces loaned by various designers. As if in a dream, we chose grown-up jewelry none of us would ever have imagined wearing. Raj, as House Quake's official representative, signed off on the jewelry.

"The collective value of these pieces is in the millions," Nina told us. "House Quake will deliver everything to your house later, Angel. For now, we're done. I'll come by later, and we'll all roll to the show together."

Incredibly, the jeweler was around the corner from The Nest, and I suggested to the girls that we go there for a quick lunch to celebrate before meeting up with the parents. They eagerly agreed, of course unaware that my real motive was getting blood. I'd already gone through Justin's stored blood, and he was right, it did taste incredibly fresh. But instead of returning to the Saucony kitchen blood supply, I wanted to try something new. Something Trad. I wanted to do Sunan.

Once settled at a table, I pulled Warren to the side while the girls were caught up in The Nest's cool atmosphere. "Cover for me while I go feed," I told him before ducking into the immortals-only section.

The waitstaff, all dressed in black, red, and white, were super friendly. When they learned I was a Council member's newborn, they ushered me into the VIP section, where I could have my own booth, much like our family's private booth in the Boston Nest.

I wondered about the magic that ensured my privacy. Luckily, since it was my first visit, the waitress made it a point to explain.

"Welcome to The Nest," she said. "We know you have other choices and we thank you for choosing us as your go-to blood supply lounge."

I didn't know there were other choices and made a mental note to ask Cici about it later. The waitress continued.

"Please be advised that due to the privacy needs of many of our customers, The Nest is infused with old, Celtic magic powerful enough to guarantee one hundred percent non-remembrance of all faces seen under its roof and within two hundred feet of its exterior walls. Furthermore, all recording and photographic devices are rendered inoperable under a separate electromagnetic spell to ensure complete privacy from paparazzi and fans. The specific spells and other details are documented in the terms of service. We are so happy to have you. What can I get you today?"

"Type A. Male. Sunan veteran."

She wrote on a small notepad. "One type A, male, seasoned donor, coming up. In the meantime,

please enjoy the entertainment about The Nest." She
handed me one of those vibrating discs you get
while waiting for your table at a busy restaurant.
"This will buzz and flash when your donor's ready.
Just make your way back here, please."

Left to my own devices, I surfed through the
channels on the flat screen in the booth. There were
a number of chick flicks, none of which I cared to
see. Soon the little buzz thing went off, and I
immediately went into the super-alert mode of a
Shimshana about to take gaddis.

My meal walked to my booth. He was an older
guy, about fifty mortal years, Asian, potbelly, my
height, and dressed in the pure-white that Nest
donors always wore. After preliminary
introductions, I told him what I needed.

"I don't want to know your name," I said in a
businesslike tone. "This is a one-time shot. Sunan.
Are you familiar?"

"Yes, I've done it before. I will keep my mind
closed."

"Great," I said, eager to start. He held the donor
timer that allowed him to press a button with his
thumb to stop the session early if he wanted. A bell,
connected to a master timer and programmed by the
staff, was set to go off once the allotted time came
to an end. Hardwired into The Nest's service
system, the feeding time was designed to protect
donors from being drained. He leaned back on the
couch, and I began.

It was heaven.

Drinking from a donor with almost zero
connection was simple, satisfying, and, most

importantly, noncommittal. It was exactly what I needed. Knowing that I would never see this donor again filled me with a sense of freedom I'd never felt with Justin.

Why hadn't I done this earlier? To be honest with myself, I must have subconsciously *wanted* Justin to come back. I shook my head, realizing that if I'd done Sunan sooner, right after Aurora first told me about it, he never would have returned. I pondered that fact while making a follow-up Sunan appointment and quickly returning to the group.

Back at the house, the sole focus was getting through all the details for the evening. After putting on music so that it piped wirelessly throughout the master suite, I showered and exfoliated with sweet-smelling lavender sugar scrub until my skin was soft and my mood was relaxed. I washed my hair and let the conditioner sit while filing my nails the way Demeter had shown me. I'd rinsed the conditioner out by the time it occurred to me....

What on earth was I going to do with my hair? "Demeter, help!"

She was in the kitchen getting something to eat with Warren, Risa, and Shay, and came quickly with her trusty tool box.

I pointed to my hair. "Perfect," she said, plugging in a blow-dryer and a flat iron. "It's still damp. D'you put anything in it?"

"Just detangler. Whad'you think will be the best style for the red carpet?"

"We're going to keep it real simple," she said. "This way we'll have the most versatility between wardrobe changes!"

She quickly applied a base coat to my nails. After a few seconds, she started blowing out my hair, which even at immortal speed took a while. My hair grew so much faster and thicker since The Change that it was now down to my butt. Outside of my go-to styles, I never really knew what to do with it. Maybe there was a hair club for immortals in the same predicament?

Finally Demeter finished the blow-out. She quickly applied a coat of blood-colored nail polish, so dark it was neutral and went well with every outfit I'd be wearing that night. The flat iron was hot, and she quickly got back to work on my hair, methodically parting it into sections and gliding the flat iron and comb through.

I was glad she'd closed the door to the suite before beginning, because if either of the girls walked in and witnessed the lightning speed at which she worked, all heck would've broken loose.

When she was done with a third of my hair, she applied a second coat of polish. She then continued flat-ironing. Then a third coat of polish. She finally applied a last layer of gel polish before plugging in an LED light device and sticking my nails into it to dry. She finished flat-ironing. I took a look.

My hair was bone-straight and longer now that she had straightened the waves, so long I could easily sit on it. She put some sort of glossing stuff on it and massaged it in. It smelled amazing.

"Pretty," I said with satisfaction. "What now?"

"Ah, that's the good part," she said with a grin. "But first let's get you into the dress so we don't smudge anything, and then I'll finish the hair and makeup!"

Good point, because the dress was hard to get on. There were pants under a sheath under a big, poufy skirt that opened in the front. On the top it fit super tightly and featured a lot of tiny diamond-like sparkles. Once she got the dress on me, she took a step back.

"Okay, we're going to need to cover up the front so we don't get it messed up!"

I started having Mahá flashbacks; half of the days-long coming-out event consisted of endless wardrobe, makeup, and hair changes. That edgy feeling that happens before my feet lift off the ground started bubbling up inside of me, but I took a deep breath and squashed it. I promised myself there'd be no drama tonight. The *only* thing I was going to do tonight was be a pop music boss.

Demeter pulled out a white garbage bag, punched holes in it for my arms and made me wear it like a crazy shirt. Then she took more bags and created an apron for me to wear over the skirt/pants.

"Now we're ready to style your hair!" She used clip-in extensions to create a look that was sleek and dramatic. My natural hair was a simple ponytail that hung down my back, and she positioned the extensions to create a dramatic pompadour that flowed around the crown of my head like a lustrous wave. She then added what seemed like a million hairpins, each with tiny pearls on the end.

It was breathtaking, but it looked like the wave was undulating in a circle around my head. After closer inspection, I realized it was.

"Demeter." She bit her lip at my tone. "Absolutely no radical illusions in the mortal world, okay?"

"Sorry," she said before quickly making the hair look like normal, unanimated hair. Next she did my makeup. She gave my face an almost nude look: no eye shadow, false eyelashes, a cat-like eye drawn with liquid eyeliner, and barely-there pinkish lip color. The nude face was a perfect foil to the dramatic hair. She did something magical to make my eyes stand out a bit more, but it still looked mortal. We took the garbage bags off and finished hooking, buttoning and zipping the dress. Finally we put on the jewelry I'd picked out for this outfit: a simple, streamlined pearl-and-diamond necklace. Cascading pearl-and-diamond earrings completed the look.

I hate fashion, but I was completely stoked to walk the red carpet in that dress.

"You look hot!" she said, handing me a crystal-encrusted clutch.

"Thanks to you." I smiled, threw my cell and business cards into the clutch and was ready to go.

We left the room in search of the girls, but each had her door closed, and was more than likely still getting dressed. Demeter went to change. And then the bell rang. Kiya answered the door, and Nina came in with Raj. Both of them were dressed in black. Nina wore a form-fitting leather dress while Raj wore a tailored suit with blingy silk tie.

"Nice suit," I said, partially because it was true and partially to help pump up his ego before what was left of it got obliterated by Jules.

"Thanks," he said with a smile. "It's Armani.
Your house is beautiful, Angel," he said, looking
around and trying to hide the fact that he was
actually looking for Jules.

LaLa came down the stairs dressed in white
leather leggings embellished with what looked like
thousands of clear-and-pink crystals. The tank top
was almost nothing but crystals, and the cropped
motorcycle jacket was white leather and bore
intricate beaded patterns on the arms and lapel.

We all complimented one another and chatted
about the awards show while waiting for the others.
Demeter re-emerged before Warren made his way
downstairs in perfectly pressed black jeans with a
smooth, long, gray T-shirt; spotless gray Nikes;
thick, silver chain necklace and bracelet; and a
black-and-white baseball cap. It was a far cry from
the granola look he sported on his first day. His
black, leather backpack had white-and-silver skulls
on it, and held emergency thermoses of blood in a
secret compartment. Risa and Shay, like Demeter,
rolled small suitcases full of work gear. The clothes
we'd picked out were already hanging in garment
bags on a rolling rack by the door, and the jewelry
was stored in locked boxes. Raj, the only one in our
group with the lockbox keys, was officially
responsible for the safety and return of the jewelry.

Everybody was ready. Well, almost
everybody...Where was Jules?

Our parents and Cici joined us and started
taking pictures. As we posed and clicked, we all
started casting anxious glances up the stairs. Risa
and Shay confirmed Jules was ready to go.

Ms. Hernandez looked worried. "Angel, will you please check on her?"

"Yes, ma'am," I said before making my way up the stairs to knock on her door. "Jules?"

"Come in," she said. Fully dressed, she was sitting on the edge of her bed.

"Dude," I said, going to sit next to her. "What's up?"

"I know Raj is downstairs. I can't face him."

I wasn't surprised at this. "Jules, we're about to go to the USAMA. We're going to actually walk the red carpet. We're going to perform with Dorito flippin' Jones and we're going to be in a theater full of some of the hottest performers in the business. But none of that is going to happen if you don't come downstairs."

"I treated him bad. I'm a horrible person."

"He's a reasonable guy. Maybe you two can talk, you know, get closure or something?"

"Yeah, you're right." She drew in a shaky breath. I heard the limo pulling up to the front of the house and Nina muttering something to Raj about a backup plan just in case Jules flipped out.

"Come on, *mamacita*. The show must go on…" I stood with determination and extended my hand to her. She took it and stood. Her dress was a white goddess gown with crystals all over the bodice, accentuating her large breasts, a source of envy from me since we were fourteen. The fabric was billowy and flowed like a gentle cloud when she walked. She looked like a princess.

Julietta was easily the most beautiful girl I knew and had the most lovely voice, but the problem was she didn't believe it. I suspected that Raj was an excuse for her flip-out, and that she was really nervous about all the things I'd just listed. She was afraid of messing up this perfect night.

I knew this because deep inside I felt it, too. The anxiety that rears its head right before self-sabotage kicks in.

I cupped her face with my hands. "You're beautiful, talented, and worthy. You can do this."

She exhaled. "I love you, girl." She sounded like she was on the verge of tears.

"Don't you dare cry and mess up that ton of makeup on your face," I said. We giggled as we left her room.

Our giggles dissolved into smiles as we made our way down the stairs. Everyone turned to look at us, and their faces at first showed varying levels of concern, before they breathed a collective sigh of relief and continued to move everything to the car.

Soon, after an avalanche of proud hugs, happy-parent tears, and good wishes, we were rolling through the nighttime streets of L.A. on our way to perform the biggest gig of our lives.

FANDOM

Walking the red carpet at the USAMA was promising to be one of the most exciting, nerve-racking, mind-altering events ever in the history of time—at least in my world.

On the way there, we made a quick stop. I'd requested that we leave super early to allow me to get a quick drink from another donor. Dad had offered to cast a spell of forgetfulness so that the mortals in our limo wouldn't remember the pit stop, but I refused, insisting that I could do it myself.

"At least let Dad make a spell that will keep your dress clean," Cici had said.

She had a point there, so I accepted the cleanliness spell.

My plan was to execute an elaborate undercover operation. Stopping the car in front of an office building a few buildings away from The Nest, I told the group that Demeter had to get backup hair extensions from her special hair connection and needed me to go with her in order to match the extensions to the hair already installed on my head. It was a Hair Emergency; and in show business, everybody—even the car's driver—knew that was no joke. Demeter and I walked into the building we'd stopped in front of, and continued to walk until we were out of sight of the car.

"I'll be here until you get back," she said. "Go ahead!"

"Thanks," I said before jetting through building walls until I came to a stop inside The Nest. I had to admit the cleanliness spell was an excellent idea. Dad even made it so there were no wrinkles.

Fortunately, the staff at the L.A. Nest had experienced similar situations—bloodthirsty performers on their way to a gig who needed blood right away or else they might kill somebody. Since I'd made the appointment earlier, they were ready to hustle me into the VIP section, where a donor was already waiting.

Fifteen minutes later, Demeter and I climbed back into the car. "You straight?" Nina asked us.

"Totally," I said, satisfied and confident about getting through the night drama-free. Demeter enthusiastically nodded her head, and we were on our way.

Nina coached us on what to expect after getting out of the car. "As soon as you put a foot out of the limo, all eyes will be on you. Get out of the car with your knees together as much as possible. There should be someone there to assist you. Wait until the last of you get out before walking together as a team, slowly, and smile a lot. There are people on the carpet whose job it is to tell you where to go. We'll connect with you at the end of your walk, somewhere on the other side. If anyone with a microphone asks you a question, any question, start by saying you're really happy to be here and you love your fans."

She made it sound easy.

The minute we got out of the car, people were yelling at us. And there was so much screaming, I thought something bad had happened, like someone was on fire; but no, it was the crowd's reaction to international pop diva Charmain. We were asked to wait until she cleared. She tossed us a look over her shoulder and a small smirk before turning her back to us and smiling at one of the many cameras.

"Whatever," Jules muttered.

It was obvious that the smirk was directed at me. There was no love lost between Charmain and me since several months ago when I'd turned down her party invite that hadn't included my girls.

"Keep your head up and keep it classy," LaLa said. We turned our heads away from Charmain and started taking in everything else going on around us.

Underneath the uproar for Charmain, my immortal hearing picked up the sound of girls screaming for Kat Trio. They stood behind a barricade fifty feet away, and a few of them held up Boston signs. I stepped into a small clearing so they could see me and started waving at them. They screamed our name even louder. Meanwhile, Charmain continued to stroll at a remarkably slow speed.

I asked the red carpet staff if I could walk away for a few minutes.

"Absolutely not!" was the reply. No one was allowed to do that.

One of the Boston girls told another fan she'd been there for over five hours waiting for a chance to see us.

"We should say hi to those girls over there," I told LaLa while pointing my chin toward the group of girls.

"They said to stay here," she said before puckering her lips.

"Yeah, I know. But look." The girls energetically waved Kat Trio signs alongside the Boston signs. "They're one of us. Probably been waiting for a long time to see us."

One girl covered her mouth when she realized we were both looking in their direction. She grabbed her friend and shook her while excitedly pointing at us. Her friend started singing the lyrics to "Get Out of Here," and soon the entire group was singing.

I'd seen enough; there was no way I was *not* going to go over there. Gathering the silk brocade of my massive skirt, I hopped over the rope of the cordoned-off area and walked across the street toward our fans, continuing to smile as Nina had instructed.

Once there, I signed autographs for them, took selfies with their cameras and thanked them for coming out to see us. LaLa and Jules joined me. When we were done, I mimed a thank you to the fans by throwing out my arms in a big air hug and blowing gigantic air kisses.

A big roar came from the crowd. I figured Charmain must still be working the red carpet, or maybe some other big star had come along, but I didn't really care. Connecting with real fans was the main reason for any of this, and being able to do that made me feel like I was levitating.

I took a quick look at my feet to make sure they were on the ground. They were.

"Oh my goodness," LaLa said. She pointed to the jumbotron. The screen showed me walking across the street, in slow motion, to the group of screaming fans. Then it played back my air hug and kiss, also in slow motion, and the hysterical reactions of the fans.

"Wow." Jules's eyes were wide.

I was speechless. The crowd was really cheering for us. I took both of my BFFs by the arm, and we walked back to the roped-off area.

"You guys can go ahead now," the attendant said with a big grin. They opened the rope, and we were suddenly on the red carpet.

There were people directing us where to walk, when to stop, and people yelling questions.

It was utter chaos. Never again would I watch people walk the red carpet on TV and think it was easy, unplanned, or that they even had enough room to maneuver.

Toward the middle we were asked questions by at least three different people from various media outlets, and I had no idea what they were talking about. I just gave a different version of the same answer Nina suggested, and it worked very well.

Then there was what I call the Wall of Death. We stood against a wall, and rabid photographers yelled at us while taking pictures.

"Hey, Angel, look over here!" yelled one.

"Over here!" yelled another.

I thought it would never end. Finally we were more or less herded to an area off the red carpet, where we connected with Nina and the others.

"Good move," she said to me, referring to the walk across the street to the fans.

"They came from Boston," I answered. "Couldn't let them down."

I'd heard this kind of feedback from her before. Nina was all about sales. Sure she was concerned for our well-being, and I didn't doubt that she would help any of us if we were, say, lying somewhere bleeding to death. But at the end of every day, Nina measured success by money shots, crowd and fan reaction, industry response, social media metrics, and the next open door of opportunity. Nina was a shark and, mortal or not, I was glad she was on our team.

An escort led us to our seats. As we walked through the theater, it was like a surreal family reunion. We saw people we recognized, but the girls wondered if they looked familiar because they were famous, or if we'd actually met them somewhere. Of course, I remembered everyone, but I pretended to wonder, too.

We bumped into people we definitely knew, including all the members of the band Elio, who we hugged like family. We'd spent many hours in Sawyer's studio with them since doing a gig together at the Boston Garden the year before. They were sitting all the way on the other side of the theater, so we compared notes on where we could catch up later, what after parties we were going to, etc. We had no idea what parties we were going to, but they assured us the place to be was the Corner Store.

I'd smelled him earlier but, for the sake of the mortals, acted like I had no idea Markus had been in the building when he came over. We all hugged and exchanged compliments on clothes. He wore a black leather three-piece suit and a black fedora.

"The tour was okay, but you've got to tell me what's going on with you," he said rapidly. "You look like you've been drinking from the vein."

"Markus, you don't even know," I replied.

"Oooh, Angel, I know you're bad."

I smiled sweetly at him with a look that said he was quickly becoming my third girlfriend.

"You guys going to Future after party?" he asked. One of his people started motioning for him to sit down.

"We'd heard the Corner Store was supposed to be good," I replied.

"Bet. Let's roll together," he said before heading back to his seat across the aisle and a few rows ahead.

We looked around as LaLa waved at a woman across the room, who was standing and waving back enthusiastically.

"I don't even know who that person is," LaLa said between smiling teeth.

"She waved first," I said, pretending to read my program.

"Girl," Jules said under her breath as she pressed Send on yet another text, "I'm just saying hello and nodding to everybody. I don't think half the people in this room know who they think they know, either." She held up the cell phone for a group selfie. We posed, she clicked, reviewed, we approved and we went back to our previous postures as she uploaded it to social media.

"So let's just be friendly to everyone," I suggested, brushing dirt off my shoes, "and that way if they turn out to be someone that we actually met but can't remember, they wouldn't know we'd actually forgotten them."

"Good idea," LaLa said, putting her hand in her hair and running it through in that way she did when she was aggravated. "And if they don't know us from Adam, they'd either look friendly back because they're thinking the same thing we're thinking, or just think we're crazy."

The thought sent us into a muted giggle fit. The lights went down, and the live telecast came into the room.

"Someone's watching you every moment, even as you sit here watching others," Nina told us. "You're 'on' until you close the door to your house tonight."

Lovely thought.

Once the cameras were live, you could feel the difference in the room. Most folks went into "on" mode as they watched their friends, colleagues, and future collaborators perform and receive awards.

Next to me, Nina was texting furiously. She'd stop and seem to be done, only to start up again, texting as doggedly as before.

Eventually she leaned over and whispered in my ear, "Angel." Her voice had that about-to-drop-a-bomb tone. I couldn't imagine what she was about to say, but my stomach clenched. I looked at her, and her face was completely neutral, but her eyes were excited and alert. Nina didn't get excited about much.

"They're in a bind backstage." Her voice was an urgent whisper. "They need someone to take the place of one of the presenters. If you want to do it, you have to get backstage immediately."

"What? Present? Me?"

"Yes." She paused. When I looked up to see why, she looked me in the eyes. "Only you." She let those two words sink in for a few seconds before picking up again in the same urgent tone. "Don't worry. They'll tell you exactly what to do, what to say. And there's a teleprompter. You'll stay back there afterward and get ready for your set." She held up her cell phone. "I just made sure everything will go smoothly for you. What do you say?"

My heart and head swam with conflicting thoughts and emotions. On one hand, the idea of presenting an award to a fellow artist on the USAMA was nerve-racking and exciting. On the other hand, I wondered why just me and not the three of us.

"What about LaLa and Jules?" I whispered back to her. "It's right before our set."

"Don't worry," she said. "I'll explain that this will benefit the group." She held up her cell phone again. "I've negotiated that they will give Kat Trio more camera time during your set in return for you stepping in at the last minute. You're doing this for the team."

"I'll do it," I said. Nina raised her finger, and an escort came over quickly and stood at the end of our row. I stood. LaLa and Jules looked at me with surprise and confusion.

"Nina'll tell you," I whispered to them while making my way, silk brocade gathered in my fists, out of the row and into the aisle.

The escort led me quickly, but not too quickly for me to trip over dress and heels. While walking through the theater, I watched other people milling and walking around while performances were going on and was surprised at the amount of activity happening during the show. Soon we were backstage, and I was led to a stage manager, Mel, who greeted me warmly. "I'll lead you to your dressing room," she said before starting to walk. "You'll be presenting the award for Best Electronic Album, along with Christopher Bing."

Christopher Bing was a popular actor who'd starred in a vampire movie. He had a following of female fans, and many had camped out overnight for his last movie's premiere, the follow-up to *The Dead of Night.*

"This is the script," Mel continued, handing me a piece of paper bearing scrawled, ineligible notes that looked like they'd been written by the person who was supposed to originally present.

"Who am I replacing?" I asked Mel.

She paused as if she was asking herself how much she could, or had time to say. "Paulia Crenshaw." She leaned in and whispered, "She got sick at the last minute."

Everything made sense now. Paulia Crenshaw was a singer known for her amazing talent, but unfortunately she was also notorious for her partying, drinking, and drug abuse.

I nodded my head, and Mel nodded, too, before continuing in the same quick, professional tone she'd used before mentioning Paulia Crenshaw. "You have fifteen minutes." We stopped at a door that had a Kat Trio sign on it. "George will come get you at the five mark. Nice meeting you!"

"Thanks, Mel," I said as she smiled and continued down the hall. My sense of smell told me that Demeter, Risa, and Shay were already in there. I opened the door, and Demeter immediately pulled me into a corner of the dressing room that was separated by a curtain and started on my hair and makeup.

"Since this is last minute, we'll just keep it the same as for the red carpet," she said. "I'm just freshening up everything. This is so exiting! I can't believe you're going to be presenting with Christopher Bing!"

I tuned out her chatter and focused on the script and lines I was supposed to deliver. It seemed pretty straightforward, and I'd watched enough awards shows to know my delivery should be upbeat and professional.

Demeter was done with minutes to spare before George arrived to lead me to the backstage area. After briefing me on where to stand and where to look once onstage, George introduced me to Christopher Bing. The actor's eyes twinkled with greeting, but once he shook my hand, those eyes quickly dropped to the floor, and his cheeks turned a deep red. He was nothing like the super-confidant guy portrayed in the media. "You can just follow Christopher," George told me. "If you let him walk slightly ahead of you, that will show you exactly where to stop and what direction to face."

They counted down, and we listened for our cue. Christopher took my hand and looped my arm around his elbow. "I'm sweating like a damn pig," he said in his British accent. I smiled, completely at a loss as to how to respond. With my other hand, I held up a corner of my dress so that I could walk without fear of my shoe catching in my skirt. They announced our names, and we walked out onto the stage to applause. The floor of the stage felt a little slippery, and I pulled on Christopher's arm to let him know I needed to walk slower. He slowed while continuing to sport his famous glower as if he were in character for his vampire role.

When we got to the designated spot, we stood for a couple of seconds as the audience continued to clap. A few people yelled my name, and I waved to the audience.

Christopher was scripted to say the first line, so I waited for him to speak while looking into the camera as instructed. He said nothing.

"Bing just froze," Mel whispered to someone backstage.

"Again?" was the response.

The teleprompter was blank, so that was no help. The audience started reacting to the awkward silence. I recalled his opening line. He was supposed to say something about it being a good night for dancing. "It's a wonderful night for dancing," I said in a breezy tone.

"Yes," Christopher said. "Yes, it is." He obviously still had no idea what to say and continued to smile.

"Well," I said, gesturing to the audience. "Should we give it a go?"

He looked at me, and his character's signature smile appeared at the side of his lips. "Be careful what you ask for," he said, delivering a line from the movie verbatim. He pulled me into his arms the same way his character did in the film, and women in the audience started screaming. "You just might get it."

I decided to go with the flow and forget about the script since my next line made no sense with what was going on. My smile disappeared, and I waxed melodramatic, too. "Show me," I said.

The audience screamed even louder as we stood there—he bending me back slightly and me staring into his eyes. He then twirled me around as if we were on the dance floor—perfectly, since his dance prowess was the reason he'd gotten the role of a dancing vampire. The crowd went wild. He ended with a deep dip that bent me way back and pulled me back up quickly to standing.

Feeling like a marionette, but relieved it had all worked out, I smiled, picked the envelope up off the lectern and handed it to him. We were back on script.

After we announced the nominees, Bing opened the envelope. "The award for Best Electronic Album goes to…"

"Terrabyte!" I announced, reading the enclosed card.

We stood there waiting for the DJ known as Terrabyte to come up to the stage. Christopher smiled at me in a way that showed he, too, was relieved with how things had turned out.

Terrabyte, wearing a pink tuxedo with tails and a pink, fuzzy top hat, finally waded through the crowd to get up to the stage. We both greeted him before following the escort offstage. Once our microphones were removed, and we were alone, Christopher turned to me.

"Angel, I'm so sorry. I completely froze."

"Happens to everybody," I lied. Judging from Mel's reaction, it seemed to happen to Christopher regularly.

He started walking away, but then turned back to me. "Are you going to the Remington Hotel for the after party? Maybe I'll see you there."

"Maybe," I answered noncommittally before George started leading me back to the dressing room. I'd just started to change when Jules and LaLa came in.

"Oh my God!" Jules exclaimed. "I can't believe what I just saw!"

"What was it like up there?" LaLa asked breathlessly.

Neither of them seemed angry or jealous. Nina must have done a thorough job in explaining the benefits of my presenting for Kat Trio. "It was wild. He was supposed to give the first line and he froze."

"I kneeew it!" Demeter was gleeful. "We were watching the monitor, and it was soooo obvious you jumped in and saved the day!"

"Yeah," Jules said. "I'm totally jealous you were up there with Christopher 'Super Hottie' Bing, but this is going to be awesome for us."

"Yeah," LaLa added. "Thanks for doing that. I wouldn't have wanted to."

I breathed an inward sigh of relief that they were okay with what had happened. We started to get ready for our miniset—THE moment I'd been looking forward to all summer.

Demeter took all the miniature pearl pins out of my hair as quickly as she could without attracting attention and transformed my updo into a chic, straight curtain that blanketed my shoulders from chin right to chin left. She added extensions to make it look more dramatic and more eye makeup while freshening up the nude look.

Our outfits were girl next door with glam appeal—beaded, painted jeans with cropped, beaded tees, and gold-plated high-tops—a far cry from the diva clothes we wore for the red carpet. The fact we weren't wearing heels (for once) allowed us to easily execute Redd's choreography, which we went over a couple more times. Our set was going to be a simple, abbreviated version of "No. 8" with the amped-up choreography that audiences expected from a music awards show.

Tonight was our chance to prove to ourselves that we were capable of performing at a high level, a level worthy of the very best of our hopes and dreams. We were being presented as ones to watch, *and* we were ready to do it all without lip-synching. We ran through the "No. 8" segment for the thousandth time while waiting to go onstage.

George came for us at the five mark and led us to the wings. We held hands and looked at each other.

"This is it," LaLa said. "The biggest gig of our lives." We bowed our heads.

"Oh God, let us do this right," Jules whispered.

"We *will* do this," I stressed. "We worked hard to get here."

"We deserve this," LaLa added calmly, squeezing our hands.

"Yes," Jules repeated with a deep breath. "We deserve this."

We collectively breathed in and out before dropping hands. Stagehands pinned on and secured our microphones, and we stopped talking.

Jules started doing tiny steps from the choreography routine to keep her mind occupied until it was time to step out. Dorito Jones was close to the end of his song. Countdown for us. We were next!

We took our places on the darkened portion of the stage. The band gave us our cue, the lights rose, and—boom—we were in the midst of Redd's sizzling choreography. It was freeing to perform onstage without heels, and the energy we danced with was more athletic than in previous gigs. We broke into the blended harmony of the first note, and the lighting flashed to dramatic.

While watching the musical notes travel throughout the theater, I felt the most amazing sense of pride. This was all me. No mind lock, none of Dad's magic, not even the relaxing effect of Justin's fresh blood. For the first time since The Change, I felt like I could handle any situation. By myself.

The joy that soaked my lyrics touched the audience: people hugged one another, cried and waved cell phone flashlights in the air.

It was the best gig of my life. And for one second I felt fear—a sense of impending doom—like something was going to happen the way it did at the Garden, the last big gig of my life.

Messed-up stuff had a way of happening to me on the nights when I was supposed to be the most happy.

Immediately I banished the negative thoughts, and returned my focus to the joy and, to my relief, our set was over so fast, the only thing it left was me wanting more. Soon we were backstage, hugging each other and dancing with glee.

"See you at the Corner Store," Dorito said to Jules with a big smile.

"Definitely." She smiled as we were led back to our dressing room to change into our after-party outfits.

I donned a short, white cocktail dress with lots of sparkly stuff going on. It was created by one of the lesser-known designers who'd sent us dresses pre-Stevidy. Strappy, glittery sandals and my own jewelry completed the look. The diamonds and pearls got whisked away for safekeeping.

LaLa chose a pair of jeans, sexy heels, and off-the-shoulder, glam T-shirt, while Jules rocked a black, sequined cocktail dress with Jimmy Choo gladiator-style sandals.

Demeter put my hair up in a sleek, sexy updo with a few stray tendrils falling in all the right places, before adding some sparkling crystal-covered pins.

And soon we were back in our seats in the audience.

Nina leaned over and whispered in my ear again. "Great job out there with Bing. It was a good thing for Kat Trio and you." She congratulated us as a group for the set, told us the energy was more than she'd expected, and gave positive notes about our dancing.

I was still excited about being a part of the USAMA, but there was also a part of me that was relieved our contribution to the show was finished and we could just kick back and relax. I became a fan at that point, clapping and cheering along with my girls for all the performers who followed us. We all squeezed hands, knowing now that not only were we worthy to be in the room and share a stage with these people, but that they thought so, too.

BLOOD AND LOVE

The USAMA were soon a warm, fuzzy memory as we piled into our limo on our way to an after party. We'd decided to go to at least two and, as Nina put it, get our faces out there as much as possible. We headed for the Corner Store first so Jules could connect with Dorito, and decided we'd go to Future afterward to meet up with Markus.

A text came in from Justin.:

> Back in L.A. See you when you get home.

It caught me off guard to see this. I knew he was coming back around now, but the fact that I hadn't drunk any of his blood over the past forty-eight hours seemed to have had a major effect on me. I felt less connected to him and realized it was the first time I'd thought straight since his return.

The Sunan was working.

We hung out at the Corner Store for a while as an uncharacteristically overprotective Nina made sure we didn't drink. Markus showed up, looking for us with his crew, including Fearmonger. LaLa was surprised to see the latter, and soon they were arm in arm like they were married.

There were plenty of stars there, and a lot of the conversations ended up revolving around what we were working on and the potential for collaborating. There was a lot of picture-taking going on. Warren had packed backup batteries for my cell, which came in handy as he was steadily uploading pics to my social media accounts.

After about forty-five minutes, Nina suggested we hit Future. We heard a lot of people saying they were going there because the Corner Store was getting lame. So everybody, including Dorito and Markus, hopped in our limo and rolled over. Inside the car, it was business as usual: Raj, sitting across from Jules and Dorito, displayed the most expressionless face; Warren monitored my social media accounts and compared notes with Nina; Risa was on the lookout for any wardrobe malfunctions; and Demeter and Shay freshened up Kat Trio's hair and makeup before we exited the car.

There was a mini red carpet and a ton of paparazzi at Future's entrance. Strolling like red carpet vets, we walked down together and stopped to let the mob of photographers take our picture.

That's when I caught his scent. Sawyer was here.

I almost collapsed. Luckily Markus was standing next to me. He swiftly caught my arm and held me up.

"I know," he murmured as we posed together for some photographers. "I smell him, too."

Fortunately, none of the rest of the crew seemed to notice what had gone down. Jules was hanging all over Dorito, and the cameras were going nuts. LaLa and Fearmonger were wrapped around each other and looked like they would stay that way all night. Risa threw a look at me that seemed to say she'd picked up Sawyer's scent as well, but wouldn't be crossing that path again.

Inside the club, the décor was ultracool, and the atmosphere was much classier than the Corner Store. Sawyer's scent was stronger.

"Stay cool, Shimshana," Markus said as we made our way into the club. "You knew this day would come."

"Yes, but not tonight! He hates awards shows; he wasn't even at the theater," My feet hovered above the floor. I drew in a few deep breaths and touched down again.

"Wouldn't be the first time someone skipped the show and went straight to the after party." Markus exuded calm. "Do your thing. Work the room and handle your business."

He was right. I was here to work. Another deep breath. And gratitude for club lighting; even if my skin was a couple of shades redder, nobody would notice.

We chatted with more people about potential collaborations. Warren gathered contact info and handed out Kat Trio cards. Demeter, Risa, and Shay were at the ready in the VIP section. Eventually I was able to let go of Markus's arm, stand unassisted and walk around on my own. I fought the urge to send an emotional SOS text to Cici.

We saw the members of Elio, who all laughed when we told them they missed nothing at the Candy Store. In fact, no one went where they said they were going to go anyway. Joy, the bass player, found that especially funny. "We spent an hour going back and forth, trying to figure out whether to go," she said. "You mean all we had to do was ask?" She cast a comical, accusing eye at the male members of the band.

Earlier, Jules, LaLa, and I had confirmed with Nina that we definitely wanted to continue working with Elio. Their cross-genre versatility was exciting. After speaking with their manager, Nina confirmed they felt the same way about the synergy between our two groups and, now that they were getting ready to record a new album, we were at the top of their list of collaborators.

Christopher Bing made his way up to us.

"Bing!" Markus exclaimed before giving him a ghetto pound and a shoulder clap.

"Wolf," Christopher said with a street vibe one wouldn't expect from a clean-cut English bloke. He greeted the rest of the group and finally looked at me. "Would you like to dance again?" he asked.

He was cute, and there was something interesting about the way he carried himself. Plus, he smelled like heaven. "Sure," I said with a small smile. Jules and LaLa shot subtle thumbs-ups before we made our way out to the floor.

The music was live, and the artist performing was one of the biggest dance music stars on the charts. Christopher started dancing, and he looked good; he was tall and moved well. No wonder women went crazy over him. For the millionth time that night, I was glad I'd stopped at The Nest earlier.

"You're a great dancer," he shouted over the music.

"Thanks. You, too." We danced until the end of the song.

"Again?" he asked. He placed a hand on my arm, but suddenly he sounded miles away. As my awareness shifted, I barely registered his gaze following the direction of my stare.

Sawyer was standing stock-still in the middle of the dance floor, and his eyes were glued on me.

I couldn't move. It was like some crazy imp had superglued the soles of my sandals to the floor. Weird paralysis took over my body as people started dancing around us.

"Sorry," I mumbled to Christopher, shaking myself out of my trance before leaving the dance floor to find a spot where I could breathe and lean against a wall.

Like a heat seeking missile, Sawyer followed close behind.

He loomed above me, despite my heels. I looked up, and it was over. Our eyes locked as everything—the crowd, the music, the room, my very breath—melted away. The only thing I was aware of was him. His scent made me feel insane, like the floor had disappeared, and I was standing on air. A quick look confirmed my feet were, surprisingly, still on the ground.

"Angel," he whispered. A question and a prayer all rolled into one. The way my name sounded on his lips brought tears to my eyes. "Can we talk?"

"Yes," I said, unable to deny him anything.

"This place is too loud," he said.

"Let's go to my place," I said quickly, thoughtlessly. "There's something I need to show you."

"Okay," he said without a trace of hesitation.

Across the room, Markus said, "Here we go."

I called for Warren in a conversational tone no mortal would be able to pick up over the music, and within a minute, he'd made his way over to where we stood.

"Go outside and hail a cab," I told him, still unable to tear my eyes away from Sawyer's. "When you get one, text me."

It didn't take long to get Warren's text with the location. I showed the screen to Sawyer. "That's right around the corner," he said. "On the side of the building opposite the entrance, away from the paparazzi."

"Meet you there," I said before watching him turn on his heel and stride through the crowd.

Under the cover of Future's strobe lighting, I rushed through the club's patrons and the walls before finding myself on the sidewalk. I shot over to where Warren waited. The cab door was open.

"What do you need?" he asked. His tone revealed concern, but his face was still professional.

"Hang with Nina for the rest of the night," I answered. "When she says the night's over, do whatever you want."

He started to turn back to the club, and I put a hand on his arm.

"I couldn't do this"—I gestured at the club— "the networking, none of it, without you. You *do* have a gift."

Something happened to Warren's face. For the first time, I saw it register pride. We both heard Sawyer coming around the corner and turned to face him. Immediately his penetrating green gaze focused on my hand resting on Warren's arm.

Warren stayed cool. "Thank you, Angel," he said before heading back to the club.

Sawyer helped me into the cab, and we took off. I could've sworn the cab was enchanted, because I honestly couldn't remember driving through the streets. In no time, we were at my front door. Sawyer paid the driver and opened my door before we went inside.

We went straight to the live studio, where I sat at the grand and began to play our ballad. I sang the few lyrics I'd written and hummed the rest as the studio became awash in the beautiful glowing colors only I could see.

Sawyer started singing in the spaces where there were no lyrics, and his hands on the keys filled in the parts of the melody I hadn't worked out. We looked at each other in wide-eyed wonder as we realized what was happening: we were completing each other's compositions. He'd worked out my empty places, and I'd worked out his. As he sang, his sensual tenor filled my senses and took me higher than any amount of alcohol or any drug could.

I'd never fallen out of love with Sawyer. I'd only fallen for him more.

"This has been the most miserable summer of my life," he said, sitting next to me on the bench. "I can barely breathe. I love you—"

I kissed him. He kissed me back. Hard and soft, wetness and fire. The heat rose.

Our ballad started to play again, and it felt like I hadn't heard its otherworldly beauty in forever. Surprised, I realized we were hearing the song's climax. It was the missing piece and it was more beautiful than anything we could've come up with on our own. It was a herald proclaiming that our love had returned and, in the wake of our love's return, the song itself was whole.

But there was one thing I needed to feel complete.

"I need you," I said.

He picked me up and headed toward the stairs as I made my weight lighter. Upstairs, we paused at the closed door to my room and he looked into my eyes. It wasn't like at the club when his eyes were like laser beams, all merciless focus. Now his eyes were soft. I felt like I was melting.

"Are you sure?" he asked.

"I want nothing, no one, but you," I answered breathlessly, decisively. It felt like my very soul was burning for him. I could think of nothing else except merging with him. Now.

He kissed me softly, tenderly and opened the door to the room. His lips still on mine, he laid me down on the bed.

But in the bed there was a massive lump. Beneath the fluffy comforter lay Justin.

WAVES OF CHANGE

I felt Justin's body jump as Sawyer unknowingly placed me on top of him.

"Oh, you're home early," Justin said, his head and sleepy smile popped out from underneath a pillow before he looked up and saw Sawyer standing there.

Justin, jumping out of the bed with immortal speed, immediately reached the far side of the room. All I could see was the look in Sawyer's eyes.

"Home?" he repeated in shock.

"Sawyer…" I rose to stand in front of him in an attempt to block his line of sight as it honed in on Justin. "It's not what you're thinking. Justin has been staying here, but it's not as bad as it looks."

It looked pretty bad.

Sawyer, eyes squeezed shut and panting with sweat and effort, stood with fists clenched and feet apart as if he was bracing himself in the midst of a storm. The sound of his now rapid heartbeat served as the rare, but undeniable herald of his loss of control. He opened his eyes, greener than mortal eyes should be, and trained them on Justin. For the first time, I felt fear—not fear of what I could do to him, but fear of what *he* might do. To Justin.

Then it happened. A massive wave of…some sort of energy rolled right through me. And then there was the unbearable pain of being burned. Sawyer was attacking me! In disbelief, I looked down at myself. There was no fire, not even heat. As I searched for the cause of the relentless burning, Justin came into my peripheral vision. He was on fire, ablaze in the corner of my room. His pain transferred to me through our blood bond. His eyes met mine as if he, too, was only just realizing what was happening, and the shock caused us both to cry out in the agony of burning alive.

Sawyer was trying to kill Justin, whom he, like everyone else, believed to be a vampire. He had no way of knowing that because of his angelic maker's power, Justin could likely burn indefinitely. Or worse, his maker, Bodiel, might appear.

"Sawyer, stop!" I screamed, shook him, tried to get through to him. But it was like he was somewhere else, similar to when he communicated with the ghosts of the dead; he was like a vacant conduit, and his eyes saw right through me. My screams became long and drawn-out—a tortured aria—until the black notes bounced aggressively through the room. Sawyer finally responded to me, to my aria, by involuntarily adding his own tortured bellows, until the three of us wailed in a strange cacophony that may or may not have resembled the sound of hell.

But the burning continued; Sawyer couldn't stop. I had to put an end to this endless loop of agony. My scream shifted to B-flat with the sole intention of stopping Sawyer. It worked. Justin stopped burning, and I stopped feeling it. Dead silence as my eyes took in Justin's lifeless form on the floor and what was left of his scorched skin and flesh.

But Sawyer wasn't thwarted; he was only diverted. "Angel, run!" he yelled. "I can't control it!"

Too late. The brute force of... something...
wrapped itself around me like the frigid hands of
death. Icy coldness surrounded me and tightened its
grip. I belted out an F-sharp to invoke heat and
counter the force that was now attacking me.
Sawyer's vacant face cried tears, but he seemed
paralyzed. Everything within my being shrieked
that Sawyer must be stopped. I redirected the F-
sharp at him. Sorrow and grief welled up from my
soul as I willed him to shut down, to retract the
tentacles, to keep his deadly magic to himself. The
windows of the rooms rattled and eventually
shattered with the force of my voice; glass flew
everywhere, cutting my flesh, but I didn't stop.

Neither did the tentacles.

I cranked the power of my voice up to a level
I'd never before unleashed in the presence of a
mortal. As the coldness continued to spread, and my
blood flowed from glass shards lodged in my skin, I
knew I was going to kill Sawyer. He screamed in
pain and crumpled to the floor.

Dad appeared in the room, his body shielded
from the flying glass and debris, and immediately
extended his hand toward me as he yelled
something in ancient Nubian. The deadly chill
diminished. Chanting, Dad then pointed a finger at
the floor, which began rippling like waves around
Sawyer's prone body. Soon the buffeting waves
tossed him back and forth until it broke the state he
was in; he became more like himself and stood. The
iciness ended as Dad continued to extend the other
hand in my direction. I stopped singing.

Dad watched me carefully. "Angel, can you hear me?"

"Yes, Dad. I can." My voice shook.

He continued to watch me until he seemed satisfied. He nodded and lowered his hand. "You were being transported into another dimension. I saw it." His voice was tinged with a combination of shock and anger. "Molecule by molecule, you were being dismantled here and put together there." He turned to Sawyer. "Your tentacles did that."

The room turned bright red. I'd never felt so angry.

"I'm so sorry," Sawyer pleaded in a tone that gave away his fear of being the target of not just me but also Dad. "Angel, it wasn't me. They have a will of their own."

"Get out." I heard my own voice as if from a distance. "You don't own me or tell me what to do."

Sawyer didn't move, but he opened his mouth. Probably to protest. Or apologize more. It didn't matter. I wanted him out—out of my room, out of my house, out of my life.

"Get out!" I forcefully sang the words, drawing them out with the intention of making Sawyer leave the house. It worked on everybody, including Dad, who turned reluctantly toward the door. Justin, already healing from having been burned over most of his body, painfully stood to walk to the door.

"Stop, Angel. Stop. I'll go," Sawyer said.

I stopped singing. Dad shook himself and turned toward me in disbelief as if surprised by the power of my voice. Justin fell limply into the nearest chair.

"Don't ever come back, Sawyer," I said, exhausted, numb.

He put his hand on the doorknob.

"I will see you out," Dad said to him. For a moment, based on what I'd seen Dad was capable of, I feared the worst for Sawyer. But that moment didn't last.

My ex-boyfriend faced Dad with resignation before turning to me one last time with dismay in his eyes. Dad clapped his hands, and they disappeared.

I turned to Justin. His clothes had burned off, charred flesh and bone was still visible in some places, but his body was healing steadily. My stomach flipped with nausea and sorrow, and my tears dropped indiscriminately to the floor.

"Don't cry." He could barely form the words with his damaged vocal cords. I directed a soft, tangerine-tinted C note toward him—the same one I'd used for Mr. C.—and his healing accelerated until flesh, muscle, bone and skin were back to normal.

He caught me in his arms as I fell, spent, backward toward the floor. The exhaustion of healing him, using my voice as a weapon, and whatever had happened to my body during Sawyer's assault, had taken its toll on me.

"Drink, Angel. You need to. I can take it."

My shimshana remained tightly coiled in my belly.

"I want to die," I said.

Justin ripped the flesh off his wrist with his teeth in an effort to force me to drink what little blood he had left. I refused, keenly aware that he needed it more than I did. His selfless love made me cry more.

But soon my grief turned to anger. Damn Sawyer! I spat every curse word imaginable until my tears returned. Waves of self-pity overtook me, and I wept because Sawyer wasn't there to hold me. I had no one to hold me! I ignored Justin's outstretched hand and wrapped my arms around my torso in a desperate attempt to hug myself as I rose to my feet.

Once I'd stood, I continued to hold myself, not caring how ridiculous I probably looked. And then something happened to me. It wasn't witchy, supernatural, or Shimshana-ish. It was simple. Human. And powerful enough to drop me back to my knees.

I felt love. Unconditional and uncompromising. But it wasn't directed at Sawyer or Justin. It was love for myself. Immediately I felt revitalized, as if I'd drunk fresh blood.

But most of all, I felt like every part of myself was loved.

Was that what Star meant? Was she telling me to love *myself* all this time?

Justin's hand slumped to his side, and I noticed his hair was growing out of his newly-formed scalp. I rushed down the hall to his room, located his suitcase and brought it back to my room. I pulled out some clothes and gently helped him to stand up. As he dressed, I grabbed blood and mortal food—

fruit, bread, cold pot roast—from the suite's minifridge and placed it all on the sitting area's coffee table. He started scarfing down food while simultaneously putting on his clothes, gingerly pulling fabric over areas of his body where the new skin was still sensitive.

Meanwhile, I sucked down blood and watched him, my heart brimming with love and gratitude. The Sunan had given me space from Justin and rewarded me with clarity. Lucidity hit me, as I truly saw him for the first time since starting Sunan; I was able to see our relationship with fresh eyes and think about it with a clear brain.

He must have sensed it, the growing distance in the midst of what had drawn us together. Now fully dressed, he devoured the last of the food and turned to me. "I can give you some blood now." Aside from the obvious fatigue in his body, he looked almost normal. "I can still give you everything you need."

He was wondering what this new feeling was. He needed an explanation…

"I've been going to The Nest." My voice was gentle. "I've been utilizing Sunan, and it's given me perspective on what we have. How you fit into my life."

I touched his hand and marveled at the new skin that had just grown there as he patiently waited for me to continue.

"Sawyer tried to kill you tonight," I said. "And I protected you from him. Because I had to. You and I are linked. And we might be forever. But for now, I choose the Sunan. I know you aren't obsessed. You proved it when you left on your own. I know you love me. And I love you, too. But I need to find out who I am independent of everyone, including you. I can't drink from you anymore, Justin."

My eyes took him in as he absorbed my words. I felt the grief welling up inside of him, and prepared myself to cry more tears of sorrow, steeled myself to argue with him about why we should stay together.

Amazingly, though, there was no argument, no tears.

"I get it." He rose to his feet. "Probably more than you know. I understand the need to separate from other people's expectations. Find what makes you...you."

He turned and slowly walked to the closet. "You're the forever type, Angel." He picked up his suitcase. "I'll love you forever."

He leaned in and kissed my forehead, letting his lips linger in my hair before he pulled himself away. It didn't feel like he was returning to his room; it felt like a good-bye.

"Stay. You're still hurting."

"Don't worry about me." His voice was soft, and his eyes caressed me, long and tender, as his hand hovered above the doorknob. "Call me when you're ready." He opened the door and left.

Again I was alone. But also gone was the feeling of despair experienced when Mom, Dad, Sawyer, the girls—all the people in my life—left me before. The need to fill myself with empty relationships was no more.

I loved myself. Nothing else was needed.

I jetted down to the Saucony kitchen. The clock on the wall said it was past three in the morning. My girls were probably fast asleep at the hotel, safe and sound, with their parents. My lips curved into a smile, and my heart lifted with happiness.

I focused on love.

I warmed some blood, poured myself a large goblet, and raised my glass to Mom's memory before taking a long drink.

"You okay?" A sleepy Cici stood in the kitchen's entranceway and barely stifled a large yawn. She sat next to me, wrapped a hand around the goblet I filled for her and savored the taste as we sat in comfortable silence.

"I heard…what happened," she said, "but Dad wouldn't let me help." Her eyes took in my appearance. I could only guess what she saw—my singed, once-white cocktail dress and my face streaked with dried, bloody tears.

But I couldn't care less how I looked.

The night had gone from being the best of the best on the USAMA stage to the worst of the worst on the stage of life. The pendulum of emotion had swung from one extreme to another and dragged my heart with it.

And I felt fine. Well, at least, I'd survived.

"What will you do now?" she asked.

"Kat Trio's got an album to finish. We have to record more tracks, collaborate with more people. Write more. Do more." I took another swig of type O. "The summer's almost over," I continued. "I'm nine months old. There's no time to waste."

Her eyes focused on her goblet as her delicate fingers slowly rotated it.

"I know what you're thinking. You're wondering why I sent Justin away. After all, he had everything, right?"

"I was thinking something like that," she conceded.

"I wanted independence. Complete. I wanted to make the break from having to depend on anyone. The Sunan gave me a glimpse of that.

"And I've made a decision." My heart found refuge in the graceful planes of her cheekbones and the twinkle in her eye. She was my sister, and I loved her as much as I loved myself. "I've decided to live an Inc lifestyle. It resonates better with who I am."

I watched her face light up and couldn't believe what I saw after a few seconds. The angles and contours of her face shifted exactly like Star's. In fact, at one point she looked exactly like our Great Mother. The sight of it made me feel as if Star herself was confirming she'd meant for me to love myself.

"I'm so happy to hear that," Cici said. She hugged me, and I hugged her back with all the love in my heart.

Focus on love—that's what Star had said. And that's what I was going to do.

"One more thing," I said. "I want to re-establish the mind lock."

"What?" She looked puzzled. "I don't understand. What about independence? How does that work if I'm back in your head?"

"Cici, I've watched you struggling to survive not being connected to me. It's been hard for you." We both laughed.

"Okay, I admit it. I got spoiled, but I fail to see how that figures in your declaration of independence."

"It matters," I said simply. "You're my family. And more than anyone—Justin, Sawyer, anyone— you will be a part of me that never takes away, only adds to the quality of my life. It'll only be for three more months, and I need to have you in my head because…I love you."

We hugged again, long and strong. Bound by blood and love in a way no one else could claim.

I was no longer the girl who had been subjected to the mind lock; I was now the woman who chose the mind lock for the love of self.

Power. Protection. Loyalty. Forever.

It was our family motto and it was also the way I chose to live my life.

THE END

EPILOGUE

JUSTIN

I closed Angel's bedroom door behind me and immediately entered cloak mode. Of all the things she didn't know about me, this ability to cloak everything—my scent, even the sound of my heartbeat—probably wouldn't surprise her. The cloaking came courtesy of Bodiel's breath, so I couldn't tell her if I tried. Even more than Shimshana, angels were real good at hiding things.

Angel also didn't know this: she thought she'd just said good-bye to me, but I was going to stay here, with her, in this house.

If Angel knew everything, the whole truth about me, would she even want me around?

I couldn't think about the answer to that. Not now…even though my heart wanted to bust through my ribcage as I thought about the look on her face when she told me she loved me.

The problem was, she didn't know she needed protection. As she wrestled with the darkness of her true nature, she was still naïve to the dangers around her.

It wasn't her fault. Her parents set her up before she was even born. Set her up to be blind to her own legacy. Now that Cleo slept, that false sense of security they'd built was crumbling. But I was going to make sure Angel wouldn't go down with it.

I made my way up to the third floor and headed to Kiya's suite of rooms. Hearing the TV through the door, I gave the knock and waited five minutes before stepping inside.

"You could have come in immediately," she said from her spot on the couch. "I'm just taking a break." Her eyes were glued on a talk show centered around paternity-test results and spontaneous brawls. She didn't even look at me.

"Angel thinks I left the house." I placed my suitcase down on the floor. "I'm not going anywhere."

"Stay here, then. More than enough room." She munched on a handful of Cheetos before offering me the bag and finally taking a look at me. "My heavens. You look like a half-dead mortal." She got up from the couch and, like a mother hen, made me lie down. She clapped her hands, and a crisply folded blanket floated to my side before loosening its tucked corners and stretching itself over me. My weight sank into the couch. "You boys will have to find a way to get along," she said.

Seeing Angel kick Sawyer's ass and then throw him out gave me no sense of victory; I was just sad to see her heartbroken. "Don't think he's in the picture anymore," I answered.

"Perhaps," she replied. Two fluffy pillows floated up to my head. She helped me sit up and lean forward before plucking them out of the air, plumping them, gently pushing me back down, and arranging them under my head. With a reluctant flick of the wrist, she clicked off the TV. "The shows these days..." She shook her head in disbelief. "It's wondrous. The stories they come up with." She continued to speak in a rapid whisper.

"I'll be gone for a little while again. Been busy with Charleston. He is a snake, but I have him."

As my mind filed through all the facts Angel didn't know about me, I figured this tidbit—that I was undercover, working B.O.R. covert operations—would probably bother her the most. She might not care too much that Kiya was an agent, and had been for a long time. I asked Kiya if our boss knew about her assertions.

"He suspected it even before you joined us. Now I will have proof. It has taken me over five hundred years, but now everyone will know that Charleston was involved in Tunde's attempt to destroy Cleopatra."

A clear glass of ice water floated over, and she wrapped her hand around it before holding it to my lips. The cold liquid soothed my throat. "I will stock the kitchen here in my suite. This time I will make sure no one sees how much you eat." Kiya was good at the mom thing, and I didn't mind because right about now I was feeling like an orphan.

"How long will you be in L.A.?" Her voice startled me. Realizing I'd drifted off, I lifted my eyebrows and widened my eyes.

"Until Angel goes back to school."

My body, underneath the blanket, rose a few feet into the air and slowly glided down the short hallway to one of the bedrooms. Air rippled along my back like a ghostly massage as the pillows floated under my head for support.

"Rest, soldier," she said as she followed behind. "The battle's only beginning."

She was right; I felt it.

Long ago, my grandfather told me to always trust my gut. "Never let ye down," he'd say in his thick Boston accent tinged with an Irish brogue. Of my family's many generations of cops, he was known as the best and he taught me all I knew.

The comforter rolled itself to the foot of the bed before my body slowly lowered to the mattress.

Always trust your gut. I didn't know why I felt Angel was in danger, but I knew I needed to act on it.

The sound of Angel's laugh erupted in the kitchen, comforting me in a way the pillow and blanket could not. My eyelids grew heavy again...

It felt good knowing that she knew my love was real, that I wasn't blood obsessed after all. And, in time, she'd know the truth about me: that I'd do anything, go anywhere on this earth, to protect her.

ABRAHAM

In all of my 1,749 years, I had rarely seen such extraordinary magical force in a mortal and had never witnessed this magnitude of potential in one so young.

The boy held his head in a vain attempt to regain control as we sped away from Angel. For mere moments after I had confused the so-called tentacles into retracting their onslaught, he had experienced complete lucidity. But no sooner had I taken him away from her, had his control once more been forfeit and the tentacles committed anew to their destructive cause. So severe was the energetic thrashing, I was forced to channel several levels of ether to stop them from harming any being or structure in their wake, as well as to protect myself from harm.

He was frightened. Frightened of what the tentacles might do next and frightened of what *I* would do to *him*.

In truth, my first instinct *was* indeed to annihilate his very being for allowing his wrath to latch upon my youngest child. In those seconds filled with all-encompassing rage, the fact that he was her beloved was forgotten. My conscious thoughts were fixed solely on fatherly duty: bring to a swift end all who hurt her and ensure the threat presents itself no more.

Nevertheless, had I killed Sawyer, the act would prove a grievous circumstance for Angel, and she would, over the centuries and forever after, cultivate hatred and animosity toward me. *That* I could not allow.

My sister Alpha, one of the most powerful and emphatic sorceresses among my kinfolk, had yet to be wrong in her observations of people—especially mortals. She had immediately read Sawyer for what she said he could possibly be. "An abiding mage," she had said. "A great and abiding mage."

I observed his posture; it spoke of his abandonment of all attempts to regain control. We were now stopped in an Aeonian Loop, an endless loop of energy contained within a magical framework. It manifested as an edgeless, empty room lacking ceiling, windows, and corners. I'd installed two such loops within Angel's house—one of which we used during her Mahá. However, of this particular loop, she—and for that matter, her older sister—was unaware. As no sound could escape it and no sight penetrate it, the loop proved to be an ideal location to preclude discovery by either daughter.

I extended my hand toward him as he lay stretched out before my feet. As before, I caused his body and the tentacles themselves to rock back and forth as if buoyed by water. The motion forced the tentacles to lose their bearing and offered Sawyer the opportunity to regain control.

And yet, his thoughts informed me of his expectation of death at my hands. He forewent the opportunity to reclaim control and lay supine in an attitude of defeat.

He had relinquished all hope.

With a wave of my hand, I invoked his body to stand. However, once he stood on his feet, his eyes remained focused on his footwear.

"Look at me," I said.

He raised his eyes, and their luminance served as a barometer of the intensity of his internal war.

"I should have had more...control." His voice faltered as the event appeared before his mind's eye, and again he was confronted with the horror. His mind recoiled as he relived the last few moments in Angel's room. He expeditiously regained a vestige of control, however, and once again stood before me, humble, apologetic, and projecting valor despite his inner turmoil.

"Control them," I commanded. "Now."

He closed his eyes. As he toiled with garnering complete control, in his heart grew the hope of having an opportunity to remedy his transgressions before I killed him. Eventually, his heartbeat returned to its normal pace, and he lifted his gaze.

I would not kill him. He was valuable, and maleficent dealings were afoot.

I had returned to my daughters, not because of complete confidence in Cleopatra's safety, but because I needed to ensure the security of our newborn. I would have arrived sooner, immediately after Cici told me of Angel's belief that she had beheld Charleston, however, there remained final, vital steps in the fortification of Cleo's resting place. Nevertheless, my distrust of the Council had ripened, and I knew in my being that they had no intention of attacking her now.

It would be foolhardy to think they had melted away so quickly in the face of my wrath. In truth, they wanted her asleep. The scattered incidents that made it appear as if the family resting place was under attack during the last couple of months were simple distractions—mere ploys to keep me occupied in Africa.

Having both parents out of the picture and away from Angel would support their devious ends.

I had heard of the Council's recruitment tactics centuries before meeting Cleopatra, before I had fallen in love with her amidst the chaos that proved to be the death throes of the Ming Dynasty. She herself could never share Council secrets with me, but I had gleaned much from her thoughts. Only hours before she fell asleep, she had revealed her deepest fear to me—that they conspired to control Angel's power to suit their own ends.

Now I regarded Angel's beloved. His heart, as they say, was in his mouth, but nonetheless he employed a breathing technique. I recognized it as a diluted version of a bygone tactic, Heart Breath, which magical beings employed to align their physical bodies with the resonance of the planet. It was clear that he was unaware of the history and thought he was simply centering himself. His thoughts showed clearly that his grandmother had presented the technique to him. Perhaps if she had educated him about what he was truly doing, aligning as opposed to confining his power, it would have, at the time he was introduced to the truth, frightened him.

However, the boy before me was no longer afraid.

"I will give you the opportunity to right your wrongs, Sawyer. Fight with me. For Angel."

"Sir…?"

"She is in danger. I am in need of your magical force, and in return for your valiance, you will be my apprentice."

At that precise moment, the sound of my daughters' laughter rang in the kitchen. He had no way of hearing it, but the fire in his eyes told me he would make a formidable pupil indeed.

Acknowledgements

I am so grateful for all my friends and supporters. First and foremost I thank Papa, Grace and all those others who continue to pave the way. Thank you Eshu, Oshun, Shango, Oya and Obatala.

Thanks to you dear readers for your emails, tweets and neverending enthusiasm. I love you!

Most of all I thank my son for being my light in the darkness. Thank you for your unconditional love. You continue to be, and will always be, my heart.

To all the readers:

Thank you for reading *Heart To Heart*. If you liked what you read, please take a few moments to leave a quick review on Amazon.com, and don't forget to tell your family and friends.

Books by Ife Oshun

Angelica Brown Series
  Blood to Blood (Vol. 1)
  Heart To Heart (Vol. 2)

Sawyer Creed Series
  tentacles (short story)

Ifè Oshun

Also look out for the first in a new series based on Justin McCarthy called *To Protect and Serve*, scheduled to appear in 2015. Stay tuned!

CPSIA information can be obtained
at www.ICGtesting.com
Printed in the USA
BVHW03s1257011018
528951BV00001B/36/P

9 780985 923556